For Jordan McLean

PROLOGUE

ONE MINUTE you're sipping on your first beer at your first bonfire party, wearing a hoodie provided by a boy you've been crushing on for months. He slips his hand around your waist, pulls you closer to him. Then he dips his head, whispers into your neck, "You're beautiful, Ava."

It's your fifteenth birthday, and you have the world at your feet, and you watch the fire blaze in front of you, watch the embers rise, float to a new existence, and you think to yourself, *This is life*.

Your phone rings, and you pull it out of your back pocket, see your stepfather's name flashing on the screen, and you end the call, pocket the phone again.

The boy kisses your neck, and you take another sip, your eyes drifting shut at the feel of his lips against your skin.

Your phone rings again.

And again.

And you ignore it every time.

Every single time.

You move to the bed of a truck, your hands in his hair, his hands on your breasts, and you're so drunk on desire it makes you high on this life.

This life.

This perfect life.

It's 3:00 a.m. when you stumble home, drunk and delusional. Your stepfather is slouched on the couch in the living room, a single lamp casting the only shadows of the night. "I've been calling you," he says, and you're too out of it to care. "It's your mother."

At fifteen and one day, you sit with your stepfather in the same living room where he waited all night for you. Night has turned to day, and unlike him, you don't look at the door, waiting. No. You look at the phone.

Waiting.

At fifteen and two days, the call comes through, and neither you nor your stepdad has slept a wink. Your stepbrother is on his way home from Texas, and you wring your hands together.

Waiting.

At fifteen and three days, you find out that the situation is so bad, they're bypassing Germany and bringing your mother right home. To you. To her family.

At fifteen and four days, your stepbrother comes home, and you look to him for courage, find it in his eyes, in the way he holds your hand while you can do nothing but wait.

At fifteen and five days, you fly to DC, and see your mother for the first time in five months. The last words she said to you were "Be careful." She smiled at you the way mothers smile at their children, and you hid the pain and fear in your chest, replaced weakness for courage, and offered her a smile of your own.

At fifteen and six days, you try to search for that smile on her face while you sit by her hospital bed, but you don't find it. *Can't* find it. Because half of her face is gone. Half of her arm is, too.

A grenade, they told you.

At fifteen and seven days, you say to yourself, "This is life." And it only took seven days for you to realize how imperfect it is.

CHAPTER 1
CONNOR

LeBron James grew up poor as hell with a single mother and zero privilege. His high school was completely unheard of before he showed up with three of his buddies and took over the league. At eighteen, a senior, he went prep to pro and was drafted by the Cleveland Cavaliers. His initial contract was $18.8 million over four years. Nike had offered him more than one hundred million off the court. This was before he played a single second of professional ball.

Talk about a game changer.

Obviously, I'm no LeBron James.

No one is.

Besides being raised by a single parent, comparing myself to LeBron would be like chasing rainbows.

Also, LeBron didn't have to change schools senior year just for the slight hope of getting noticed.

I walk back down the driveway for the millionth time, sweat pouring from every inch of my body, and blink away the fatigue from driving all night. Dad's at the rear of the rental truck unloading the last of the boxes we managed to stuff in there. After this, we only have *all* the furniture to unload. Fun times. I pick up a large, heavy box and ask, "Where to?"

"What does it say on the box?" Dad huffs. He's struggling more than I am.

I look down at the box, at the *somewhere* written in Dad's handwriting. "It says *somewhere*," I tell him, rolling my eyes.

He chuckles. "That must have been when I started to lose my mind. If only I'd had someone to help me pack."

I shrug. "I was busy." *Lazy.*

"Just dump it in the living room, and we'll go through it later, but I gotta go."

"Where?" I stop halfway to the house and look at the truck, then him, and back again. "Who's going to help me unload the furniture?"

"Just take the small stuff for now. I'll be back in a couple hours."

Sweat drips into my eyeballs. "A couple *hours*?" I drop the box, use the bottom of my shirt to wipe at my eyes, then search for a hose so I can drown myself. Maybe I don't even need the water. I could just use my own self-pity. There's sure as shit an abundance of it. I look over at my dad as he struggles to open the front door with his foot while carrying *two* boxes. *Shit.* I need to suck it up and quit complaining. He's given up a hell of a lot more than I have, and besides, he's here for me, no other reason. I rush to hold the door open, then I plaster on the most genuine smile I can muster. "No worries, Pops. Take your time. I got it."

"Don't overdo it, Connor. Just the small stuff."

When he leaves, the first thing I do is try to lift a three-seater couch on my own. Because I'm a shit of a kid and I don't listen apparently.

"Yo, you need a hand?" a guy calls from behind, rushing to lift the other end of the couch before it falls off the back of the truck. He asks, "You thought you could lift this on your own?"

I'd be annoyed by his words if he wasn't laughing when he said them. Besides, the guy's huge. If Shaq had a long-lost son, he would be it… so it's probably best not to start off on the wrong foot.

"Apparently so," I murmur.

With his help, we get the couch into the living room within seconds.

"Hey, man. Thanks for that." I throw out my fist for a bump as we walk out of the house.

"Nah, it's nothing." I expect him to leave, to go back to wherever the hell he appeared from, but he simply walks back to the truck, jumps in, and comes out with a mattress.

"Dude, honestly, you don't need to help."

He jumps down, then lifts the mattress onto his back as if it's air. "I got nothing going on."

"I can't, like, *pay you*... or anything."

He shakes his head. "Man, shut up with that." Then he motions to the rest of our shit in the truck. "But I'm not doing this on my own."

"Right."

An hour later and the entire truck is empty. I'm completely drenched in sweat. So is Trevor—whose name I just asked a minute ago. "I'd offer you a drink," I tell him, rolling down the truck door, "but we don't really have anything."

He looks over at my house. "You got AC?"

I nod. "I assume so."

He slaps my arm. "Get it on. I'll be back."

A minute later, AC blowing in the living room, he returns with two beers and hands me one. I take it without a second thought, down half of it in one go while he makes himself comfortable on the couch. Legs kicked up on the *somewhere* box, he says, "I live next door by the way."

I sit on a desk chair opposite him. "I figured. Hey, I can't thank you enough. My dad had to run out, so you showed up at the right time. Or wrong time for you, I guess."

He chuckles, his voice deep, low, when he says, "I wouldn't have offered if I didn't want to."

"Well, thank you. *Again.*"

He lifts his beer bottle in a salute motion, looking around the room. "So, you're here with your parents?"

"Just my dad."

"That him walking up your porch steps right now?"

I look through the window behind me, and sure enough… and I'm too late to remember the beer in my hand because it's the first thing Dad spots when he walks into the house.

The second is Trevor.

"This is Trevor," I tell Dad, standing, trying to hide the beer in plain sight. "He lives next door."

Dad clears his throat, takes the beer from my grasp. "Nice to meet you, Trevor," Dad says. "And I assume my son didn't mention he was a *minor*."

"Oh, my bad." Trevor gets up to shake Dad's hand. "To be fair, I didn't ask."

Dad simply nods, enjoying the ice-cold beer that I once called mine. "You help him bring all this furniture in?"

"Yes, sir."

Dad opens his wallet.

I cringe a little on the outside, and a *whole lot* on the inside.

Dad tries to hand him a twenty, but Trevor shoves his hands in his pockets, declining. "You're good, sir. I just saw him trying to lift more than all our weights combined. Didn't want him hurting himself, you know?"

"Well, thank you. I appreciate it."

Trevor eyes me. "A *minor*, huh?"

I nod, face heating with embarrassment.

"High school?"

"Yep."

"West High?"

"Nah. St. Luke's Academy."

Trevor's eyes widen. "Oh yeah? That's my old stomping ground." He takes a quick glance around our two bed, one bath, paint-peeling-off-the-walls rental, and all our belongings, focusing a few seconds on the framed Larry Bird jersey. When his eyes meet mine again, he's smirking. "Let me guess. Basketball scholarship?"

"Yeah," Dad and I answer at the same time. Dad asks, "You play ball?"

Trevor looks down at his feet. "Football. Well, I used to. Not so much anymore."

"You in college?" Dad asks him, and I hold back from doing the whole *ohmygod Dad stahhp, you're so embarrassing!* thing and keep my mouth shut.

"Nah," says Trevor. "I just work full-time now. Got my own company." He pulls out a card from his wallet and hands it to Dad. "Electrician. If you need anything, my number's on there."

"You got it," Dad asserts.

Trevor smiles at the both of us. "It's been fun, but I gotta get going. Hope y'all settle in all right."

"Hey, thanks again," I tell him.

Dad says, "Are you sure you won't take any—"

Trevor lifts his hand, already halfway to the door. "I'm good."

"Well, if you won't take money, maybe come around later this week. I'll grill some steaks for us."

Trevor stops, his hand on the door, and turns to us, his grin from ear-to-ear. "Now *that* is an offer too good to refuse."

He's gone a second later, his footsteps heavy on the porch.

Dad waits for him to be out of earshot before stating, "Good kid."

"Yeah."

"Good beer, too."

I clamp my lips together.

He laughs. "Come with me?"

"Where?"

He places the empty bottle on a box labeled *Boy Spawn* and heads out the door.

I follow as he leads me to a hunk of metal on four wheels.

"So…?" Dad asks, his eyes wide and waiting. It doesn't take long for his face to switch from his usual overtired, overworked, over-the-every-day-struggles-of-life frown into a full-blown grin. All it took was a twitch of my lips, a semblance of a smile. "Do you like it?"

He's asking the wrong question, because honestly? Do I *like* it? No. The car's a piece of shit. Way beyond its expiration. Beaten to death and then brought back to life only to be beaten again. Rust forms the majority of the two-door's roof. Door handles have been replaced with what I assume are coat hangers. The rear windshield… well, there is no rear windshield. There's just black plastic in its place, so… again… do I *like* it? Fuck no.

Do I *appreciate* it? Hell yes. "Dad, are you serious?" My grin matches his now. "You didn't have to. I mean, you shouldn't have. Things are hard enough with the move and—"

"Connor," he cuts in, shushing me with one hand, while a finger of the other runs along the dirt of the car's hood. "It's my job to worry about what's too hard and what isn't." His shoulders heave with his inhale as he focuses on the perfectly clean line he's just created. When his gaze meets mine again, I can see the exhaustion in his eyes. He's worn out. *Done.* He tries to cover it up with the same smile he's kept on, but I can tell it's waning. Slowly. Surely.

I inspect the car closer. Or at least pretend to. Because my mind is elsewhere, running on empty, doing a play-by-play of every possible scenario my future has waiting for me. And not even my entire future. Just *tomorrow*.

The first day of senior year is daunting for anyone, but the first day as the new guy in a new school full of rich kids who I'm sure can sniff a poor, scholarship kid from a mile away? Yeah, tomorrow's going to suck. And showing up in this car? It's going to be hell… but there's no way I'm telling Dad that. Or anyone else. Because the truth is, I don't *have* anyone else. It's 598 miles from Tallahassee, Florida, to Shemeld, North Carolina. Physically. But for my so-called friends and teammates back there, I may as well have moved to Mars. The second rumors started to spread about my moving for a better chance at my dreams was the exact second the invites and phone calls stopped. In one breath I was the team hero, and in the next, I was getting a stream of *Fuck you, Traitor* text messages.

What a time to be alive.

I grip the makeshift handle and pull up, cringing at the sound of metal scraping metal.

"She'll get better. Don't think she's been used in a while," Dad says, kicking at the tire. The hubcap separates from the wheel and falls to the ground in a circular motion—around and around—and I watch it, feel the chuckle building in my chest. I clamp my lips shut and try to contain it because the last thing I want to do is offend him.

His laughter starts low from somewhere deep inside him, and a moment later, he's in hysterics, a belly-rumble type sound that has me doing the same. "Goddamn, it's a piece of shit," he murmurs, trying to compose himself.

"It's not," I assure.

It is.

"At least this way, you'll be sure to get to school and games on time. Besides, it's all for the end game, right?"

I nod. The "end game" is what we call the plan for my future, and St. Luke's Academy is the first step. My agent, Ross, suggested the move, and Dad and I agreed early on that whatever Ross says goes, and he says to "trust in the process."

So... I trust in the process.

Ross had organized everything. All I had to do was show up, play ball, keep my grades up, and he'd make sure I'd get into a D1 college.

Four years.

Graduate.

NBA.

End game.

Ross—he's not big on the four-year part of the plan, but Dad's adamant on it and in a way, so am I. A pro-athlete can only maintain the physical demands for so long. Besides, one injury could end it all and then what?

I catch the keys Dad throws at my chest.

"You need to drive me back to my car."

"What? You ain't worried about ruining your street cred by being seen in this?" I joke.

"Boy," he mocks, pulling open the passenger door. "Being seen with *you* ruined my street cred a long time ago."

CHAPTER 2
Ava

THE CORRIDORS of school are deserted, first period already in progress. Through thin walls and solid doors, teachers speak loudly, authoritative tones used to impart their knowledge and wisdom on the students in front of them.

St. Luke's Academy is the most prestigious school within a fifty-mile radius, and I'm lucky to be here—just ask the faculty.

I descend the main staircase, past the words etched into the mahogany above the doorway: *Vincit qui se vincit.* Translation: He conquers who conquers himself.

Basically: master yourself, and then master the world around you. What's written between the lines, though, is this: St. Luke's will mold you to perfection, then throw you out into the real world and hope you know what the hell you're doing.

On the ground floor, I look left, look right. It's the same down here as it was above: deserted. The air conditioner above me whirs to life, blowing chills across my skin. Posters and flyers flap at the edges. The largest one spans across an entire wall, from one classroom door to another. *Wildcats! Wildcats! Wildcats!* There's a significant divide in this school, with only two segments: jocks and academics.

My stepbrother fell into the jock category.

Two years ago, so did I.

Kind of.

Now, I don't fit in either. I'm a loner, floating on the outskirts, discarded and unseen.

Invisible... until I'm not.

The long, narrow, empty hall stretches in front of me. Even with the air conditioning creating goosebumps on my flesh, making the hairs on my arms rise, sweat builds on my neck, at my hairline. I hold my psychology book to my chest and keep my head lowered. One step. Two. The walls seem to close in, but there's no exit in sight. I stop just outside the classroom door and freeze. I pray for an escape while I will myself not to press my ear against the heavy timber and listen in. A short breath in, out. I ball the note in my hand: a message from the school's psychologist excusing me from my tardiness with words so articulate, I struggle to understand them even though they're written about me. It's as if she tries to hide the truth that everyone already knows. It should just say: *Be nice. Y'all know what she's been through.*

I take one more deep, calming breath before I press my shoulder to the door and start to push, but the door gives way, and I'm falling forward, my shoes squeaking against the marble floor as I try to brace myself.

"Miss Diaz," Mr. McCallister booms, his hand on my arm to help keep me upright. Heat forms in my cheeks as I quickly hand him the note. Around me: silence. Not a single word, not even a whisper. Mr. McCallister doesn't bother reading the note; he simply places it on his desk and motions to the classroom.

"Please swiftly find a seat so we can continue."

My phone vibrates in the hidden pocket of my school skirt.

Ignore it.

But I can't. I start to reach for it at the same time Mr. McCallister clears his throat. "Now, Miss Diaz."

I swallow my nerves and glance up through my lashes. I can feel every set of eyes on me, but I refuse to meet them.

It's a miracle my feet move at all, and they lead me to the only empty seat left in the room.

I drop my bag by the desk and climb into the chair, the lump in my throat the size of the random basketball by my feet.

Mr. McCallister turns his back, his focus already on writing down the semester's syllabus on the whiteboard. It takes a second for the class to follow, fingers busy tap, tap, tapping on their keyboards.

"Hey," a male voice whispers from next to me. I have no idea who he is, and I don't look up when he says, "I'm Connor."

I open my textbook to the first page, ignoring the dampness on the side of the pages from where I'd been gripping it.

"I'm new here..." my desk-mate says, his voice trailing as if waiting for a response.

In my mind, I say, "Hi, I'm Ava. Welcome to my personal hell. The only reason I'm here is because guilt forces me to be."

Out loud, I say nothing.

Soon enough, he'll know everything there is to know about me.

CHAPTER 3
CONNOR

The car didn't stall once.

A miracle, really.

I got to school early this morning, about a half hour before I was supposed to be here. I thought it might help with the whole car situation. Not that I'm embarrassed by it, because I'm not. But you know what they say about first impressions. I didn't want to go into the year being "that kid."

It was pointless, though. One car in the parking lot, one kid on campus. Put two and two together, and you get my dumb ass.

I spent some time on the court alone, getting used to the hardwood that would become my playground for the next year. About twenty minutes in, my new teammates started to show.

Rhys, the team captain, was the first to greet me. His lackey, Mitch, was next, and then the rest of the guys. Everyone but Rhys seemed more interested in my car than in me, and when Rhys told them to quit raggin' on me, they didn't listen.

The first official practice of the season sucked. I'd spent so many hours during the summer learning the plays and memorizing my positions. I thought I had it down. I was wrong, so fucking wrong. I lagged. Hard. Balls flew past my head faster than I could catch them, names were called, threats were made. And that was just from Coach Sykes. Besides Rhys, no one said a word to me in the locker room afterward. This was all before the first bell, and my introduction to the shitty elite side of St. Luke's Academy.

And then first period started, psychology, and things just went downhill from there. No one sat next to me, and other than a few girls with coy smiles, I was ignored.

Then *she* walked in, like a baby bird leaving its nest for the first time—a discombobulation of limbs flapping around. Thing is—after the morning I had—I thought people would laugh at her, but no one did. Maybe because things were taken more seriously off the court, or maybe it was because the girl was crazy hot; all naturally tanned skin and legs upon legs beneath her school-issued skirt, and I never thought I'd have a kink for the whole school-girl uniform thing, but hey...

She made an entrance, that's for sure, or maybe it was just me that was paying attention. Maybe a little *too much* attention. She sat next to me, the only available seat... and said and did nothing. Even when I calmed my thoughts enough to introduce myself... nothing. While the entire class was busy taking notes, she stared ahead, picking at the desktop with her fingernail.

It's not until the bell rings forty odd minutes later that she finally moves. We face each other as we gather our things. Our eyes meet. Hold. Her irises catch the sunlight streaming through the windows, a light brown—so similar to the maple I spend my days shredding. Her lips part and my gaze glues to the motion. I try again, this time extending a hand. "I'm Connor. It's my first..." I trail off because she's already making her way to the door.

I turn at the hand landing on my shoulder. Rhys is behind me, his gaze following mine. "She's unavailable."

With a shrug, I tell him, "I wasn't interested."

He shakes his head. "No. I don't mean she's unavailable because she's seeing someone. I mean, she's unavailable"—he taps at his temple—"because she's checked out."

"No longer part of this world," Mitch adds, stepping up behind him. He rotates a finger around his ear—the universal sign for crazy—and whispers, "Certifiable." He eyes me up and down, stopping at my worn-out sneakers. "Actually, you'd do just fine together. Ghetto with ghetto. A perfect match."

I should punch him. Once for me. Then two more for the girl-with-no-name. Instead, I walk away, convince myself that people, in general, can be dicks, but people in high school? They fucking thrive on it.

Besides, I'm not here to make friends.

I'm here to make plays.

CHAPTER 4
Ava

Healthy Ways of Coping with PTSD and Anxiety.

I read the title of the pamphlet for the umpteenth time, shaking my head in disbelief. I'm not the one with PTSD, and maybe if the school psychologist had given me reading material about how to cope *with* people suffering *from* PTSD, I'd have a different reaction. I didn't feel like I needed to see her, but Trevor had spoken to the principal about how to "make sure my final year runs as smoothly as possible" and this was one of the many, many things on the list. So, every Monday and Wednesday I had to sit in an uncomfortable chair for a half hour and spill my guts about everything that was going on, all the emotions I was experiencing, and what I was doing to *cope* with it all.

I had nothing to say regarding any of those things, so I spent the entirety of our appointment trying to convince Miss Turner—a woman not much older than myself—that I was *fine*. Perfect, even. That my home life did not affect my school life, my grades, my future.

Vincit qui se vincit: He conquers who conquers himself.

I am a conqueror.

I am.

I am.

I flick the ring around my thumb.

I am.

I am.

I wish it to be true because those are the last words my stepdad, William, said to me before he walked out the door. *"You're a conqueror, Ava. You got this."* I didn't respond to him. I simply held the front door open and watched his truck pull out of the driveway and disappear down the road. I didn't ask where he was going. I didn't care. And I didn't ask why he was leaving me, leaving *us*. I already knew. He didn't love us, so he left. Love should make people stay. Love should make you want to keep the people who hold that love near.

Until one day when you open the bathroom door, and the scream that erupts from your throat forces you to understand. At that moment, I fell to my knees, soaking in crimson while clinging to hope—and I knew why William left. Because sometimes, love isn't enough. And neither is a school motto that teaches you from the day you enroll to the day you graduate that you must *conquer all.* Always. And when the tears blur your vision and your hands shake uncontrollably, and your throat aches with the cries that have consumed you, and you pick up the phone and question who to call, who to save you… you fail.

You don't dial 911 as you should.

Guilt seeps into my veins and through my airways, making breathing a task.

I flick the ring again.

I am not a conqueror.

I am a fucking failure.

I am.

I am.

At around five thirty a car door slams, and I pack up my homework scattered on the kitchen table and get started on dinner. Heavy footsteps enter the house, his head lowered, tools in one hand, work hat in the other. I watch from the kitchen doorway as he slumps down on the couch by the front door of our tiny three-bedroom house and starts unlacing his boots. Shoulders slouched, messy hair and tired eyes, the man is a picture of exhaustion and responsibility, and I hate that he's here. Hate that he's taken us on when he should be living his dream: playing football and finishing his degree at Texas A&M.

I don't ask him how his day was; I already know.

"How was your first day?" he asks, never once looking up.

"Good," I lie.

He nods, not asking anything more. He looks across the living room at a bedroom door—behind it: *our* reason and *his* responsibility. He murmurs words I can't decipher. When he looks up at me, he offers a smile that shatters my heart and adds layers to the constant knot in my throat. Heat burns behind my eyes, and I choke back my weaknesses. "Dinner will be ready in ten minutes."

He sighs, "Thank you, Ava."

I want to yell at him. I want to tell him that he shouldn't be thanking me for anything. That I'm the one who's thankful, that I'm forever in his debt. I want to tell him that I love him.

But if my stepdad leaving has taught me anything—it's this:

Love is not a noun.

Love is something you *do*.

Something you *prove*.

Something you work hard to *create*.

Love is not something that simply exists because you say it.

Love is not a noun.

Love is a verb.

CHAPTER 5
CONNOR

IT'S ONLY BEEN a week since school started, and I'm already counting down the days until it's over. I'm sure things will get better. They have to. Once the season starts, I'll be able to focus all my energy on ball. But right now, I'm feeling… stuck. Somewhere between my old life and my new one. I'm struggling to navigate the hallways, not just geographically but socially, too. The kids are different, the classes are harder, the teachers are stricter, and the girls… the girls are on another level. I've been approached more in the past week than I have in my entire life. They know what they want, and I'm sure they're used to getting it. I could lie—tell them that I have a girl back home. Truth is, I'm out of my damn element, and every morning when I wake up, I feel like I'm drowning.

I tell Dad all this while lifting weights in our garage.

"It could be worse," Dad offers.

"Yeah? How?"

He helps me settle the bar onto the rack before handing me a water bottle. Then he raises his eyebrows at me as if to ask *do you really want to know?*

I down half the bottle and shake my head. No, I don't want to know. I've heard it too many times before. Dad's a paramedic, so he's seen it all. He was lucky enough to get a job here doing the same. The downside? He works nights.

I admire him for what he does. Honestly, I do. But sometimes I wish I could just complain about things and not have it thrown in my face. Sometimes I want to vent without feeling guilty for having those thoughts.

And sometimes I want to go back to my old school and play ball as if our future wasn't riding on it. To be fair, he's never made me feel as though that responsibility was mine.

But that doesn't mean I don't think it.

Going pro isn't just the end game. It's our ticket out. Our saving grace. Being a single parent is tough enough but raising a kid whose goal in life is to be a paid athlete—that's a whole other level. Training camps, uniforms, gear, gas to and from practices and games—games that up until a couple years ago he never missed, the time off work, the food. Goddamn, I eat *a lot*. I'm surprised he still somehow affords the roof over our heads.

"It's just a year, Connor. Do the work. Stay focused. No distractions—"

"Like girls?" I cut in, smirking.

"It only takes one," he mumbles, removing a weight off the bar.

His words hit me hard and fast. I lower my gaze and say, repeating his words from earlier, "It could be worse."

He crosses his arms. "Yeah? How?"

I shrug. "I could be nothing more than a stain on your bedsheets."

He says, his tone filled with regret, "That's not what I meant, son."

"Yeah? Because that's not what I heard, *Dad*."

CHAPTER 6
CONNOR

I WAS AN AWKWARD KID, a loner, anxious, with barely any social skills. On the advice of my teachers, Dad had me trying a bunch of things to help build my confidence and make me feel like I was part of something. Anything. Looking back, I know he went above and beyond to help me find my place in this world, to make me feel as comfortable as I could in my own skin. For most of my life, he'd played the part of both parents, which I'm sure comes with a level of difficulty I can't even imagine. He'd always been there for me. *Always.* Which I guess is why when he says things like he did last night—things in passing that aren't meant to offend—it cuts deep.

Deeper than I'll ever let show.

Anyways, the point is I spent a good year of my life trying everything: baseball, football, soccer, karate, Scouts, *sewing*. You name it, I was there. But I didn't love any of them, and nothing stuck. Not until I touched a basketball for the first time when I was ten years old, and something just… clicked.

My coaches said I was a natural-born athlete, which makes sense, I guess, given my genetics.

A lot changed in the years that followed.

The harder I worked on the court; the easier things became off of it. Throw in a growth spurt that didn't seem to end, and I started to get attention from all over. Girls included. Luckily for me, Dad was always there to remind me of my never-ending list of priorities, and dating… it wasn't even in the footnotes.

So, with that said, it's no real surprise that my experience with those of the opposite sex is limited to a few make-out sessions at post-win celebrations. I'd never been in a relationship. Never even dated. And so the aggressiveness of the attention I was suddenly getting was intimidating, to say the least, and uncomfortable as hell. Especially when it's constant. Like this girl, Karen, who's somehow managed to find me at my locker every single morning. There's no doubt she's cute, in the kind of way that money can buy attractiveness. Perfect make-up to go with her perfect skin and perfect hair and perfect attitude. And I'm sure she's perfect for a guy who's just as perfect for her. But for me? I'm not interested in her, at least not in that way, and I sure as hell don't have the time to try to match that level of perfection. Or the time at all… just ask my dad.

Monday morning. First period. Psychology. And guess who's in my class?

Karen.

Karen… who's currently staring at me from across the room. Or maybe she's looking at the girl next to me; Ava—whose name I worked out through other people because she still won't talk to me even though she sits next to me every psych class.

She's a goddamn enigma.

I've never seen her outside of this class, not even in the cafeteria. Not that I've been looking. *Lie.* Unless she's conspicuously making a grab for her phone under the desk, she shows no other signs of life. It's as if she lives in a bubble, and everyone accepts that.

Sometimes, sitting next to her like we are, I wonder what it would be like to burst that bubble.

"One thing I forgot to mention—" Mr. McCallister's voice booms, pulling me from my thoughts, "the nature versus nurture paper you're all going to submit will be done in pairs. You have three seconds to choose your partners."

Across the room, Karen's eyes widen and zone in on me. Chairs scrape, students move, and panic fills my bloodline. Instantly—*stupidly*—I reach for Ava's arm at the same time she stands. Not a second later, Karen's in front of us, her gaze switching from me to Ava to my hand on Ava's arm. Ava's wide-eyed as she looks up at me, then at Karen, then to our touch. Behind me, a throat clears. It's Rhys, and he's looking at all three of us with unmasked confusion.

"Ava," Karen says, motioning to me. Ava's shoulders rise with her intake of breath, and she pulls her arm from my grasp. My eyes drift shut, embarrassment heating my cheeks. *What the hell was I thinking?*

"Ava?" Karen repeats. Firmer. Stronger. There's a hidden question there, one I can't decipher.

Rhys asks, "You good, A?" It's the first time I've heard a student speak to Ava this way, as if they care, and I sure as shit didn't expect it from him.

Ava swallows, nervous, her eyes flitting to mine quickly before moving away. "I'd rather work with Rhys," she says, so quiet I barely hear her. But I do, and there's a sudden knot in my gut, a flashback to my past. Awkward, anxious, loner. I bite my tongue, physically and metaphorically, and try to push down my insecurities. I feel like I'm being judged, and it sucks that the one person in the entire school who's paid absolutely no attention to me in the past is the one doing the judging.

"Groups of two, not four," the teacher yells, waving a hand toward us. "And since none of you can take basic direction, I'll make the choice for you. Ava and Connor. Rhys and Karen."

Rhys curses under his breath, his lips pressed tight as he eyes Ava. "You going to be okay?"

"Jesus Christ," I murmur. "Way to make a guy feel good."

I watch Ava for a response, but I don't get one. At least not to me. Rhys does, though, in the form of a painstakingly slow nod from her.

In front of me, Karen stomps her foot, spins and walks back to her seat, Rhys following after her.

I turn to the girl next to me, my insecurities switching to annoyance. "I'm not stupid."

Her gaze locks on mine, her head shaking slowly. "I'm sor—"

I interrupt because I don't need her sympathy. "No, *I'm* sorry. I'm sorry to disappoint you before you even get to know me." I take a breath, try to regain some composure. "I'm not stupid," I repeat, calmer. "Just because I'm new and I'm here on an athletic scholarship doesn't mean I'm a dumbass. I'll work just as hard as you, if not more, because I have something to prove. I don't expect you to carry the weight if that's what you're thinking." I keep my eyes trained on her, watching the confusion settle across her face.

"It's Connor, right?"

"Yeah…?"

"Let's just get this clear, *Connor*." She spits my name. "I have no assumptions about you at all because I haven't thought of you once. Not even for a second. And I don't care enough about you to judge you. So, let's just get to work." She slaps a sheet of paper between us and scrawls my name and hers across the top, then glares up at me. Daggers upon daggers. "Do you think it's nature or nurture that has you believing that your woe-is-me attitude isn't just another form of self-entitlement?"

My head spins, but I can't come up with a retort. Not even a decent response. All this time I spent wondering what it would be like to burst her bubble, and now here she was… completely obliterating mine.

CHAPTER 7
Ava

ONE OF THE only two friends I have left belongs to my brother. He was there the first day I met Trevor—when I was nothing but a kindergartener in a bright purple dress and rainbow-colored socks. He's been there pretty much every day since. From grade school to middle school to high school, wherever Trevor Knight was, so was Peter Parker. Yes, that's his real name.

When he and Trevor graduated, they both took off to Texas A&M. It's safe to say we all grew up together, but the four-year age difference meant we experienced things at different times. While they hit freshman year of high school, I was in fifth—and back then, I was trying to decide between Harry Styles and Justin Bieber while the *Glee* soundtrack blasted from my bedroom.

The point is, now that I'm older, wiser, and the experiences of my life have forced me to grow up, the four years between us don't seem so vast anymore.

Peter comes from the "right" side of town, the same side where Trevor and I grew up before we had to sell the house to cover my mother's medical bills. The same side with the fancy, big houses and boats in their yards. His parents usually go away for the summer, a new country every year, and every year he'd join them. Until last year. Last year, he spent his summer helping Trevor with his business. Trevor's offered to pay him what little he can. Peter refuses every cent, knowing we need it more than he does. He's become a good friend to me, a solid wall of dependency that for so long, I refused to believe I needed.

And that's the difference between Trevor's friends and mine: when our worlds came crashing down, Peter stood by our sides. My so-called friends stopped coming around, too afraid of the woman with the half face and stub for an arm.

Soon enough, they stopped calling altogether.

"I like what you've done with the place," Peter jokes, throwing his entire weight on the couch next to me. "It's very—"

"Thrift store chic?" I finish for him.

He shakes his head, placing the bowl of popcorn on my lap. He's home for the week, and when he found out Trevor was out quoting jobs after hours, he offered to come over so I wouldn't be home alone. "No," he says, "It's got bits of your personality all over the place." He grabs a blanket from behind us and places it over his lap. "Like this." He rubs the blanket between his fingers. "It's very... *boho*."

"You mean homeless?"

With a chuckle, he throws his arm on the couch behind me and gets comfortable. "So, Ava. Tell me everything. What's been going on with you?"

"Same old, really. Just counting down the days until school's over." I hit play on the remote, but keep the volume muted.

"You'll miss high school when it's over," he tries to assure.

I scoff. "I think your version of high school and mine are very different, Peter."

"Yeah, I guess." After grabbing a handful of popcorn, he asks, "You still friends with that Rhys kid?"

Nodding, I stare at the opening scene of the horror movie he's got us watching.

"Is he still helping you out at school? Getting you notes for your missed classes?"

"Yeah," I reply through a slow exhale.

On TV, a blonde girl climbs the stairs toward the killer.

"Good," Peter says, nodding. Then adds, "He's a good guy, Ava. He's just not good enough for *you*."

"Okay," I mumble because it doesn't really matter what he thinks.

"Ava?" Peter asks, his leg brushing against mine. He's closer than he was only minutes ago, and discomfort swarms in my veins, beating against my flesh.

I manage a "Yeah?"

The warmth of his breath floats against my cheek as his heated fingers brush along the skin of my shoulder. It's not the first time he's acted like this. It won't be the last. And it would be so easy to use him this way, to be with someone who understands without explanations, who forgives without excuses.

I swallow, nervous. "If Trevor knew what you were thinking right now, he'd kill you with his bare hands."

CHAPTER 8
CONNOR

THE WAY STEPHEN CURRY puts his defenders off balance with a simple behind-the-back crossover is history-making. He's proven that a killer jump shot can make or break a team's final score, making him arguably the best ball handler in the NBA.

Me?

I can't even catch the fucking ball when it's thrown directly at my chest.

It's the day after Ava tore me to shreds, and I'm in the locker room following another pathetic practice, staring down at my hands trying to reason with them. For years, I've lived and breathed this sport. I dreamed about it even when I was awake. The amount of shit I've broken in the house because I couldn't *stop* thinking about it is enough to fill a whole other house. Every lawn I mowed to earn money to replace those things—worth it. Every grounding—worth it. Every single hour I spent watching game tape or studying plays or fantasizing about what it would be like to play at Madison Square Garden was *worth it*.

But here? Now? I'm second-guessing it all.

"You ever watch that movie *Little Giants*?" Rhys asks, flopping down on the bench next to me. I thought I was the only one left in the locker room, but apparently, I was wrong.

I slam my locker shut and face him. "That one with the reject kids playing football?"

He nods. "There's this line in it that I always think about whenever I have bad days. Football is 80% mental and 40% physical."

I glare at him, my brow bunched in confusion. "That makes no sense."

He taps at his temple. "Get out of your head," he says, squeezing my shoulder. "The rest will follow." I force out a breath as he comes to a stand. He adds, "You know Miss Turner?"

"No."

"She's the school psychologist."

I shake my head. *Is this kid serious?* "I'm fine."

"I've made an appointment for you after school tomorrow."

Frustration knocks on my flesh from the inside. "Dude, I don't need—"

"Trust in the process," he cuts in, and I'm reminded of Ross, of my dad, of the weight of expectation balancing on my shoulders.

He starts to walk away but stops just by the door. "And hey. Not that I'm assuming this has anything to do with you sucking—because you might just be a shitshow—but the whole Ava thing? Try not to take it personally, okay?"

◇◇◇◇◇

Try not to take it personally.

It's 3:00 a.m., and Rhys's final words are plaguing my mind. Like a scratched record stuck on repeat. Over and over. Again, and again.

The thing is, I *did* try.

Just like I tried to forget what Dad had said.

And just like I tried to ignore the fact that I've made zero connection whatsoever with my new life.

◇◇◇◇◇

The next day drags, every second filled with anxiety. By the time I sit my ass outside the psych office, I'm a ball of nerves. My knee bounces, my palms sweat, and there's a throbbing between my eyes that won't fucking quit. Elbows on my knees, I lower my head and pinch the bridge of my nose for some form of reprieve. I try to blame it on the lack of sleep, but I know the truth. I've been here too many times not to know.

The door opens, and I look up just in time to see Ava standing in the doorway.

"My door is always open," a younger woman who I assume is Miss Turner tells Ava. "Whatever you need."

Ava doesn't respond to her because she's too focused on me, her head cocked, eyes narrowed.

Great, now I'm the "self-entitled" new guy with *issues*. But she's here, too, which means…

I try to offer a smile.

She returns it with a scowl.

Awesome.

◇◇◇◇◇

"Tell me why you're here," Miss Turner asks.

I settle my hands on my knees to stop the shaking and take a breath. Her office is nothing but white walls and empty bookshelves. I squirm in my seat, unease filling my bloodlines.

"Sorry," she says. "The seats aren't very comfortable." She waves a hand around the room. "As you can tell, I'm waiting on more funding to get my office up to scratch."

"I'm sure the parents of a few kids here could throw you some loose change," I remark, my gaze catching the files on the desk in front of her.

Connor Ledger. *Beneath that:* Ava Diaz.

"Sure," she says, swiping both files together and placing them roughly in a draw. "But the parents here aren't as interested in their kids' mental health so much as their grades, or in some cases their triple-double stats."

My eyes lift to hers.

She smirks. "So why are you here?"

I shrug. "My stats suck, and I guess my team captain wants to figure out why the hell I'm at this school."

"Do you ever wonder why you're here, Connor?"

Every damn minute of every day. "Nope. I *know* why I'm here."

"Enlighten me then."

"Because some people think I'm good enough."

"And you don't?"

Another shrug.

Her sigh echoes off the empty walls. "Let's start from the beginning," she says, grabbing a pen from a cup in the shape of a unicorn. "Tell me about your home life."

Here we go…

◇◇◇◇◇

The time with Miss Turner did nothing for my nerves. If anything, it just made things worse. By the time I finally make it out of the damn building, my heart is racing, sinking, and my mind? My mind is questioning what all she had to say about me in her too-messy-to-make-out notes that went on for *five* goddamn pages. I'm almost positive it'll be the same generic diagnosis of everyone else before her.

Connor Ledger has a good head on him, but he lacks self-confidence due to his fear of abandonment.

At the end, she asked if I wanted to schedule another appointment. I imagined getting out of my chair and throwing it out the window, I was that exasperated. Instead, I politely declined, told her I'd do "better." I don't even know what I meant by "better," but it sure as shit seemed to suffice.

In the student parking lot, my car is the only one left. By now, every single person knows who it belongs to, so there's no shame left, and even if there was, I have absolutely zero fucks left to give.

I make it halfway to my car before I hear a "Hey!" from somewhere behind me. I assume it's Miss Turner, but it's not.

It's Ava.

She's standing a few feet away, her hands gripping the straps of her bag. I stop in my tracks as I watch her approach. And I mean *watch* in every sense because as much as she might despise me, *goddamn*, there's still an attraction to her I can't seem to shake, and maybe…

Maybe Rhys is onto something. Because as hard as I've tried to deny it, what Ava said affected me in ways I don't truly understand.

"Is that your car?" she asks, looking over my shoulder.

So those fucks that had disappeared? They're back, and they're plentiful, and they're causing the heat forming in my face.

"Yes," I answer, but it comes out a whisper. *Jesus.* I clear my throat, try again. "Yeah, it's mine."

"Cool…"

Then I pull out the last remaining semblance of confidence I have left. "Do you… I mean, do you need a ride somewhere?"

◇◇◇◇◇

Sitting next to Ava in class is one thing. Having her sit in the tiny space of my car? Whole other story. Besides giving me directions, she doesn't speak, but I hear every sound. Every breath, every swallow, every shift of her skirt against her thighs…

And my eyes… my eyes can't seem to focus on the road because they're too busy focusing on her.

"Just here," she says, her voice pulling me back to reality.

I pull over in front of a diner and watch her looking out the window, her index finger flicking the ring around her thumb. It's too big for such small, delicate fingers, and I wonder who it belongs to. The sun reflects off the bright red stone, and when I look closer, I see the words *United States*—She closes her fingers around her thumb, blocking the ring entirely. With her other hand, she reaches into the pocket of her skirt and pulls out her phone. Her thumb moves swiftly across the screen as she types out a text, but she doesn't make a move to get out.

I strum my fingers on the steering wheel.

"You got somewhere you need to be?" she asks, not looking up.

"I'm good," I tell her, then swallow my nerves. "Listen, about yesterday…" I wait for her to say something, and when nothing comes, I continue, "I think we got off to a bad start. I shouldn't have snapped at you the way I did, and I guess I just wanted to apologize." *There.* I said it. And as soon as the words are out of my mouth, I feel the tension lift off of my shoulders.

"We all say things we don't mean," she mumbles, shrugging, and it's as genuine as the slight smile she offers me. A smile that has my stomach twisting. She adds, "That includes me. I shouldn't have said what I did, either."

I bite my lip, contain my grin, and take the apology one step further. "So… *friends?*"

She turns to me, and the corner of her lips lift just a tad. "I'd make a horrible friend."

I settle in my seat, my back against the door to give her my full attention. "To be honest, you could be the absolute worst friend in the world, and you'd still be the best one I have."

Her smile fades, concern dripping in her words. "But you have the team, right?"

My eyes widen in shock. *Busted.* Caught in a lie. "I thought you hadn't thought about me, not even for a second?" I tease.

"Just because I don't listen, it doesn't mean people don't talk," she rushes out, a blush forming on her cheeks. Shaking her head, she blinks hard. Once. Twice.

"Anyway," she says, scrambling for words. "You're a good-looking jock. You don't need friends when you can have girls."

"Wait." I sit up higher, my heart racing. "You think I'm good-looking?"

Those small hands of hers cover her entire face. "Jesus. That's not—I didn't mean—what I meant is that… I gotta go!"

CHAPTER 9
Ava

I PRACTICALLY RUN AWAY from Connor's car, past Trevor's truck with the *Knight Electrical* decal plastered on the side. When I enter the diner, I keep my head down but my eyes up, searching. I spot Trevor almost immediately, working on an old jukebox. Pressing my hands to my cheeks, I try to feel for any visible signs of the blush I'm positive I'm wearing. I could blame it on all the people I'm sure are staring, but it's not them. The *real* reason just drove away after letting me escape so I could yank the foot out of my mouth. *You're a good-looking jock...* God! What an idiot! Who even says that?

I kick the heel of Trevor's shoe when I get to him and wait the few seconds for him to pop his head out from behind the jukebox. His eyes widen when he sees me, and I tap my imaginary watch on my wrist. "Did you forget about me?"

"Shit, Ava. My bad. I got caught up."

I drop my bag and sit in the booth next to his tool bag. "It's cool. I just hitched a ride from some beefy dude with full-sleeve tats and a ferret named Roger."

Trevor rolls his eyes. "I'm guessing he had a blacked-out van?"

"Motorcycle actually. Cool guy."

He focuses on his work again. "Where was the ferret riding?"

"Shirt pocket. *Obviously.*"

Chuckling, he swaps one tool for another. "I'm almost done here. Grab a drink if you want."

"I'm good."

A few minutes later, Trevor's being handed a check by the diner owner, and we're on our way. Walking side by side toward his truck, he nudges my shoulder. "Guess what?"

"What?"

"We got the Preston job."

"Trevor!" I squeal, stopping in the middle of the sidewalk. "Are you serious? That's amazing!" I wrap my arms around him, my laughter unconfined. God, we needed this. Even without the extra money or job security, we *needed* this; a tiny ray of light to help clear the darkness.

He returns my embrace with the same enthusiasm, and when he releases me, he asks, "Honestly, though, how did you get here?"

"Some guy from school gave me a ride."

"Some guy?" he asks, eyebrow quirked.

I shrug, try to play it cool. "Apparently, I'm his new best friend."

◇◇◇◇◇

I haven't stopped smiling since Trevor delivered the news, and neither has he. "So, tell me everything!" I all but shout, moving around the kitchen like it's my job. Around us, music blares, filling our souls with a semblance of hope.

Tomorrow we'll go back to worrying, to eating ramen and potatoes. But tonight? We celebrate. Tonight, it's a three-course meal with all of Trevor's favorites. He deserves it every day, but we've never been in a position to splurge like we are now.

Trevor sits on the counter, his legs swinging as he licks the wooden spoon from the cake mix I've just made. "The contractor they used for all their electrical work retired, so they were after someone new. I applied, went in for the interview with Tom Preston, told him about our situation—"

"You used our sob story to land the job?"

His brow bunches. "I did what I had to do, Ava. This job gives us an iota of breathing room, and it's something we really need right now."

"Oh, I know," I assure. "I don't blame you. I would've done the same." Hell, I would've thrown in some waterworks if it guaranteed us the job. Everyone in town knows Tom Preston is a giant softy, especially when it comes to matters of family.

I shove the cake tin in the oven, slam the door, and turn to Trevor. He's wearing a shit-eating grin, and I think I know why. "So…" he sing-songs, rocking back and forth. "Who's the guy?"

I turn my back to him, pretend to be engrossed in the salad I'm spinning. "What guy?"

"What guy?" He repeats, mocking. "The guy who's got you in a daze since you walked into the diner."

"Pshh. What are you talking about?"

He points at me. "You think I don't know you, Ava…"

True. He knows me well. Too well. I throw a piece of lettuce at his head. He ducks it, of course, and doesn't bother with the cleanup.

"So?" he pushes.

"Trust me, there is no guy. And even if I were interested in someone, it's not like I could—"

"You could."

"Could what?"

"Date."

"No." I shake my head.

"Why not?"

"Because," I snap. And even though I know he's just teasing; I can't ignore the microscopic ball of disappointment settling at the pit of my stomach. "Because I'd be the world's flakiest girlfriend, that's why." And I can't help comparing myself to the type of girl Connor could easily attain. I mean, the guy's a god. And I don't know why I've never noticed him in that way before because his presence is pretty hard to ignore. Well over six foot, eyes so blue you'd mistake them for puddles. His hair, that unintentional blend of messy perfection, parted in ways that let you know he spends many seconds running his fingers through it. His body—God, it's a wonder the girls at school haven't devoured him to pieces and spat out his remains. And don't even get me started on his dimples. I didn't even know he had them until I was riding in his car. But I think the thing I'm most drawn to is the way the blood rushed to his cheeks and his eyes lit up when I mentioned he was good-looking. I mean, he has to know, right? If the mirror doesn't show him, then there are plenty of girls, and even guys, who would tell him, who would be more than happy to *prove* it to him.

When I saw the car in the lot, I put two and two together and assumed it was his. In a way, I was kind of hoping it was. I imagined what it would be like to sit with someone who (hopefully) knew nothing about me or my past or the moments that led me here. It felt like a blessing. Until I was sitting in that confined space with no way out, and I couldn't ignore the way his forearms looked beneath his rolled-up sleeves or the way his large hands wrapped around the wheel. And I definitely couldn't ignore the way his eyes drifted from the road, lower, lower, until they focused on my legs, and guh!

It's so pointless. Stupid, really.

"No, you wouldn't, Ava," Trevor says, hopping down from the counter, and I can feel his pity from across the room. "You'd make a great girlfriend because you're a great girl. You just—"

"I just what?" I interrupt. "I just need to find a few extra hours in the week, so I can make time to hang out, go on dates... no. It wouldn't work. And I don't *want* it to, so there's that."

Trevor watches me warily. One second. Two. Then he nods, slow, as if afraid to say anything else.

I make my way over to him and place my hands on his back, pushing him toward the living room. "Will you please go and relax. Let me do something for once."

He grabs a beer from the fridge before taking my instructions.

We eat dinner at the table—just Trevor and me—and we laugh, and we talk, and we go back to who we were *before*. Before the weight of uncertainty and responsibility crashed into us, wave after wave of hopelessness and desperation. We become people again, individualized by what little hopes and dreams we have for the future. And when we're washing up at the sink once we're done eating, I look outside, see the fireflies glowing like embers searching for freedom.

"They'll be gone soon," I murmur, motioning toward them. "They're so beautiful."

Trevor takes a moment, watching them with me. Then he settles his hand on my shoulder, presses his lips to my temple. "I'm glad she was here to see them this year, Ava. I'm glad we all were."

◇◇◇◇◇

Trevor's fallen asleep on the couch, hands on his chest as he breathes to a steady rhythm. But even with his eyes closed, muscles relaxed, his brow is bunched, as if his troubles never truly leave him. There are electrical plans scattered on the coffee table, his laptop sitting atop them. I go to close it but freeze when my gaze catches on the screen. There's a picture of his ex, Amy, with another guy's arms wrapped around her. She's smiling as if their heartbreak had no history. I look over at Trevor again, at the stress lines that mar his youthful face, and my chest tightens. Heat burns behind my eyes, my nose, and I cover my mouth, so my single sob doesn't wake him.

Amy had been his girl two weeks into college, and if I ever doubted that true love existed, I'd go to them. When my fourteen-year-old self questioned life, I'd go to them. Not just one or the other. But both of them. They were a team, a fortress, a love so strong I thought nothing could break them. But *I* did. *I* broke them. I still remember listening in on Trevor's call to her—he here and she in Texas—the way he struggled to get through his words without his voice cracking. "I can't come back," he'd told her. "And I can't hold *you* back because of it."

I sat in my room that night, tear after tear, cry after cry. Hopelessness swam through my veins, pulsed through my airways.

I see the empty bottles of beer on the floor, and I fight to keep it together, to contain my emotions. To *conquer* them. Tears stream down my cheeks, and I hold back my cries. But it's useless. I'm too far gone, and I wasn't built with the strength my mother holds. Trevor wakes, and he's quick to sit up. To notice my anguish. "Hey," he coos, his arms around me like a shield. A protector. Always. "Ava, it's okay. What happened?" I cry into his chest, tears of self-loathing soaking into his T-shirt. I can't speak; I can't say the words.

Remorse.

Regret.

Guilt.

He holds on to me—my *Knight*—and I try to remember why it was I called him. Why amid the darkest and most terrifying moment of my life, I couldn't fight my need for him, for anyone, just so I wouldn't have to go it alone. It had been a year since his father had walked out, a year of Trevor calling every other day to check in on me when he had no real reason to. And so when I look back on it—at the crimson life seeping into my hands, the way the liquid pooled on the glass layer of my phone, making it impossible to see—as if the tears weren't enough, as if the scene in front of me wasn't enough to force my eyes shut… I know I should've called 911.

But instead, I called Trevor. And I gave him no other choice but to come home and carry the burden of what should have been his father's. The difference is, Trevor stayed.

Because for Trevor, love is enough.

Love is everything.

He is the conqueror.

He is.

He is.

CHAPTER 10
Ava

In my desk drawer lives a check.

A check for six figures.

Signed by Peter Parker.

The sum is enough to put my mom in a treatment center full-time.

In my mind,

I wonder what it would be like not to have to worry as much as we do.

In my heart,

I try to imagine what it would feel like to *abandon* her like that.

The check is made out to me.

I can take care of you, Ava,

Peter said.

But it's our little secret.

I wonder why he didn't offer it to Trevor.

But in my heart,

I already know.

In my desk drawer lives a picture.

Me and Mom surrounded by fireflies.

When the world is at its darkest,

that's when the magic appears,

my mom says.

So, in my mind,

I question if the check is a form of magic.

But in my heart,

I believe that *hope* creates the magician.

CHAPTER 11
CONNOR

'D BEEN KILLING it during practice. Every shot, every play, every move of my feet had been perfect. I was back to the old me, or as the team saw it—a *new* me. And then *she* walked into the gym, and I forget who I am and why I'm here.

The girl is something else. Even beneath her school blazer, those knee-high socks and completely modest skirt, I could tell she was hiding things some girls go above and beyond to flaunt.

I'm staring.

"Ledger!" someone calls out a split second before a ball hits the side of my head, knocking what little sense I had right out of me.

I take a time-out and head for my water bottle.

Still staring.

Because I can't not.

"How's that going for ya?" Rhys asks, motioning to Ava as he slumps down

She's at the corner of the gym now, picking up a random backpack I didn't know was there. "Huh?"

"You got a little drool," he says, chuckling, and hands me a towel.

I wipe at my mouth because I'm too far gone.

Bending down to tie his laces, he says, "She told me you gave her a ride yesterday."

"She did?" So, she and Rhys are friends. *Noted*. I clear my throat, try not to sound too… inquisitive. "What—I mean, what else did she say about me?"

He all out laughs now, coming to a stand. Shaking his head, his gaze floats between Ava and me. His hand on my shoulder tells me *"You poor, pathetic little dude"* but his words—his words say, "She said you make her uncomfortable."

◇◇◇◇◇

The first class I ever had at this school was psychology. After doing everything I needed at the office to register, I was late. It was only a minute, but it was enough to make my already anxious mind go into overdrive. When I walked into the room, there was only one desk free, two chairs, and so I took what was offered. A few people watched me walk through the rows, but no one said a word. It was a relief. A few minutes after that, Ava walked in. Initially, I thought she might be new, too, but I didn't see her in the office and going by how the teacher spoke, I figured she was just late.

Now, I was walking toward that same room, and I wish I were late again. Or better yet, I wish the floor would swallow me whole. Unfortunately, I can't come up with an excuse or some form of sudden chronic illness that would excuse me from attending classes for the rest of the year, so I grab the door that someone holds open for me and make my way into the room.

She's here, in her seat, a textbook in front of her, staring into the abyss. You know, *Classic-Ava*. I walk painstakingly slow, but not slow enough because I still end up next to her. My chair drags as I pull it out, causing her to glance up, then right back down.

I clear my throat, and with my voice low, I ask, "Is it okay if I sit here?"

Her eyes lock on mine. Hold. She offers a smile filled with pity and laced with what I'm sure is disgust. "Of course," she murmurs. "Why wouldn't it be?"

"I don't know," I breathe out, taking the seat. "The last thing I want to do is make you *uncomfortable*."

A sound falls from her lips; a squeak of sorts. And she turns in her seat to the person behind us.

Rhys.

She shakes her head at him, her eyes wide.

Rhys laughs. *Fucker.*

And me? I spend the rest of the day in *Classic-Ava* mode.

CHAPTER 12
Ava

"**Y**OUR GRADES ARE FANTASTIC, Ava. Your GPA hasn't dropped once since you started here. There are a lot of colleges that would be lucky to have you," Miss Turner says, an assortment of catalogs spread out on her desk. "UNC, Duke, NC State. Given your circumstance, I assume you'd like to stay local?"

She's only half right. I do plan on staying local; I just don't plan on furthering my education—much to Trevor's dismay.

I don't tell her this, though. I simply nod, watch the minutes tick by. I don't want to be here a second longer than I have to. I want to get to first-period psychology early enough to get a few words in with Connor, if he'll even listen to me.

"Have you thought more about where you're going to apply?"

One minute until the warning bell.

"Everywhere, anywhere," I rush out.

"Well, that's great, Ava!" She beams. "I'm glad you're—"

"I have to go," I say, cutting her off. I stand quickly. "I have a thing I need to do."

◇◇◇◇◇

Connor's already in his seat when I walk in, his head on the desk, arms folded beneath it—a vision of hopelessness.

There's a sudden sinking in my gut. An ache so strong it has me frozen to my spot. Around me, students swarm, bumping into me with zero apologies. My feet drag when I make my way over to him. Standing beside him, I whisper, "Hey."

Tired, tormented eyes lock on mine. One second. Two. Then he goes back to his original position.

My heart drops.

"Take a seat, Ava," Mr. McCallister says, walking into the room. "Are you with us, Connor?"

Connor sits up, grumbles under his breath, "Unfortunately."

Mr. McCallister waits for the rest of the class to settle in, and when enough silence descends, he announces, "It's your lucky day, people. My laptop has decided to die, so you'll be working on your nature versus nurture assignment, and since it's such a lovely day out, I'm going to let you partner up and work wherever you like. Within reason, of course."

A flurry of excitement fills the room. Beside me, Connor groans. "Jesus. No."

Connor silently, reluctantly, agrees to follow me outside. With his backpack in one hand, a basketball in the other, his feet drag as he tracks behind me.

I take him to the school gym.

"Here?" he asks, moving to the center circle. "You want to work *here*?"

I shrug. "I figured it's where you're most comfortable."

Dropping his bag by his feet, his eyes take in the surroundings: from the championship flags strung off the ceiling to the retired jerseys hanging on the walls. I try to make small talk. "First game of the season's in a few weeks, right?"

He eyes me sideways, a rush of air falling from his lips. I watch the way his shirt shifts beneath the muscles of his broad chest, strong shoulders, and I look away, hoping he isn't witness to the heat forming on my ears, my cheeks, my entire damn body. "So, I think we should talk about—"

"The paper," he interjects.

"—what Rhys said," I finish.

He drops the ball, sweeps it up again, his bottom lip caught between his teeth. "So, this paper..." he says, deflecting. "I've taken some notes. Hopefully, it'll be enough to give us a starting point." After reaching into his bag, he pulls out a few sheets of paper and holds them out between us.

Okay.

So.

He obviously doesn't want to deal with what happened, and I'm clearly not going to get anywhere.

I step into the circle so I can take the notes, flipping through them without actually reading a word. My mind works in overdrive as I try to come up with a way to fix things for us, *for me*. I need a way to settle my guilt. "I was thinking," I start, needing a moment to catch my breath. It's as if we're in his car again. Close. Almost *too* close. And there's no one here but us. "I was thinking..." I repeat, coming up with a plan on the fly. It's a selfish plan, one that will help me find a way to gain his forgiveness. "We should maybe put our own spin on it."

"How?" he asks, and when I look up, I catch him watching me. He averts his gaze a moment later, focuses on the ball in his hand.

"I thought we could make it more personal? Have an actual test subject rather than resources we find online so it's not the same old, same old, you know?"

He bounces the ball. Again and again. Contemplating. "You have a subject in mind?"

"You."

His eyes widen. "Me?"

I nod.

"And what exactly would that entail?"

"You have to tell me about you. Genetics versus upbringing."

He takes a step back, shaking his head. Jaw tense, a fierceness flickers in his gaze, a wall dropping down between us. It's as instant as it is intense. He closes his eyes, slowly, his dark lashes fanning across his cheeks. By the time he opens them again, all emotions have been wiped. "I wouldn't be the best subject for this," he says, his voice flat. "We should use you."

"Hell no." A giant *Fuck No*. There's no way I'm willing to reveal the details of my life.

Not yet.

Not to him.

"Well, I'm out."

"But—"

"But nothing, Ava. We're not doing this," he says, his voice firm.

"But you need the grades, right? To play, I mean. This is the perfect—"

"I said no!" His voice echoes off the walls, and he cringes at the sound. Annoyance fills his every word. "Just leave it alone."

I shrink into myself. I hate being spoken to like this. Being yelled at. "Jesus, what's your deal?" I snap, combative. "I'm just trying to get to know you here, and you're—"

"I'm what?"

"You're fighting me."

"Fine!" he barks, frustrated, and looms over me. "I can't do what you're asking because I don't know shit about my mom." His voice cracks on the last words.

My breath catches on an inhale, my stomach giving out. I lower my gaze, wishing for a damn shovel to dig a hole that I could crawl into. I stumble through my speech. "I'm so sorry, Connor. Did she, umm… did she die or…?"

"No," he breathes out. His voice softer, calmer. "I mean, I don't know. She abandoned me when I was young."

I look up again. Right into his eyes already focused on mine. "As in, she left?"

His lips part, but nothing comes out. A sharp inhale. Steady exhale. His throat moves with his loud swallow, but he doesn't break eye contact. Finally, he speaks. "As in she drove us to the airport parking lot on a hundred-degree day in the middle of July, made sure I was buckled in nice and tight in my car seat, kissed me goodbye, and walked away. She walked away, and she never came back. So no, Ava, she didn't just 'leave me.' She fucking *abandoned* me."

CHAPTER 13
CONNOR

MY EARS FILL with the sound of the ball bouncing off the hardwood, the backboard, the rim. Again and again. Echo echo echo. My shoes scrape. Muscles in my arms, my legs, my heart burning. Sweat pools, drips down my face, but I can't stop. Won't stop. I push harder, further. It's the only way to get out of my head, to stop the memories from flooding in.

I remember looking down at my hands, at the sweat that pooled beneath the two toy cars I held on to. Lightning McQueen in my right. Sally in my left. I took them everywhere with me, even in my sleep. "You're my reason, Connor. Don't ever forget that," she said. She kissed my forehead, and I'd kept my gaze down, watching my three-year-old legs kicking back and forth.

I remember the heat.

The way the sun filtered through the open door, burning my flesh…

Right before she slammed the door shut between us.

No other words.

No warnings.

I watched her walk away, step by step until she disappeared between the rows of cars.

Minutes passed, and I started to worry.

She'd never left me before, not for that long.

I struggled to breathe.

It was so hot.

I kicked at the back of the front seat in frustration, dropping Lightning as I did.

I tried to reach for it, but my belt was on tight.

So tight.

So hot.

That's when the tears came.

I remember the way the belt cut into me when I kept reaching for the car, over and over.

I squirmed.

I screamed.

I remember how my tears felt on the palms of my hands. Warm and wet.

I remember the marks those tears left on the windows. Handprints dragged down in desperation.

I remember the pain in my chest, the ache in my throat from crying her name, over and over.

Mama! Mama! Mama!

I remember the heat.

God, I remember the heat.

Like a fire burning inside me.

I remember the thickness of the air in my throat.

The sweat in my eyes.

And I remember the exact moment my body started to shut down.

To give in.

Give up.

I remember the heaviness of my eyelids.

The weakness in my limbs.

The anguish.

The despair.

I remember those last moments.

The world as a blur.

Right before it was coated in darkness.

I'm in a daze when I come to, eyes wet and weary as I watch the ball bounce away from me and into Ava's arms. *Fuck.* I'd forgotten where I was, and worse? I'd forgotten who I was with.

I fold in on myself, exhausted, every muscle in my body screaming for reprieve.

But I'm not ready.

Not yet.

One hand on my knee to keep me upright, I extend the other. "Give me the ball, Ava."

"No."

I grind my teeth, irked beyond reason. "Not right now, okay?"

She shrugs. "Okay."

I stand taller. "So give me the damn ball."

She holds it behind her back. "Come and get it."

I'm in no fucking mood for these mind games. Shaking my head, my eyes on hers, I take several steps to close in on her. But as soon as I'm near, she throws the ball away, and the next thing I know, her arms are wrapped tightly around me, her nose to my chest. I feel the heat of her breath against me, the way my shirt stretches across my torso from the strength of her hold.

"I'm so sorry, Connor," she whispers, and everything inside me stills.

Breaks.

Shatters.

My inhale is shaky. My exhale the same. I close my eyes, take in the moment. Bask in it. If only for a second. "What's this for?" I ask.

She looks up at me, liquid sorrow coating her eyes. "It just looked like you needed it."

I reach up and palm the back of her head, hold her to me. Because of all the things I hoped could heal the memories of my past, the human touch and a single moment of compassion weren't it. Maybe it was because it was never offered to me before. Or maybe it's because it's coming from her.

When I feel her start to pull away, I bring her closer. Hold her tighter. Because her touch…

…her touch is like fire.

Only this time,

I don't mind the burn.

CHAPTER 14
CONNOR

DAD GREETS me at the door when I get home. It's been a solid two weeks since we've seen each other in more than just passing. By the time I'd get back from school, he'd be asleep, and by the time he'd leave for work, I'd be getting ready for bed. "Can I help you?" he asks, hand pressed to my chest to stop me from going inside.

"What?" Confusion clouds my mind.

"Do I know you? I mean, you *look* like my son, but it's been so long I can't be sure."

Chuckling, I swat his hand away and force my way inside. "Haha. You became a comedian overnight." I start for my room.

"I ordered pizza," he calls out after me.

"Can't wait."

In my room, I drop my bag and ball on the bed, dock my phone on the speakers and hit play on Kendrick Lamar. In my mind, I'm at Toyota Arena wearing number 13, James Harden, and I've just sunk a killer fadeaway against the Nets. In the real game, Harden walked away with one hand out pretending to hold a bowl, the other holding a utensil to mimic stirring the pot—his signature celebration. In my bedroom, I do the same while the imaginary crowd chants my name, *Led-ger! Led-ger! Led-ger!* I nod, hold my hand to my ear to encourage them. *Louder! Louder! Louder!* My eyes close, and I take in the moment, remember the feel of Ava's body against me. The way her eyes locked on mine. *Connor! Connor! Connor!*

A stupid grin sweeps my entire face.

"Connor!"

My eyes snap open. Dad's at my door, his hand on the knob. He eyes me sideways, looking from me, to my speakers, and back again. Shaking my head, I move to the speakers and switch off the music.

Dad says, "Pizza's here."

I walk past him and toward the kitchen.

"I take it you had a good day," he muses.

I shrug. "Same old." Then I ask, only slightly embarrassed, "How much did you see?"

"Enough to know you'll never be able to grow a beard as majestic as Harden's."

I rub my chin, and for a split second, I wonder if Ava likes beards. "I could grow a beard."

"So…" Dad says, settling in the chair opposite me.

I pick up a slice of pizza, take half of it in one bite. "So?" I mumble around a mouthful of food.

He throws a napkin toward me. "So, tell me everything. We haven't had a real conversation since school started. How are the classes?"

I swallow. "Good."

"And the team?"

"Also good."

"Welp. I'm glad we had this talk," he jokes, standing. He opens the fridge, eyeing the drink selection. I watch his every move, waiting for the right time to bring up what went down today. Besides the people who were there that day and my dad's parents, no one else knows what happened to me. Until Ava. I figure I should ease into it, so I say, "So, I met a girl…"

His shoulders tense. "Oh yeah?" he says, refusing to turn to me.

"Yeah," I edge. "She's uh… she's in my psych class. We're working on a paper together."

He moves again, and just when I think I can proceed, he asks, "Psych, huh? What's that like?"

I ignore his question, sit higher in my chair. "Her name's Ava."

"Right." He turns to me now, his eyes trained on the floor. "Just remember we need to keep focused on the end game, Connor."

Irritation fills the emptiness inside me. "*We?*"

"You," he sighs out. "I mean *you*."

Puffing out a breath, I slump in my chair, throw the napkin in the almost full pizza box. I'm frustrated. It's obvious. And the truth is, I've *tried* to understand why he's like this. Why he seems to have a distaste for *all* women. In all the years post-Mom, I've never known him to date, or even have a random hook-up. I guess, in a way, I get it. The one woman he loved enough to have his child left, abandoned not just me, but him, too. Only he wasn't there. What happened to me didn't happen to him. I'm the one who should have his level of hatred and distrust. Because in truth, as much as I hate to think about it, she only *left* him. But me? Me she wanted *dead*. And that's a hard fucking pill to swallow no matter how I try to spin it. I inhale deeply and swallow all those thoughts. Bury them deep inside me. Like always. "It doesn't matter," I say, mask back in place. "I'm pretty sure she's not interested in me."

Dad nods. "That's probably for the best."

"Yeah." I stand, done. "Thanks for the pizza… and the talk, I guess." I start to leave.

"Connor," he calls after me.

"It's fine."

◇◇◇◇◇

I knew going into this year that the schoolwork would be hard. I thought I was prepared. I was wrong. The workload is insane, which is okay for now, but once the season starts, I'll probably have to give up sleep. It's my only option. Most of my free nights I split between studying game tapes, memorizing plays, and doing homework. But tonight, I can't seem to focus on anything. Well, anything besides the girl who appears to have infiltrated my mind. I know it's wrong to be this infatuated, and I'm not one to be making moves on a girl. And *I won't,* I assure myself.

Unless…

Sitting at my desk, I reach into my bag and pull out the team folder. The first page has a list of numbers, including the coaching staff and all the players. My finger moves down the page until I find the one I want. I stare at the name, flip my phone in my hand. Then I stand. Pace. Convince myself that *surely* even James Harden had moments like these growing up.

I type out a text.

Connor: Hey.

Rhys: Who's this?

Connor: Connor.

Rhys: Hey man, what's up?

I stop pacing.

Start again.

Drop my phone on the bed.

Pick it up.

Suck it up.

Connor: Do you have Ava's number? I need to talk to her about the psych paper.

Seconds pass.

Then minutes.

Fricken *eons*.

When he finally responds, he has her number attached and the words:

Rhys: Remember: whatever she does, don't let it affect you. And whatever you do, don't fucking hurt her.

Connor: Thanks... I guess?

I go back to pacing. Preparing—*out loud*—the first message I'll send. "Hey... Hi, it's Connor... Hey, it's me, Connor... Yo... Yo, it's Connor from school..."

Dad opens my door without knocking, interrupting my absurdity. "You okay?"

"Yeah."

He taps on the door. "I'm heading out..." he trails off, the tension from earlier hanging between us.

"Okay."

⋄⋄⋄⋄⋄

Connor: Hey, it's Connor. From psych. I had an idea about the paper.

The swiftness of her response has my stomach flipping.

Ava: Hi Connor from psych :) What's your idea?

Connor: I think I've come up with a subject that might set us apart.

Ava: Go on.

Connor: Serial Killers.

Ava: Dude

Connor: No? Too much? Too dark?

Ava: It's fucking genius. I'm obsessed with true crime.

Connor: Me too! You should check out some podcasts. I listen to them on the way to and from school.

Ava: Shut up! Me too. Casefile is my favorite.

Connor: Mine too! The narrator…

Ava: So intense.

Connor: So good.

Ava: Lol

Connor: Cool.

Ava: Cool.

Connor: So.

Ava: So…

Connor: How are you?

Ava: Oh, you know, living the dream.

Connor: Money.

Ava: Money?

Connor: I don't know. I'm trying really hard to sound cool here.

Ava: lol. What are you doing?

Connor: Homework.

Ava: Want me to let you go?

Connor: Hell no.

Connor: Wait.

Connor: Are you busy?

Ava: Not at all. I was doing the same. Could use the break.

Connor: Yeah?

Ava: Yeah.

Connor: So.

Ava: So.

Connor: We're nailing this whole conversation thing.

Ava: I know, right? It's… dare I say… money.

Connor: Are you teasing me?

Ava: A little. Don't hate.

Connor: I couldn't if I tried.

Ava: Yeah? Because for a minute there, I'm pretty sure you did.

Connor: When?

Ava: The whole Rhys thing?

Connor: …

Ava: About how you make me uncomfortable…

Connor: Ohhhh! You mean *that* thing.

Ava: …

Connor: So what exactly did you mean by that?

Ava: You don't want to know.

Connor: I mean… I asked, right?

The three dots on the screen appear, disappear. Again and again. My anxiety builds. And builds. To the point of—

Ava: So these serial killers…

Shaking my head, I smile at her response.

Connor: What's your middle name, Ava?

Ava: I have two. Elizabeth Diana.

Connor: Like, the Royal family?

Ava: lol. Yes. My mom was a little obsessed. What about you, Connor? What's your middle name?

Connor: Jordan.

Ava: As in Michael? Lol. Did you have your whole life planned out before you were even born?

Connor: I'd love to say yes, but no. Just a fluke, I guess.

Ava: Got it.

Connor: Yep.

Ava: So…

Connor: So…

Ava: I should probably get back to this homework.

Connor: yeah, I should probably do the same.

Ava: See you at school?

Connor: Yep.

I drop my phone in my desk drawer, slam it shut. Keep it away from temptation. Because sending her useless, one-word texts is the second-best time I've had since I moved here. The best was when she was riding shotgun in my car.

I try to eat.

Try to study.

Try to sleep.

Nothing flies.

Hours pass, and I'm still wide awake, tossing and turning when my phone goes off in my drawer.

A text.

I stare in the general direction of it. It might be Dad, but he calls, not messages.

It goes off again.

And again.

Hope fills my chest—*please be Ava*—and I reach for it without getting out of bed.

Ava: Hey, I hope this doesn't wake you.

Ava: I've just been thinking about you… about what you told me today. And I have a question but feel free not to answer.

Ava: I was just curious. Do you remember any of it… what happened to you?

My response is swift. Easy to formulate. Because I give her the same answer I've given everyone before.

Connor: Not a damn thing.

CHAPTER 15
Ava

FOUR THIRTY A.M. comes around quick.

After a hurried shower, I check over the notes that Krystal, Mom's in-home caretaker, had provided. She's here Monday through Friday, from 7 a.m. until I get home from school. On the weekends, it's just Trevor and me. Or just me, most of the time. Trevor doesn't like to leave me alone with her so much, but he works, and now and then I force him to go out and live a normal twenty-two-year-old life.

We're so lucky he was able to pick up the family business when his dad left, and it only took him a couple of months to get certified. If he'd let me, I'd have dropped out of school and worked, too, but for him, that wasn't an option. For him, it was vital that we look further into my future than just tomorrow.

Breakfast is already on the table when Mom appears from her bedroom at 5 a.m. sharp. No alarm clock needed. Years in the military can do that. "Mornin'," she greets, kissing me on the cheek. She adjusts the hood of her robe to hide most of her battle scars as she takes a seat at the kitchen table.

"Morning, Mama. Did you sleep well?" I ask, even though I already know the answer. No screams in the night mean no flashbacks or memories of her real-life nightmares, and I'm grateful for that always, but last night especially because I couldn't sleep.

My mind was too inundated with thoughts of Connor.

And me.

Not Connor and me.

At least not like that.

But, I'd thought about him a lot, all day and night, and I kept replaying what he'd told me.

I wondered if everyone remembered traumatic experiences the way I do. Vivid and powerful and intense. As if I were reliving the moment again and again. Maybe he was too young. Or maybe he blocked it out completely. Sometimes I want to ask my mom if she remembers any of it, but I'm too afraid of her answer.

Sometimes, I'm afraid of *her*.

"I slept like a baby," she says, a slice of toast halfway to her mouth. She watches me watching her and places the bread back down. Using her one good arm, she scoots back in the chair and comes to a stand. "Ava?" she asks, her tone flat.

I swallow, apprehensive of her next move. She stops in front of me, her eyes shuffling between each of mine. "Ma?" I whisper.

Her head tilts.

I dig my heels into the floor, my muscles taut.

Ready.

Waiting.

Of all the injuries and affects her "accident" caused, the toughest ones to deal with are the ones no one sees. And while this entire town was running scared from her physical trauma, not one of them ever thought about the invisible scars. PTSD, reassimilation, agoraphobia, and short-term memory loss to name a few. Sometimes I worry that she'll wake up one day and have no idea who I am, that she'll forget about me altogether.

Mom smiles, a vision that has me exhaling with relief and warming me from the inside out. "You look so exhausted," she says, holding my face in her hand. "But you're still so damn beautiful, Ava."

Please, please don't ever forget me.

CONNOR

The sun is just beginning to rise when I finish my weekly six-mile run. Out of breath, I slow to a jog as I turn into my cul-de-sac and take in my surroundings. All the houses on the street are the same, but different in their own right. All in various levels of upkeep. Ours is at the end, one of the more *modest* ones on the block, a simple cottage style with a centered door, a window on each side, and a rotting porch Dad and I plan to fix sooner rather than later.

I spot Trevor's truck in front of his house, the *Knight Electrical* sticker on the side a giveaway. I should follow through on Dad's invitation to have him over for dinner, but when I check the time, it's too damn early to be knocking on doors. I go back to the house, shower, then sit on the couch with *Forensic Files* on in the background. An hour passes, and all I've done is read through my text conversation with Ava too many times to count.

Ava

One of the more apparent effects of Mom's injuries, besides the physical, is dysarthria. She's still wholly understandable, at least to me, but the trauma to her brain left her with a slight slur and slowed speech. The doctors said that her mind processes everything normally, but the signal from her brain to her mouth is just a little more… crooked.

Mom works on pronouncing the words on her flashcards Krystal had prepared while I start on the meal prep for the upcoming week. She's improved so much since we started the speech therapy, but I can tell how frustrating it is for her. Not only is she relearning a skill she attained while still in diapers, but she has to do it in front of *me*, and I think that's the hardest part for her. For her, being my mother was always the priority. Everything else came second—even the Marines. But for me, she'll always be the woman who held me through my first knee scrape, my first loss of friendship, my first heartbreak. She'll always be the one to teach and guide me with more patience than I deserve. The least I could do is be the same for her.

CONNOR

"Oh, my God, I'm so fucking bored," I whisper, throwing my ball in the air for the fiftieth time. On my back, in my bed, I blindly reach for my phone under the pillow.

Connor: Yo, are there any pick-up games I can walk in on?

It takes a good ten minutes for him to respond.

Rhys: Yeah, man. The team's got one going right now.

I balk at his response, read the text again and again.

Rhys: You want in?

Connor: The team?? Thanks for the invite.

Rhys: Want a spoon?

Connor: *What?*

Rhys: For your cry-about-it soup?

Connor: *Whatever*

Rhys: It was a joke. Seriously, you want in?
Connor: I'm good.

Ava

My phone vibrates in my pocket, and I'm quick to check it. I try to hide my smile when I see his name.

Connor: Jeffrey Dahmer, Ted Bundy, Richard Ramirez.

Ava: I'll take men I'd actually be caught *dead* with for two-hundred please, Alex.

Connor: Ah. So you're not just a pretty face. You got jokes, too.

My stupid heart does a stupid pitter-patter, and I bite down on my lip so my grin doesn't split my face in two.

Ava: You think I'm pretty?

Connor: Of course I do. But so would Ted Bundy so…

Ava: I think we change Richard Ramirez for Blanche Tyler Moore.

Connor: Who's that?

Ava: She was a serial killer in the early 1900s who met her victims via newspaper (aka text messages). She promised them love (told them they were good-looking), then when they came to see her (psych class paper), she'd poison them, chop them up into pieces and bury them on her farm. Then she'd take whatever life insurance and money they had.

Connor: Ha! Joke's on you! I have no money :(

I cover my mouth, stifle my laugh.

Ava: What are you doing on this fine day, Connor?

Connor: I have a multitude of dates.

Ava: Do you now?

Connor: Yep. First with my basketball, then with my laptop, and later, if I'm feeling frisky, with some leftover pizza. So, yeah. Not much. You?

Ava: About the same.

Connor: You play basketball?

Ava: Not even close. I can throw a mean spiral, though.

Connor: You're into football?

Ava: It's a family thing. I don't have a choice.

Connor: Right.

"You got that list for me?" Trevor asks, hand out waiting.

Dropping my phone, I quickly fish the list from my pocket and hand it to him.

"What's with your face?"

I touch my cheeks with the back of my hand. *Fire.*

Trevor smirks. "Are you texting *some guy from school*?"

"What guy from school?" Mom asks from her spot on the couch.

I look out the window. "It's such a beautiful day outside…" I deflect, even though it's true. The sun's out, leaves are starting to turn orange. If only I could leave…

"This guy who—" Trevor starts.

But I interrupt, "Don't skimp on my chocolate. I've got cramps."

"Dammit, Ava, I don't need to know this shit," he grunts, recoiling away from me as if he'll catch The Menstruation.

"It's such a heavy flow!" I yell after him.

He slams the front door shut.

I laugh harder.

Mom says, "Don't you think that boy goes through enough?"

I shrug. "I have to get my kicks where I can." Then I turn to her, my smile fading. "You think you might want to try wearing your prosthetic today? Just for a little bit?"

"Not today, Ava."

"But Krystal—"

"No." She turns away from me, her facial scars in full view. "We've been through this before—"

"But—"

"But *nothing*. It's not growing back, so there's no point in pretending like something's there when it's not!" She's quick to stand and march to her room. Before kicking the door shut, she mumbles, "I have one good arm; it's all I need."

CONNOR

Of all the things my dad and I are, handymen are not it. I searched the entire house and garage for a measuring tape and came up empty-handed. Now I'm on the porch measuring the fucker with a 12-inch ruler. A bunch of kids rides past on their bikes, no older than ten, and I watch them, feeling a pang of childish jealousy. They dump their bikes and start throwing a football around. I check for Trevor's truck, but it's not there. When I'm done with the measuring, I head back inside, get on YouTube and spend the next hour watching old men build porches from scratch. I thought we'd just have to replace the top; turns out, it could be the foundation, which means getting under there. With a grunt, I get my ass back up and out but freeze when I see the kids messing with Trevor's house. Rolls of toilet paper in each of their hands, they make quick work of stringing that shit all over the front chain-link fence, giggling maniacally at their masterpiece.

"Hey!" I shout, at the same time Trevor's truck pulls up to the curb, brakes screeching.

He hops out. "Get the hell out of here!" he yells, chasing after them at a speed much slower than I know he's capable of.

The boys bolt to their bikes, cursing, and I take the steps down to meet him on the sidewalk.

"What the hell was that about?" I ask, helping him remove the toilet paper.

Trevor shakes his head. "Just dumb kids being kids," he murmurs, pulling on a longer piece. I watch his face, the tension in his jaw, the frustration in his brows. "What's been going on? How are you settling in at St. Luke's?"

"As well as can be expected." I hand him all the trash I've collected. "You know anywhere good to eat around here?"

"Yeah." He balls up all the toilet paper with both hands. "Best place on a Saturday is the sports park. They have a bunch of food trucks. Take your pick."

"Sports park?"

"Yeah, there are batting cages, basketball courts, sometimes they put up the rock-climbing thing. It's pretty cool. You should check it out."

Nodding, I push away my awkwardness and ask, "You want to come with?"

His eyes widen, and he offers a crooked grin. "Yeah?"

I shrug. "On me."

Pointing to his truck, he says, "Let me just bring in the groceries." He hands me the toilet paper. "Take care of that for me?"

"Got it."

He gets a few bags from his truck while I get rid of the trash.

When I get back to the sidewalk, I notice a note stuck on his mailbox, no doubt put there by the same kids—*Insane Asylum*. I look at the house again. The blinds are open, but the sheer curtains stop me from seeing much else.

When Trevor comes out, he notices what I'm looking at and rips it off before pocketing it.

"What's that about?" I ask.

"Like I said, dumb kids…"

The sports park is insane, and I've dubbed it my new playground. And Trevor? He's a cool dude. I would even consider him a friend. I learned that he lives with his stepmom and sister and that he used to play college football but blew out his knee and gave up on it. I also learned (the hard way) that Trevor is a natural-born athlete. Put a ball or a bat in his hand, and it's like he was specifically built for it. He even gave me a hard time on the court, almost put me to shame until I realized I was taking it a lot more casually than he was. I amped up my game, gave it a hundred, and he assured me I'd have no problems getting into a D1 school, giving me the confidence I'd been struggling to find.

By the time I drive us back home, the sun's already beginning to set. I would have stayed longer if Trevor didn't have to get back. Hell, I would've stayed all damn night. "Thanks for hanging out," I tell him, standing on the sidewalk. "It hasn't been the easiest making friends, you know?"

He settles with his back against his fence, his hands in his pockets. "It'll get better. You're a good kid with a good head on you." He glances toward his house. "Right now, your team probably sees you as a threat because you're good, Connor. Like, *really* good. And people… people fear what they don't know."

Ava

Ava: Sleeping?
Connor: It's, like, 9:30. Lol
Ava: Hey, I don't know. Maybe playing with your balls all day got you tired.
Connor: Dirty girl.
Connor: I like it.
Connor: What's up?
Ava: Nothing, just researching these serial killers. It's a little depressing.
Connor: I know. I had to stop after a while, too. It's kind of messed up that we're so intrigued by it all.
Ava: Because people fear what they don't know.
Connor: You're the second person to tell me that today.

Ava: Really? Strange. But I think that's why it's so intriguing, right? The more we know, the less afraid we are of it all.

Connor: That makes sense. No wonder you're taking this class.

Ava: Why are you?

Connor: Not gonna lie, I thought it would be easy. Why are you taking it?

Ava: I think it might be something I'll want to get into more when I'm older. Not necessarily a career, but… I don't know. It would be nice if I could help turn someone's bad day into just a bad moment.

Connor: That's… that's a really great way to look at things, Ava. For real.

Ava: Also because the human mind intrigues me. Makes me curious…

Connor: Uh oh. Why do I feel like those ellipses are a segue to something else… about me?

Ava: Because they might be…

My eyes widen when Connor's name flashes on the screen. I clear my throat, sit up in bed. "Hello?"

"I figured it was easier to talk than text." His voice… I never really paid attention to it before, but now that I hear it, and it's all that I hear… holy shit. Deep and smooth and so intense… he could easily host a podcast, and I'd listen to it regardless of the topic.

"Ava? You there?"

"Yeah." I swallow. "Yeah, I'm here."

The speaker distorts with his light chuckle. "So what's up? What about me has your curiosity piqued?"

I pick at the blanket covering my thighs and stare at the wall opposite me, trying to find the courage, the words… "It's about what happened to you."

A loud sigh from his end. "Yeah, I figured. I mean, *I hoped* it wasn't that, but here we are."

"Do you not like talking about it?" I ask.

"It's not that I don't *like* it, so much as… it's not really something I've shared with anyone besides professionals, you know?"

"Wait. I'm the first real person you've told?"

"Well, yeah. I guess."

"But why—"

"I don't know, Ava," he says through an exhale. "It just kind of came out in frustration."

"Because I pushed you?"

"A little."

"I'm sorry."

"It's okay."

Moments pass, neither of us saying a word. I listen to him breathe, and I wonder if he's doing the same.

Finally, he says, "I don't know what happened to her if that's what you're wondering."

It was *exactly* what I was wondering.

He adds, "There was no evidence she got on a plane, at least under her name. And there's been no evidence of her existence since."

"Do you—" I start, my voice cracking with emotion. "Do you remember when you stopped looking for her?"

"It happened when I was three. The last time my dad ever mentioned anything about it, I was in third grade. That was probably when we stopped looking. But looking and *hoping* are two very different things."

I want to ask him when he stopped hoping, but I'm almost afraid of the answer. I get through each day searching for hope, so the idea of losing it the way he has…

"Connor?" I whisper.

"Yeah?"

"I just wanted to tell you that I'm sorry."

"For what?"

"For so many things. But mainly… I'm sorry about what happened to you. About *how* it happened, and what that must've felt like. I think, as kids, all we truly need are our parents, and your mom—I think I feel the sorriest for your mom… because she missed out on you."

CHAPTER 16
Ava

"**W**HERE THE HELL IS MY WALLET?**"** Trevor's walking around the house as if we have all the time in the world.

"Did you check your pants pocket from the last time you remember having it?" Krystal offers.

"I don't even know when I had it last!" he grumbles.

I put my hand on the doorknob, twist. "Hurry up!"

"Ava," Mom scolds. "Give him a minute."

Trevor walks out of his room with three different pairs of pants, patting down each pocket.

"I'm going to be so late," I mumble.

Now Trevor's looking behind the TV because *of course* it's going to be there. "Why do you have to get to school so early, anyway?"

"Because *someone*," I say glaring at him, "made me see the school shrink,"

"Ava," Krystal admonishes. "We don't use that term."

"Sorry." I lower my gaze, my voice. "I didn't mean that."

"Where the hell is it!" Trevor utters.

"I'll be outside," I announce to whoever is listening. I open the door.

Freeze.

On my doorstep is Connor, one hand raised, ready to knock.

"Connor?" I shriek.

"Ava?" He looks as confused as I feel.

"What—" My voice is too high, too loud. My pulse thumps wildly, beating on my eardrums. I try again. "What are you doing here?"

Trevor shoves me to the side.

Connor lifts Trevor's wallet, but his eyes are glued to me.

"Thank you," Trevor says, relieved as he grabs for it. "I've been looking all morning."

"You left it in my car," Connor tells him. To me, he asks, "What are *you* doing here?"

I say, "I live here."

Trevor laughs. "I'd introduce you both, but it seems like you've already met."

"Wait," replies Connor, his feet planted on our porch. "You *live* here?"

Now Trevor's pushing me out the door as if he's the one in a rush. I stop inches short of slamming into Connor, while Trevor shuts the door behind him.

I'm practically sniffing Connor's shirt; I'm *that* close to him.

"I told you I lived with my sister," Trevor says, moving past us and down the porch steps.

I ask, "How do you know each other?"

Trevor answers, "I told you about him, no? He just moved in next door."

He told me we had new neighbors. He didn't mention him by name or give *any* other information.

"Your *sister*?" Connor asks, confusion evident in his tone. "But you're…" he trails off.

Trevor quirks an eyebrow, holding back a smile before saying, "Black?"

Connor's cheeks flush red.

"Stepsister," Trevor and I respond at the same time.

"Oh."

We all three make our way down the driveway.

"Hey," Trevor says, turning back to us. "Do me a favor? Drive her to school? I might be able to grab a decent breakfast before work."

"Sure," says Connor.

I reply, trying to get out of it, "No, wait." Because the last time I was in the confines of Connor's car I almost lost all my senses. "His car…" I get stuck for words and idiotically come up with: "His car *smells*…" But it comes out a question, and I wish I could rewind time, or I don't know, disappear into thin air.

"My car does *not* smell," Connor says defensively.

"I'm sorry, I don't know why I said that," I admit. "It doesn't."

Trevor's eyes narrow. "How do you know what his car smells like?" Then his face lights up with a stupid shit-eating grin. "Wait, is Connor *the* Some Guy From School?"

"Trevor!" I screech. "Shut. Up!"

Trevor laughs, his head thrown back as he opens the door of his truck. "Go easy on her," he tells Connor. "She's on her period. Apparently, it's a heavy flow."

I die.

Right there.

On my driveway.

Dead.

◇◇◇◇◇

The first thing Connor does when we get into his car is reach for his gym bag in the back and spray deodorant *everywhere*. I die my second death of embarrassment and cover my face with my hands. "Sorry. Your car doesn't smell!" I laugh out.

"Uh huh. Sure," he responds. He's smiling, though, eyeing me sideways as he starts the car. Then he coughs, waves a hand in front of his face, the deodorant getting to him. He winds down the window. I try to do the same. "Yours doesn't work," he says, clearly proud of himself. He sprays the can directly on me.

"Connor!" I squeal.

He does it again. "Sucks to be you."

Another spray.

I attempt to shield myself, but it's useless. "I said I was sorry!"

His chuckle reverberates throughout my entire body. "Okay," he says, dropping the can on his lap. He offers me his pinky, giving me the same deep-dimpled smile that had me losing my mind the first time I saw it. "Truce?"

"Truce," I respond, linking my finger with his. His touch is warm, soft. I'm almost tempted to take his entire hand and hold it in mine. But that... that would be crazy. Right? Right.

We stop at a red light, and he turns to me. "I researched that Blanch Tyler what's-her-face."

"Moore."

"Yeah, her. Man, she's..."

"My hero."

"Your *hero*?" he asks, incredulous.

"I don't know. There's something about having that level of control over men that makes me..."

"Insane?" he finishes, his back pressed against the door, as if afraid of me.

His reaction makes me giggle.

And the spray of deodorant makes me stop. "You called a truce!"

The light turns green, and we're moving again. "I value my life more than a truce," he murmurs, and resprays me.

I reach across the car to grab his forearm, but he's too strong, and he damn well knows it. "Give me that stupid thing!"

"Ava, you're going to make me veer off the fucking road," he laughs.

"No, *you* are. Give it!" I can't stop laughing.

"Fine," he says, handing it over.

I throw it out his open window.

He hits the brakes so fast my seatbelt catches. Then he turns to me with a seriousness that has me clamping my lips together to stop from busting out a cackle. "That's littering, Miss Diaz." He motions his head outside. "Off you go."

He has a point. I roll my eyes but open the door. There are no other cars on the road, thank God, and so I quickly find the can, pick it up, and start back for his car, gripping the can tight. No way I'm letting him have it again. I place my hand on the handle, but the car moves forward a few feet. "Are you serious?" I yell, jogging forward to keep up. I reach for the handle again. He drives off again. This time farther. "Connor!" I can hear him laughing, see him eyeing me in the rearview. This happens three more times, his laughter getting louder, and mine becoming more uncontrollable. It's been years, *years* since I've felt this way. Laughed this hard. Felt this free.

I don't bother moving when he does it again. Instead, I stand still, my hands on my hips, my foot tapping. "I don't mind walking," I shout. A lie. Fuck walking. I'd sooner call Trevor to pick me up.

The car roars to life, and just when I think he's going to bail, I see him reach across the car to open the door for me. "Truce," he yells.

"Your truces mean nothing!" I shout back.

"Triple truce!" he counters.

I walk toward the car slowly, anticipating his next move. When I get to the open door, I see him watching me, his head dipped, his bottom lip between his teeth. I gracelessly sit and quickly shut the door, deodorant still in my hand.

"You're an asshole," I say playfully, spraying him with his chosen weapon.

He chuckles, starts driving again. "What can I say? I like to watch you run."

⋄⋄⋄⋄⋄

It turns out Connor comes to school this time on Mondays because he has a short practice. I tell him the truth about why I do, to see Miss Turner. He simply nods. When I ask if he's curious as to *why* I was seeing her, he shrugs, says, "I mean, it's pretty obvious you're a sociopath."

I spray his entire body.

He laughs it off, cranks his window up, and breathes it in as if it's fresh air.

If anyone's a sociopath here, it's him.

◇◇◇◇◇

Connor and I walk together to Miss Turner's office, as it's on the way to the gym. "Thanks for the ride," I say, my hand on the doorknob. I twist. Push. Nothing happens. Connor laughs, peels off a note stuck on the office window.

Miss Turner is ill. No sessions today.

"Seriously?" I groan, slamming my open hand on the door. And because I'm an idiot, I try the door again, my forehead touching the timber. "Doesn't she know about texts or emails?"

Connor says, sticking the note back up, "Yeah, you sure seem like you could've used that extra hour to sleep in, *cranky*."

I narrow my eyes at him, backhand his brick wall of a stomach. "Go to your stupid practice."

He feigns hurt, only for a second, before asking, "What are you going to do?"

"Sit in the stands and shout *boo* every time the ball comes near you."

Laughing, he says, "Why are you so mean to me?"

I hasten my steps to keep up with him. "Defense mechanism."

"For what?" he asks.

To stop me from falling for you, stupid.

I shrug. "I don't know."

CONNOR

Ava comes through on her word. She sits front row center, in the gym stands. And as promised, the second a ball is in my hand, she shouts, "Boo!" Which garners looks from the other players, coaches, and the few spectators crazy enough to watch a half-hour practice session first thing Monday morning.

I shake my head at her, but she simply raises her eyebrows, a smirk on her lips, lips I'd love to—

"Ledger!" Coach Sykes yells. "This isn't a teen soap opera. Get to work."

"Boo, Ledger!" Ava shouts, and now she's laughing, silently, but I know it's there because I can see her shoulders shaking with the force of it. I'm too busy watching her that I don't even notice Coach Sykes approaching me until the ball slams against my chest.

Ava laughs harder.

"You get one," I tell her and decide that if she's here to watch me, then I may as well give her a show.

The practice is nothing more than basic drills. But when the coach asks for suicides, I'm the first on the line. When he wants to work on ball handling, I'm using two balls, behind the back, reverse, between the knees, ankle breakers. When he asks for lay-ups, I'm power dunking—one after another.

"Damn, Ledger! Where the fuck have you been hiding?" Rhys shouts.

"Quit showing off!" Mitch yells. "We get it; you're good."

"He's better than good," Coach Sykes retorts. "In fact, every practice I want you all to come in with the same amount of power and precision that Ledger has! Got it?"

I throw Ava a smirk.

She gives me the finger.

◇◇◇◇◇

Psychology may be my favorite subject in the history of forever. Scratch that. *Ava* is my favorite subject. Sitting side by side in class waiting for the teacher to arrive, she asks me questions:

Where am I from?

Why did I move here?

Who do I live with?

What's my favorite murder?

I answer each one with truth, minus the murder one because I don't even know *how* to answer it. Mitch walks past us, sniffing the air. "What the hell is that smell?"

We burst out in childish giggles. She says to me, "You were not *at all* impressive this morning. I just want you to know that in case you think otherwise. In fact, you pretty much sucked."

Mr. McCallister enters the classroom saying, "You may spend the first ten minutes of class discussing your partner paper. Use that time wisely."

Ava and I turn to each other at the same time, our knees knocking painfully. Ava groans, reaching for her knee, but I beat her to it, grimacing. I rub at the spot I think I hit, while we both apologize. Dipping my head closer to hers, I whisper, "So I worked on the outline like we said."

She moves closer again. So close I can feel the heat of her cheek on mine. "Why are we whispering?"

"Because I don't want anyone to hear our plan and steal it."

"Got it."

"Hey, Coach said you have to be at every game from now on. Says you're my lucky charm."

Ava pulls back to look at my face, then rolls her eyes. She says, her voice still low, "You're going to need it if you don't take your hand off my leg."

It's not as if I'd forgotten it was there. I was just hoping *she* wouldn't notice. Or if she did, maybe she wouldn't mind. With a confidence only she brings out of me, I squeeze her knee, tell her, "I'm just trying to give you an *actual* reason."

"For what?"

"To say I make you uncomfortable."

"Oh, I've come to terms with the fact that you're a creep."

"Oh yeah?" I laugh.

She nods, brings her head closer again, our faces almost touching.

I ask, "You want creepy?"

"Oh, no," she backpedals.

If she wants to play, I'm here for it. "Your eyes are possibly the prettiest things I've ever seen." And it's the truth. Whenever I picture her in my mind, her eyes are the first things I see.

I hear her swallow, loud, and I know she's feeling *something*. When she pulls away, her eyes search mine, her cheeks flushed. My heart is racing, my mind spinning. Because never in my life have I wanted a girl more than I want her. And not even in the physical sense. But just talking to her or being around her. To feel *this* all day, every day. It feels like my soul's on fire, and she's holding the match. "Yeah?" she starts, a threatening lilt to her tone. She opens her mouth. Closes it. Opens it again. Finally, she stutters, "Well... well, your smile could melt panties." The second the words are out of her mouth, her eyes widen, and she covers her face. I think she mumbles, "Too far, Ava. Too fucking far." But I can't be sure.

I finally remove my hand from her knee so that I can tug at her wrists and uncover her face. And then I smile my—and I quote—panty-melting smile, just for her.

She shoves my face away with her entire palm. "Stop."

"Psst!" Rhys hisses from behind us.

We both turn to him.

He says, "Quit eye-fucking each other. It's making *me* uncomfortable."

I rip off a sheet of paper from my notebook and draw a large spoon, then hand it to him, my smile widening. "For your cry-about-it soup."

CHAPTER 17
CONNOR

"So, how's school?" Dad asks.

"Good."

"And the team?"

"Also, good."

Dad looks up from his meal and drops his knife and fork on the plate. "I feel like we have this same conversation every day."

"Because we do," I murmur. "But I don't know what else to tell you."

"Well, I don't know, Connor," he says, running his hands through his hair. "Why don't we talk about something else then? I feel like… I don't know. Ever since we moved here, we've become so disconnected."

Shrugging, I take a sip of my soda. "Remember that girl I told you about?"

Dad inhales, long and slow, and I already know what's coming next. "Don't let a girl distract you from—"

I rub at my eyes, frustrated, cutting him off.

"Connor, this is serious," he says.

"I know, Dad. I *know* how serious this is. I'm the one who feels the pressure of it," I rush out, then take a calming breath and regroup my thoughts. "But you want to sit here and have a non-mundane conversation with me; this is what I want to talk about. This is what's happening in my life right now. This is what I *want* to tell my dad. I'm seventeen, and I'm interested in a girl. And I'm allowed to be. But my wanting to spend time with someone doesn't take away from my other priorities. I know how important *the end game* is. For both of us."

Dad's silent a moment, his heavy breaths filling the small room. Finally, he nods, his eyes locked on mine. "You're right," he sighs out.

And I exhale, relieved.

"You're absolutely right, Connor, and I'm sorry I haven't been what you needed me to be." The corner of his lips lift. "So, this girl… her name?"

"Ava."

He smiles. "That's a pretty name."

I relax in my seat, let the words flow through me. "She's a pretty girl."

"I bet. Does she go to your school?"

"Yeah. Well, we met at school."

"Psych paper, right?"

I nod, shocked that he remembers. "Turns out she lives next door."

"No way!" he says, his enthusiasm genuine. "So, have you been hanging out outside of school?"

"Not really, I mean not yet. But she's a cool girl. Remember that Trevor guy who helped me move in all the furniture?"

"Of course, yeah."

"She's his stepsister."

"Ah, I see." Then his face falls as if his mind suddenly became consumed by something else.

"Dad?"

"Which uh… which house? I mean, which side does she live on?"

I point in the general direction of Ava's house.

"I see," Dad mumbles, his gaze distant.

"What just happened right now?" I ask.

He gets up, picking up his half-eaten meal. "What do you mean?"

"It's like something triggered you about her house. What… what do you know?"

Dad empties his plate in the trash, then dumps it in the sink. With his hands gripped to the edge of the counter, facing away from me, he says, "I've just heard things…"

"What things?"

He huffs out a breath but stays quiet.

"What *things*, Dad?"

He turns to me now, his arms crossed as he leans against the counter. "It's not something I'd normally mention, but if you like this girl as much as you say you do, it's probably important you know—"

"Dad, just spit it out already."

His lips part, but no words form, and he's looking everywhere but at me.

I push my plate away.

Dad rubs the back of his neck.

The clock tick, tick, ticks, the only sound in the room.

"Look," he starts, crossing his ankles. "When I told Tony—"

"The guy you ride with?"

Dad nods. "When I told him where we moved to, he mentioned the house next door. Apparently, there was an incident a while back with the mother there. I don't know if it's your friend's mom or—"

"What *incident*?"

"She's a war veteran, the mom, and I guess she got injured in Afghanistan. A grenade went off too close, and she lost an arm and part of her face."

"Jesus Christ," I whisper, my thoughts racing—every one of them on Ava.

"When she got home, things were pretty bad for her. People around here—

they're not used to seeing someone in that state. Anyway—and I'm only going by what he told me…"

I'm all ears now.

All in.

Dad takes a breath. And then another. Preparing. "Apparently, she went into a store one day, and maybe she overheard a couple of guys talking about her… no one really knows. But she lost it. Completely. She went through the aisles knocking products off the shelf, screaming and yelling and threatening people with whatever weapons she could find. They say she was inebriated because she was unintelligible, slurring her words and whatnot, but Tony thinks it might be a side effect of some form of head trauma from her injuries."

I press my palms against my forehead, waiting for the pounding to stop.

"The kids around here call her the town drunk or the loony lady…"

I stand, my fists balled, and recall those punk kids messing with their house. *Insane Asylum.*

Dad adds, "They even call her two-face."

"Enough." I'm angry, furious, but beyond that, I'm fucking devastated. I picture Ava smiling, hear her laughing, and I wonder how the hell it's possible she still manages to do any of that when her life… I don't even know anything about her.

"There's more, Connor," Dad says, but I'm done listening.

"*I don't…*" I don't want to know.

"Look, I just think it's important for you to know everything before you get involved with someone like her."

"*Someone like her?*" I spit. "What the hell is that supposed to mean?"

"It means that if you take things further with her, it can and will get complicated. There's so much more I haven't even told—"

"With all due respect, *if* we decide to take things further, that's *our* decision. And if there's more to the story, I'd rather hear it from Ava."

CHAPTER 18
Ava

Connor: Where the hell do you hide every lunch break?

CHEWING MY LIP, I contain my smile and think twice about letting him know. For a while now, I've been coming to the same spot, living in isolation. I've enjoyed it, so I thought. But I enjoy Connor's company more. I reply with a picture of what's in front of me, set my phone down, and wait.

It only takes a couple of minutes for him to appear, long legs on the bright green grass of the football field. His eyes keep shifting from his phone to the field, again and again, no doubt looking for exactly where I might be.

He spots me within seconds and strides up the steps, taking them two at a time. He sits on the bench in front of me, legs bent, feet next to mine.

I point to the ball under his arm. "You take that with you everywhere?"

He shrugs. "Habit. I sleep with one, too."

"No, you don't," I chide.

Another shrug. "I get lonely at night."

He dribbles the ball next to his knee, higher, lower, again and again. But he doesn't speak, doesn't even look at me.

"What's with you?" I ask.

He doesn't skip a beat. "What do you mean?"

I grab the ball, hold it behind my back. "Is everything okay?"

"Mmm-hmm." He holds out his hand, asking for the ball, but I shake my head.

"Your words say mmm-hmm, but your face says something's going on."

He smiles, but it's fake. "You know my *faces*?"

"I watch you through your bedroom window. I see you more than you know."

A forced chuckle from him to accompany his flat words. "My bedroom's on the opposite side of your house."

"Who says I watch you from my house? I'm standing outside your window," I say, my attempt at a joke that doesn't seem to fly.

"And you say I'm the creep?"

It's our usual back-and-forth, but the tone is off. Even if I couldn't see it in the dullness of his eyes, I can feel it in my heart. "Connor, what's going on?"

He runs his fingers through his hair, then tugs at the end. "I just…" He peeks up at me through his long, dark lashes, his bottom lip caught between his teeth. "I was telling my dad about you last night…"

Said in any other context, I'd be surprised and maybe a little flattered, but here? Now? I just feel… like something horrible is about to happen. "What did he say?" I croak.

He waits a beat, his words unsure. "He told me about your mom or stepmom…"

I nod, already knowing the fate of the conversation. "*My* mom," I tell him, heat burning behind my eyes. "What did he say about her?"

"Nothing bad," he assures. "He just told me what he heard from a guy at his work. And it's not like gossip or anything. When Dad told him where we lived, he mentioned—"

"The guy warned him about her?"

"No," he's quick to say, sitting higher. "Ava, it's not like that."

I look away, afraid he'll see the tears threatening to fall. I just wanted a friend, and I thought I found that in Connor. But I *knew*, as much as I tried to ignore it, I knew he'd find out eventually, and knowing the truth would take him away from me. I push down the lump in my throat. "What did he tell you exactly?"

Connor sighs. "He told me about the incident at the store, about how she… she…"

"Yeah, I'm aware of what happened," I murmur. I remember getting the call at school and rushing to the store to get to her. I remember the stares, the whispers as I walked by the witnesses. By the time I saw her, the cops had her detained in the storeroom. She was crying, belligerent and afraid, and then William appeared, and I could see it in his eyes: he'd lost the fight to fake it. He was gone soon after that incident. And I was left to pick up the pieces. I try hard not to blink, not to let the liquid heat fall from my eyes, but I fail. A single tear rolls down my cheek, and I swipe it with the back of my hand.

"Ava," Connor sighs, and I can feel the breath of sympathy and guilt filling the space between us. I imagine my life two weeks from now, when he starts to make excuses for not returning texts, or not sitting next to me, or not acknowledging my existence at all.

I already miss him, and he's sitting right in front of me.

It's my fault, I tell myself. It was stupid of me to get attached. To crave him when he wasn't around.

"Is it true?" he asks.

I nod. "Whatever you heard, it's all true." I don't bother asking what was said or how he feels. None of it matters. I flick the ring around my thumb, over and over. I say, my heartbreak falling from my closed lids, "You know the court ordered her to be on twenty-four hour supervision after that day, so she has a caregiver while I'm at school, and I have to be there all the other times, so it's not really a big deal that, you know… that you can't—or don't *want* to—be friends anymore. It's probably better that—"

"Wait," he interrupts. "Is that what you think this is about?"

"What else can come of this, Connor?"

He gets up to sit next to me and pulls my chin toward him. I resist, not wanting him to see my complete devastation. He lets me go but moves closer until his arm is touching mine.

I face the field.

He does the same.

"I'd like to meet her," he says, and my heart stills.

My entire body turns to him. "Why?"

He replies, his eyes holding mine, "Because regardless of what you think of me, or how you think I'd react, I'd still like to get to know you more, and I feel like she's a big part of who you are."

I wipe at my cheeks again, feel the wetness soak my palms. My exhale is shaky while I wait for all the broken parts of me to calm, still cracked, but settle. "I don't think that's a good idea."

"Oh," he says, looking away.

He's taken it as a rejection, so I try to explain, "She doesn't really remember it, what happened that day. She has problems with memory loss, but I think she's aware that *something* happened, because afterward, whenever she'd go out, people would treat her differently. Worse than they did before. It wasn't bad enough that she was ashamed of the way she looked, and the things people said about her and the names they called her…"

Connor nods, listening intently.

"She doesn't leave the house anymore, and she doesn't like having people there."

"I understand," he says, gentle and comforting.

"But… I can ask."

His face lights up. "Really?"

I nod. "I can't promise anything."

He smiles, genuine, for the first time since he got here. "I'd really like that, Ava."

I really like *you*, Connor.

◇◇◇◇◇

"So, I have this friend…" I tell Mom when I get home from school. I'm sitting on the couch with her on the floor in front of me while I braid her hair, something she used to do for me.

"Uh huh," she responds.

Today is what Krystal and I call a zero-day. We scale Mom's moods and actions between -5 to +5. When things are good for her, when she's a fragment of the woman I know as my mother, we go into the positive. The negative… well, that's obvious. Today is a zero-day. A day when she scrapes by, barely any emotion or recollection of who she truly is.

A zero-day is probably not the best time to be having this conversation, but waiting for a positive day might take too long, and a negative day… I don't think she even hears me on those days.

"He's new in town…" I say.

"He? So, a boyfriend, huh?" she asks, her tone void of any emotion.

"Not a *boyfriend*, but a friend boy."

"Go on."

"And he said he'd like to meet you."

"When?"

"Whenever you're up for it."

"Hmm."

"You don't have to if you don't want to."

"Not tonight," she mumbles. "But maybe tomorrow."

"Okay," I say, but I don't believe it. Believing would create hope. And hope has no home here. At least not on zero days.

CHAPTER 19
Ava

I TAKE the bus home the next day because Trevor has a job and Connor has practice. I'd love to watch, jeer him from the sidelines, but it's been a long time since I've wanted to do any after-school activities, so Krystal only works the set times I'm at school.

The moment I enter the house, the smell of freshly baked cookies hits my nose, filling my heart with nostalgia. "Ava!" Mom calls from her bedroom.

I drop my bag by the door and rush in to see her, panic swarming my insides. Krystal's sitting on the bed, while Mom stands in front of her dresser. Dressed in a floral skirt and pale pink cardigan, she holds up two different necklaces against her chest. "Which one?" she asks.

"Mama, you look so pretty," I croak out, my pulse settling to a steady strum. "What's the occasion?"

She lowers her hand, eyeing me questioningly. "For your friend's visit? Remember?"

Jaw unhinged, I look over at Krystal. "She's been talking about it all day. She's very excited, Ava. She even baked cookies."

"You did?" I ask, my gaze back on my mother.

She's nodding, smiling.

Pride fills every empty space of my being. "He's at practice right now, but he'll be done soon."

"Okay," Mom chirps. "We can wait."

"Okay," I agree.

"So?" she asks, lifting the necklaces again. "Which one?"

◇◇◇◇◇

Ava: **CONNOR!**

Ava: CALL ME AS SOON AS YOU FINISH.

Ava: IT'S URGENT.

I throw my phone on the bed and strip out of my clothes. Then I stand there in my underwear, trying to decide what to wear because, besides my school uniform, I live in sweats. It's been way too long since I've had to dress for the outside world, and even though I'm still at home, it's Connor... Connor is coming to my house and—

And—

Calm down, Ava.

I slip on a pair of jeans and a Texas A&M T-shirt, and then rip off the T-shirt and get into a fitted tank, something a little more *feminine.*

I tidy up the house a little, ignoring Mom watching me. She's sitting on the couch with a magazine on her lap, smirking, and how is it that she's so calm and I'm the one in a panic?

My phone *barely* rings before I answer it. "Hello?"

"What's wrong?" Connor rushes out. In the background, I can hear a bunch of boys hollering, their voices echoing. He's still at school, in the locker room. "Ava! What happened?"

I run to my room, close the door, and lean against it. "My mom wants to meet you…"

He huffs out a breath, static filling my ears. "Is that it?"

"What do you mean *is that it*? She wants to *meet* you. This afternoon. Like, now, Connor."

"Jesus Christ, Ava, your text sounded like something *bad* happened. Calm the hell down."

"I'm sorry."

"It's fine. Hey, what should I call her? Like… something military or…"

"I don't know. Miss Diaz will do."

"Cool. I'm on my way."

I lower my voice so my mother can't hear me. "Okay, but hurry, because I don't know how long she'll be like this."

Connor chuckles. "I'll break every speed limit."

"And text me when you're leaving your house. Don't knock. Knocking gets her—she gets—"

"I'll text."

"And remember what I said about her short-term memory, she might ask the same—"

"I got it."

"And don't stare when you first see her because—"

"Ava, I'm not a fucking asshole."

My eyes drift shut, my phone held tight to my ear. I release a staggering breath. "I know, I'm just… just…"

"Nervous? And scared?" he asks quietly.

I nod, even though he can't see it.

"It's okay to feel like that. You have every right to. The world hasn't been good to you guys, and I get that. But I wouldn't have asked if I didn't think I could handle it. So, don't worry, okay? I'll see you soon."

I swallow the lump in my throat and whisper, "Please hurry."

"I'll travel through time to get to you."

◇◇◇◇◇

Connor's on my doorstep, freshly showered, dark jeans and a light blue Henley to match his eyes and *damn, boy*. He ignores me standing right in front of him, his smile purely for my mother. "Ava didn't tell me she had a sister."

Mom giggles—*actually giggles*. "Ava didn't tell me how handsome you were. Come, come," she orders, moving toward the kitchen.

Connor says, stepping into the house, "I should've brought flowers or something. I wasn't thinking."

"It's fine," I assure, the panic over their first meeting lifted. "You being here is enough."

He settles his hand on the small of my back, guiding me in my own house. Dipping his head, his words just for me, he says, "You look nice, Ava."

I pull back so I can take him in again. My initial thoughts haven't changed. "You look… *okay*, I suppose."

"It's milk and cookies," Mom announces proudly, standing behind a chair at the kitchen table. On the table are a giant plate of cookies and three tall glasses of milk. "I used to do this for Ava's friends whenever they'd come around. They were a lot younger then, though." Her eyes shift from Connor to me, a wistfulness in her gaze that sets my soul at ease. "You remember that, Ava?"

"Yeah, Mama," I answer, my voice cracking with emotion. "Of course, I remember."

Please don't ever forget me.

She smiles, but it's sad, and I wonder what's going through her mind. I wonder if the memories of *before* haunt her or heal her. "I know you're seventeen now, but I don't know what else to do…" She looks at Connor. "When I left Ava for my first deployment, she was only ten years old and so…"

Connor rolls up his sleeves, looks directly at her with the same gentle softness in his eyes he carries with him everywhere. If he's at all shocked or deterred by her appearance, he doesn't let it show. "I'm here for it, ma'am," he says. "I mean, who *doesn't* love milk and cookies?"

We sit at the table, all three of us, sipping on milk and munching on cookies while Mom asks Connor about himself. "How tall are you, Connor?"

"Not as tall as I want to be. Six-five right now, but I'm hoping for a growth spurt," he jokes.

Mom says, "Kobe Bryant's only six-five and look at him."

Connor's eyes widen.

Mom adds, "And Chris Paul's six foot even. That never stopped him."

Connor drops his cookie on the plate. "Damn, if I don't like a woman who can talk ball."

Mom laughs.

I tell him, "Mom played college ball."

"No way!" Connor doesn't even try to hide his surprise. He stuffs an entire cookie in his mouth. "These cookies are so good, Miss Diaz."

The conversation moves from him, to the paper we're working on, to me as a kid, me as a baby, and even though some of Mom's stories are embarrassing, I can't wipe the smile off my face. Because I realize that she remembers all the important things, all the events that made me who I am, who *we* are as a family. She remembers the camping trip we took together right before she deployed, the tent leaking, the marshmallows I loved to watch being set ablaze right in front of my eyes. She remembers the fireflies. The magic. "And we sang that song, remember?"

I nod. "'Fireflies' by Owl City."

"I love that song," she hums. "It brings it all back, doesn't it, Ava?"

Another nod, because I can't speak through the knot in my throat. There's an ache in my chest, but the right kind. The kind that reminds me of why I'm here, of why I wake up every day at 4:30, and why I feel absolutely no jealousy when I hear about the parties over the weekend or the games I've missed or see the public displays of affection from the kids at school.

I'm here because *she* is.

Mom refills Connor's milk. "How tall are you, Connor?"

And just like that, my stomach sinks.

Connor says, not skipping a beat, "Not as tall as I want to be. Six-five right now, but I'm hoping for a growth spurt."

Mom smiles. "Kobe Bryant's six-five and look at him."

Under the table, Connor taps his foot against mine. "That's true."

Mom adds, "And Chris Paul, he's only six foot and that never stopped him."

"Also, true," Connor says. Then adds, "Did I mention how good these cookies were?"

Mom's smile widens. "I'm glad you like them."

The front door opens, and Trevor appears, sniffing the air before even stepping foot in the house. "Is that Mama Jo's cookies?" he asks no one in particular. Connor and I watch as Trevor turns his back to slide off his shoes, talking to himself, "I love me some Mama Jo cookies. Mmm-mmm."

Connor stifles his laugh.

When Trevor turns around, he sees Connor at the table and halts momentarily. Slowly, as if stalking his prey, he makes his way over to us and picks up a handful of cookies. His glare shifts between Mom and Connor. Once. Twice. To Connor, he says, "These are *my* favorite cookies…. and you're in *my* seat."

Mom and I bust out a laugh.

Today…

Today is a +infinite day.

◇◇◇◇◇

Ava: Thank you.

Connor: For what?

Ava: For giving me a part of my mom I thought I'd lost.

Connor: No, thank you.

Ava: For what?

Connor: For letting me be witness to it.
Ava: You're something else, Connor.
Connor: You're something MORE, Ava.

CHAPTER 20
CONNOR

"**I**s your dad tall?" Ava asks, walking along the bleacher bench, bouncing my basketball.

"He's a few inches shorter than me."

Ava spins, goes back the opposite direction—long, tanned legs moving swiftly. I could watch her all damn day. "Is that where you got your height and athleticism from?"

"Height is from his side, but he doesn't have an athletic bone in his body. Apparently, my mom ran college track, though."

Ava stops completely, the ball held to her waist. Lips parted, she tilts her head, as if contemplating. The girl's got an inquisitive mind, I've realized, and I wonder what questions are floating through her head. "Huh" is all she says.

I laugh under my breath and stand, take the ball from her. "Ask, curious girl."

She snatches the ball back. "I was just thinking you got split genetics."

"I guess."

"Do you know much else about your mom?"

"I kind of remember what she looks like, but it's a little hazy. And I don't know if it's from memory or because I saw a picture of her once," I admit. "In a drawer in Dad's side table. They were both wearing FSU sweatshirts, so I assume that's where they met."

"He hasn't told you about her?"

"Nah. He doesn't really talk about her or what happened, and to be honest, I kind of prefer it that way."

"Aren't you at all curious?"

"About?"

"God, so many things," she says, eyeing the sky. "Like where she is or what she's doing, or I don't know… *why* she did it."

I run my hands through my hair, replay her words. Lightheartedly, I reply, "Maybe she was a sociopath."

Ava jumps down off the bench and stands in front of me, her head tilted back so she can look me in the eyes. "I'm serious, though, Connor. I mean, if she had some form of mental illness then she should get help."

I swallow, painfully, and try hard to not let her thoughts consume me. "I get where you're going with this, Ava. I do. But my mom and your mom—they're two completely different situations."

"Because something *happened* to my mom to make her that way?"

"I don't know. I guess."

"Maybe your mom was born like that."

"Or maybe…" I start, grabbing my ball. I spin it around on my finger, so I have something else to focus on that isn't her. "Maybe it's a lot simpler than that."

"Like what?" she asks.

"Like maybe she just didn't want me."

◇◇◇◇◇

For the next few days, Ava and I ride to school together when our schedules align. She hasn't invited me over again, and besides the few text messages we send to each other at night, we don't really interact. Psych class and lunch are the only times we see each other, so we make the most of what we get. At least I do.

We sit in the bleachers away from the crowds and talk, learn more about each other. She finds new ways to get under my skin, and I find new excuses to touch her.

"Why are you hanging out with me?" she asks out of nowhere.

I push aside the so-called "food" attained from the cafeteria. School this rich, you'd think they'd supply something a little more… edible. "What do you mean?"

She picks up her sandwich—turkey on rye, the same as always—and takes a bite. With her mouth full, she says, "Shouldn't you be hanging out with your team?"

"Eh." I shrug. "You're nicer to look at."

She flicks her shoulder, rolls her eyes. "I mean, *obviously*."

"Modest, too."

She laughs, the kind that starts deep, comes out low and slowly turns higher and higher. It's my favorite of her laughs, and I pity the world for not hearing it as often as it should. "Honestly, though. Don't they wonder why you're not part of the jock-patrol?"

"I don't really click with anyone on the team as much as I do with you."

"You haven't made friends?" she asks.

"No, *Mom*. I haven't. I told you the first time you were in my car. You could be the suckiest friend in the world, and you'd still be the best one I have. And, to be honest, you're pretty fucking sucky."

"Shut up," she says, shoving my shoulder.

"Nah, the guys aren't too bad. Rhys seems like a decent dude, but talking to him is like talking in circles—which yeah, is basically like talking to *you*—but with Rhys comes Mitch and—"

Ava makes a gagging sound, cutting me off. "Yuck."

"You're not a fan?"

"That guy's a self-entitled dick."

"Hey, remember when you called me self-entitled?"

She stretches her arms in the air, then settles them behind her. "I remember it fondly." Nose in the air, she adds, "It was the morning of August—"

I reach over and cover her mouth, gently push until she's on her back, another new excuse to touch her. "You're such a smart-ass."

"You love it," she mumbles beneath my palm.

With her heavy breath against my hand, our eyes lock, stay. And I don't know why my mind chooses *now* of all times, why the urge I've held on to for so long is at its strongest.

I want to kiss her.

In so many ways.

For so many hours.

My gaze drifts to her throat, the movement sharp as she swallows.

I could kiss her there.

"Connor?" she whispers beneath my touch, her eyes drifting shut.

I could kiss her there, too.

She reaches up, yanks at my wrist to uncover her mouth.

I could kiss her there the most.

"We can't do what you're thinking right now."

My heart sinks. "Why?"

Hand pressed to my chest, she pushes me away and sits up. She refuses to look at me when she says, "Because we *can't*."

And I have no other words but a repetition of "Why?"

"Because," she starts, looking out onto the field, then down at her feet, at her hands, anywhere but at me. "Because my life is complicated enough as it is."

"I'm not here to complicate things, Ava. If anything, I want to help."

"I'm not a charity case."

I shake my head. Sigh out loud. "That's not what I meant."

The warning bell sounds, and I curse under my breath.

Ava's quick to stand. "We should go."

◇◇◇◇◇

I don't see Ava for the rest of the day, and she doesn't respond to my texts all afternoon. I'm tempted to go knock on her door to finish our conversation, but I remember what she told me about her mom's reaction to knocking, so I force myself to let it go until the next morning.

Sleep eludes me, and just when I've tossed and turned for the millionth time, legs kicking out in frustration, my phone goes off.

> *Ava:* I can't date. I don't even know what the meaning of dating is for people our age, but I know that I can't do it. My life outside of school is… my life. My priority. I can't be that girl for you. I can't be the girl on the sidelines cheering you on. I can't be the one you hold hands with when you go out to celebrate all your wins or commiserate all your losses. I can't be the one you bring home to meet your dad or the one you call when you have off days. I can't be anything more than I am right now. Which means *we* can't be anything more. And as much as I hate it, as much as it hurts, I know in my heart that's what you deserve. And it doesn't matter how much I want you or how hard I've fallen for you. Because I have, Connor. In all the possible ways that absolutely terrify me, I've fallen for you. But nothing good can come of this. There'd be no happy ending to our story. There'd be an intense beginning, a shaky middle, and then heartache. And we've both been through enough heartache to last a lifetime.

CHAPTER 21
Ava

I SPENT first period in the girls' bathroom because I was too afraid to face Connor.

This is my life now.

After I sent him the wall of text last night, I switched off my phone and managed to get a total of two hours sleep. I didn't want to see what he had to say or fight him on my decision. It had taken me hours to come up with something I felt was worthy enough to send. I gave him the answers he needed, and with it, I gave him every piece of painful truth.

I was falling for him.

And I couldn't do anything about it.

But even saying all that, it still hurt when I turned my phone back on this morning and there wasn't a response from him. I know he'd read it, the proof was there, so maybe that was it for us.

The story of Connor and Ava: *over before it began.*

It's what I wanted; I convince myself. It's what I *asked* for, really. It doesn't mean I won't miss his friendship, or his banter, or the way he puts up with me… or the way he *looks* at me.

My stomach drops as I stare out at the football field. I pick up my phone, see that it's been ten minutes since lunch started, and the ache in my heart doubles. Triples. I lock the phone, stare at the wallpaper: a picture of Trevor, my mom, and me on my last birthday. A zero-day. I can see it in her eyes, remember it like it was yesterday. There were no candles on the cake. No poppers. No singing. But there was *us*. Our mismatched little family; a gradient of skin tones. Trevor being the darkest, then mom, and then me. My *reason*.

"Sorry I'm late," Connor shouts, practically sprinting up the steps. "I was stuck on a stupid conference call with Coach Sykes and my agent, something about UCLA. I don't know; I tuned out."

My mind does a double take.

My heart does a double flip.

"What are you doing here?" I breathe out.

His steps falter. "Are we…" He eyes me sideways. "Are we not allowed to be friends anymore? Because I swear, I read your text, like, eighty times, and there was no mention—"

"I wasn't sure if you'd still want to be," I cut in. "Friends, I mean. I didn't…"

He sits down on the bench in front of me, a step down, his usual spot. "I'm kind of attached to you, Ava." He sniffs at whatever food the cafeteria has supplied him. "You gotta work harder if you want to get rid of me."

I'm *beaming*, and I don't even try to hide it.

He chews the corner of his mouth, his eyes on mine. "Ten bucks says I can wipe that smile off your face in less than five seconds."

Impossible. "Do your best, Ledger."

"I always sit *right here* because I can see up your skirt."

I kick his chest, my mouth open in shock. "You jerk!" Then I cross my legs.

"Red today," he laughs out. "Green yesterday. Did you buy a rainbow-themed bulk pack?"

"I hate you!"

"You owe me ten bucks."

"Fuck you, you didn't earn it." I try to kick him again, but he grabs my ankles, settles them on his lap. I should kick him there, but I don't know… he'd probably make a good dad one day, I suppose.

"Speaking of fuck you," he says, hands still on my ankles. "Rhys invited me to a party this weekend. It's the last chance to let loose before the season starts, so I guess the team is getting drunk and I don't know… trading *yachts*?" He releases my ankles and starts massaging his shoulder.

"What happened?" I ask, motioning to his shoulder.

"I think I tweaked it at practice."

I put my lunch to the side and say, "Come here."

"What?"

"Come here," I repeat.

He leans forward.

"Turn around, you dumbass."

"You have the strangest love language," he mumbles, scooting so his back is facing me.

I press my fingers into his shoulder, feeling the muscles shift beneath my touch. I realize I've never touched him before. Not like *this*. I try to ignore my body's reaction to the heat of his flesh, the strength of his muscles, the sound of his groan when his head rolls forward. I silently clear my throat, reclaim some form of sanity. "Are you going to go?"

"Huh?"

"To the party… are you going to go?"

"I don't know. Do you think I should?"

I keep working his shoulder, below his shirt, skin on skin, up his neck and to his hairline and back again.

He moans. "Ava?"

"Huh?"

"Do you think I should go?"

"Probably. Team building. Blah blah blah."

He chuckles.

I work on both shoulders, watching his muscles contract beneath my touch. Then I move up his neck, run my fingers through his hair.

"Goddammit, Ava," he grunts, his hands covering mine, stopping me. "You're making it really fucking hard."

"What, being *just* friends?"

"Yeah… that, too."

CHAPTER 22
CONNOR

I'VE NEVER FELT MORE out of place than I do standing in Rhys's living room. There's a Solo cup in my hand filled with beer, given to me by a server who clearly works for a company that gives zero shits about underage drinking. I thought it was just a team thing, but it looks like the entire school is here. Minus the one girl I wish was.

I sent Ava an SOS two minutes after I got here, but she hasn't responded. And no matter how much I look at my phone, Karen doesn't get the hint. She's on my arm, practically hanging on for dear life, and I don't even know how I got in this situation. "So, you totally should come!" she shouts over the music.

"What?" I yell.

"Next week. To my party. On my boat." She narrows her eyes. "Have you been listening to me at all?"

"Yeah," I lie, point to my ear. "It's just hard to hear you with all the—" My phone vibrates, and I'm quick to check it.

Dad: No drinking tonight, and if you do, no driving. I mean it, Connor. I don't feel like peeling your brains off the concrete.

Connor: Don't stress. I'm not drinking.

A tip I learned a while ago is that people tend to leave you alone if you have a drink in your hand. Nobody checks if you're drinking it. And I'm not stupid enough to drink and drive, especially since Dad has enough stories of car accidents to scar me for life.

"So, you'll come?" Karen asks.

"Hey, where's the bathroom?" I need out. Of this conversation *and* this room.

She points in the general direction of a large staircase, and maybe she's beyond drunk, because in a house this big, there has to be at least five down here.

"I'll catch you later, all right?" I don't wait for a response. Instead, I make my way through the already half-drunk party and start for the stairs where I know I can at least get some room to breathe. At the top are two hallways, and honest to God, I wonder if one of them leads to the servant quarters because the house is that big and that lush that it wouldn't surprise me if they had full-time help. And also, where the hell are Rhys's parents? Where the hell is Rhys?

I open door after door looking for the bathroom just so I can shut myself in and get a moment of peace. It's not like I'm not used to partying; I had my fair share back home, but they weren't like this. I find the bathroom, but it's occupied. Mitch has a girl pushed up against the counter, his pants down and her legs around him. "Sorry!" I shout.

"Ledger! What's up, man?" Mitch laughs. "You want in? I don't mind sharing." There's not enough eye bleach in the world to stop me from slamming that door shut.

The next door I open is an empty bedroom, thank fuck. Illuminated by a single lamp on the nightstand, I do a quick sweep of the room before declaring it safe. I close the door behind me. Lock it. And sit on the edge of the bed.

I look at my phone. Still no message.

Then I look around the room again, at the navy-blue paint and the *Wildcats!*

Wildcats! Wildcats! poster. My eyes narrow, trying to adjust to the darkness. My gaze catches on a large framed picture on the wall. It's the basketball team, Rhys front and center. Realization sinks in. I'm in his room. And because I'm bored, and maybe a little curious, I start to snoop. I scan the books on his shelf and the clothes in his closet that's the size of my room. The guy's got good taste in kicks, I'll give him that. He owns every pair of Jordans ever released, but only in the classic colorways. Not going to lie, I'm a little jealous. I wonder if he'd notice a pair or two missing...

I look over his desk, boring, and then the massive pinboard above it filled with photographs. Mainly of him. Not surprising. I scan the pictures, one by one. His parents are in them, along with a girl I assume is his sister. And right in the middle, the largest picture there... I look closer, but it's dark, and my eyes... my eyes might be deceiving me. I unpin it from the board and take a closer look. He's in his JV jersey in the middle of the court with a girl in his arms. She's wearing a cheerleader uniform, her hair braided to the side, with his jersey number painted on her cheek. He has his arms around her waist, her arms around his neck, and I fight the urge to rip the picture in half.

A twist in my stomach has me searching for somewhere to sit. I find the edge of his bed again, flop my ass down, my eyes glued to the photograph. She's the same Ava, but she's *different*. Smaller. Younger. Less... *broken*.

My eyes snap up at the sound of the doorknob twisting. I stand, hide the picture behind my back, and gear myself for whoever comes through the door. "Why the fuck is this locked?" I recognize the voice as Rhys's, and I mentally punch myself for getting caught.

The knob jiggles, and a second later the door's open and his head's poking through the gap. "Connor?" he asks, switching on the light.

I blink away the brightness. "Sorry, man. I got lost and... I just needed a little time out."

Stepping into the room, he eyes me suspiciously as he closes the door behind him. "Are you stealing from me?"

"No," I say quickly. "Jesus. *No.*"

His eyes span across the room, looking for evidence.

Please don't look at the giant empty space on the board. Please please please.

But he does, and he sighs out loud. "What's the deal with you guys anyway?" he asks, moving closer.

"What's the deal with *you* guys?" I counter.

He chuckles. "I'm not interested in her in that way if that's what you're thinking. At least not anymore. Has she not told you about us?"

And because I suck at hiding my jealousy, I say, "She hasn't mentioned you *at all.*"

"That's not surprising," he murmurs. "We didn't exactly have the best timing."

"What does that mean?"

"It means…" He rubs the back of his neck, contemplating. Then he opens his blinds, motions for me to look out the window, to which I comply. "See that house?" he says, pointing to a house only slightly smaller than his.

"Yeah?"

"Three years ago, Ava lived there."

My eyes widen, move to his. "No shit."

He nods. "I was so afraid to talk to her at first, because… well, you know what she looks like. She was so intimidating, and she had this fierceness to her like she wouldn't take shit from anyone. When I found out she was crushing on me, too, I lost my damn mind."

I know that feeling, *I don't say.*

"We did a lot of back and forth trying to navigate our feelings. We were only fourteen at the time, so it was all kind of new to us."

I don't know if I want to hear anymore, but I nod regardless.

"Anyway, you know Karen?"

"Yeah."

"She and Ava were best friends back then. Karen threw her this rager of a bonfire party for her fifteenth birthday, and I finally found the courage to shoot my shot."

"So, you dated?" If this is all he wants to tell me, he should just say it. I don't need the details.

Rhys shakes his head. "That night we uh… you know…"

Well, now I know, but I wish to fuck I didn't.

"It was the same night they got the call."

"What call?"

"About her mom."

"Oh." *Shit.*

Rhys exhales loudly. "We tried to make it work. Or at least *I* did. I gave her as much as I could, but she… she had *so much* going on, Connor, and then when her stepdad left them and—"

"I uh…" I cut in. "I kind of would prefer to hear her story from her if that's cool."

He nods, understanding. "I just want you to know that whatever goes on between you guys, I'm not your enemy or your threat or whatever. When it comes to Ava, I'm here for the same reason you are. I *care* about her. *Truly.*"

I'm having an out-of-body experience; I'm sure of it. Because I can't seem to process a single thought. It's as if I'm watching Ava's entire life play out and there's no pause button, no rewind. I don't know what to say or how to react, so I mumble, "I appreciate it."

I need to go. I need to get out of here. And I need to go to *her*. "I'm going to take off," I say.

We bump fists, and I start to walk away but stop when he calls my name.

When I turn to him, his hand's out, palm up. "Can I have the picture back?"

I reluctantly hand it back to him and then make for the door. When I go to close it, he's staring at the picture, his mind no doubt filled with memories.

I stand there, watching him, wondering how much time will pass before I start doing the same.

◇◇◇◇◇

The second I'm in my driveway and out of my car, I send Ava a text.

Connor: Everything okay? I haven't heard from you all day. Just checking in.

I'm halfway up my porch steps when I hear the notification, but it's not coming from my phone. I send another one.

Connor: Ava?

I hear it again and hit reverse on my feet. Down the steps and down the driveway, my focus on Ava's house. It's pitch-black, no lights.

I hit dial on her number and hold the phone to my ear. It rings twice on my end before hers goes off, and I follow the sound, see the screen light up.

Ava's sitting on her porch steps, her phone on her lap. She doesn't make a move to answer it, and it's too damn dark to see her clearly.

Slowly, carefully, I make my way up her driveway until I'm standing in front of her.

She's staring straight ahead, her eyes wide.

"Ava," I whisper.

She doesn't respond.

I look up at the house again, but there are no signs of life. So, I sit down next to her, keep my voice low. "What are you doing out here?"

She doesn't look at me when she whispers, "The fireflies are gone."

"What?"

She turns to me now, and lit only by the moonlight, I see her face clearly. Wetness trails down her cheeks, remnants of the tears she's been shedding.

My chest tightens at the sight, and I reach for her hand, link my fingers with hers.

Heartbreak forms in her words even though her features are void of emotion. "Mom says that when the world is at its darkest, that's when the magic appears." Anguish falls from her eyes, and she doesn't make a move to wipe them away.

"But there's nothing but empty darkness and negative numbers and… and the fireflies are gone, and I'm finding it really fucking hard to believe in magic right now."

I wish I knew the right thing to say or the right thing to do. But I don't. I let her words settle through me, every single one echoed in my mind. I hold her hand tighter, letting her know that I'm here, with her, for however long she needs me. Time passes without meaning, and I hear every one of her breaths, each one claiming a part of my heart.

"I was dead," I tell her, my voice calm. "There was a couple on their way to their honeymoon who spotted me in the car. A couple who just *happened* to be first responders. Apparently, they tried waking me by knocking on the window, and when I didn't stir, they smashed it open with their luggage. I wasn't breathing…" I pause just so I can push down the knot in my throat. "They got me out of the car, and the man did CPR while his wife called 911. They worked on me for ten whole minutes before I coughed out my first breath. *Ten minutes.* And who knows how long I was out before they got to me. I was barely conscious by the time help arrived."

Ava squeezes my hand, moves closer to me.

"What are the odds? What are the chances that the people who saw me were the right people at the right place and the exact right time? They brought me back to life, Ava." I turn my body to hers and gently place my hand on the back of her head, bring her ear to my chest, right above my heart. "Do you hear it?" I ask. "My heartbeat?"

"Yes," she whispers, her tears soaking through my shirt.

I blink back my own and try to stay strong, for *her*. "If you need proof that magic exists, I'm right here."

CHAPTER 23
Ava

Connor's grin is stupid, and I wish it didn't give me butterflies like it does. "You made me lunch?"

"It's not a big deal," I say, adjusting my school blazer over my knees, so we don't have a repeat of previous days. "You won't shut up about how bad the food is here, so…"

Swear, his dimples have never been so deep. "So, you made me lunch?"

"I didn't *make* it for you. It's leftovers. It would've just gone to waste."

"Uh-huh," he murmurs, devouring a mouthful of last night's lasagna. "I'm sure Trevor would've loved a second serving."

I wince. "Yeah, maybe don't tell him."

"What? That you *made* me lunch?"

"You're such a pain in my ass."

He chuckles. "And yet, here we are."

I spend a few minutes just watching him eat, a comfortable silence shared only between us. But I have questions. So many of them. And somehow, he picks up on this, because he says, "Yes, I met the couple who saved me. Yes, I keep in contact with them. They're retired now, but they send me a birthday card every year. Dad and the guy became close friends. He actually helped Dad become a paramedic."

Eyes wide in surprise, I open my mouth, but nothing comes.

"I can read you like a book, Ava."

I lean forward, look right into his eyes.

"What are you doing?" he asks, rearing back. "You're creeping me out."

"I'm trying to read your mind," I mumble. "Stay still."

With a laugh, he says, "I don't think that's how it works, but here—" he leans forward, his nose an inch from mine, bright blue eyes staring back at me "—do your best." His hands are on my knees, moving higher and higher. My breath catches, the tension between us building and building. Then his gaze drops, a slight change, but one I notice. One I *feel*.

"You're scared," I whisper.

Defensively, he asks, "Scared of what?"

Of me, I want to tell him. He's afraid of the same things I am. That no matter how hard we try to fight it, we can't stop the momentum. We're getting closer, and these feelings we harbor are just getting stronger and stronger.

I pull away.

Look away.

And come up with a lie. "You're scared about your first game tonight, right?"

Connor huffs out a breath. "Yeah," he admits, sighing heavily. His entire body seems to deflate with that single admission. "I actually am."

Pouting, I say, "I wish I could be there."

He nods. "I know. I understand why you can't."

"Do you want to talk it out?"

With a shrug, he replies, "I'm just nervous, I guess, which is weird because the game has always come so naturally to me. But I feel like I have a lot more riding on it now than I did before. I mean, we picked up our entire lives and moved to another state just for the chance to be seen, and God, Ava, if I don't succeed…"

"I'm sorry," I tell him honestly. Connor was right; I *am* a sucky friend because I'd never really thought about it before. I never stopped to think about the pressures of his life that might weigh him down and keep him up at night. All this time we've spent together and all the stupid questions I ask about his past, I never once asked about his future. Shame fills me. "That must be hard, to feel like all that is riding on *your* shoulders."

"It's all for the end game, right?" he mumbles.

"Well, it's good that your dad supports you with it. He moved here for it so…"

His eyes drop, his hand flexing around his basketball. "Yeah, I guess," he says, but his eyebrows are drawn, and there's a sadness in his expression that has me scooting forward just to be closer to him.

"Is he, like, pressuring you to be something you don't want to be?"

"No." He shakes his head, adamant. "No," he repeats. "I want to go pro. Obviously. And it's not like he'd disown me if I didn't make it, but… I don't know." He pauses a beat. "I feel like I have to *be* something. Something greater than average. Something big, because…" he trails off.

"Because why?"

His nostrils flare with his heavy exhale. "Because there has to be a reason I survived that day."

"Connor," I whisper. "You're putting way too much pressure on yourself."

He shakes his head, his eyes on mine. "What if I fuck it up, Ava? What if it was all for nothing?"

I suck in a breath, hold it there. And I think about my life before Connor, and all the emptiness I felt from scraping through each moment in my own version of zero-days. I sit down next to him, facing away from the field. Then I take his hand in mine, squeeze it, and hope that it gives him the same level of comfort he'd offered me. "What if it was something else entirely?"

"What do you mean?" he asks, spreading my fingers with the tips of his. Our hands are mismatched, his too big and mine too small, but when our fingers entwine, there are no empty spaces, no room for anything more.

"What if five hundred miles away, there was a girl… a girl who was barely holding on to hope… a girl so close to giving up. And you just *happen* to move next door to her? Just *happen* to sit next to her in class. And you form this friendship with her, not knowing how badly she needed someone *exactly* like you, at *exactly* that time, to help piece her back together. To help heal her. And to show her that magic exists and… and maybe it's not the NBA," I say, my voice hoarse, throat aching with the force of my withheld sob. "And maybe it's not what you imagined your purpose to be…" I look up at him, at his red, raw eyes holding mine hostage. "Would that be enough?"

He settles his hand on my jaw, then places the gentlest of kisses on my forehead, making my eyes drift shut. "So, this girl you speak of…" he starts, his lips still on me. "Is she hot?"

CHAPTER 24
CONNOR

"**Y**OU GOT EVERYTHING?**"** Dad asks, poking his head through my bedroom door.

"Yeah." I adjust the strap of my gym bag across my chest and take one more look in the mirror. Nervous anticipation crawls through my skin, and I wish Ava were here. I wish she'd hold my hand like she did today and calm the anxiety inside my chest, building a fortress, creating a home.

"You okay?" Dad asks, walking behind me toward the front door. "Pre-game nerves always get to you, but once you're on the court and the ball's—"

"I'm fine, Dad," I interrupt. I don't need a pep talk, at least not from him. I just need to stay in my head, stay focused.

I open the front door and freeze momentarily. There's a single, sad looking balloon hanging off the porch railing. Bright orange, like the team colors. And written in black marker, a large *#3*, my jersey number. I notice more writing on the other side, and so I flip it between my hands and take a closer look. A laugh erupts from deep in my throat. *BOO!*

◇◇◇◇◇

My back squeaks against the hardwood as I slide a few feet, leaving a trail of sweat in my wake. The crowd that'd been deafening all night is suddenly quiet. I start to raise my hand to shield my eyes from the bright gym lights, but Rhys stands over me, blocking them. He offers me his hand, and the crowd goes crazy. His grin matches mine when I use his hand to help me get back on my feet. "They're going to keep knocking you down until you can't get back up!" he shouts into my ear.

I make my way to the free-throw line, hands out for the ball. "They can keep trying," I yell back. "But I can go all damn night!"

I sink both shots without even trying.

"All damn night, baby!" Rhys whoops, ruffling my hair.

From the sidelines, Coach Sykes calls out to me, "Are you done?"

"Not even close!"

My opponent stands beside me, hands on his knees. He's the sixth one to cover me tonight, and he's *done*. Roasted. Me? I haven't even warmed up yet. He turns to me, shaking his head. "Where the hell did you come from, Ledger?"

I shrug. "Florida."

"Well, go the fuck back."

◇◇◇◇◇

"You killed it tonight, Ledger," Oscar, a sophomore says, punching my shoulder while I sit in front of my locker.

"Thanks, man."

"Yeah, way to show us up," Mitch calls.

I ignore him, but Rhys doesn't. "Last I checked, basketball was a team sport. Go run track if you want to get noticed, or I don't know… up your fucking game."

Mitch scoffs. "You cup his balls while you're down there kissing his ass?"

Rhys laughs. "No, but your mom does."

I grab my phone from my locker, the post-win adrenaline spiking when I see the text from Ava:

Ava: Triple double on your first game? Way to show off, #3.

Connor: Stalk much?

Ava: What can I say? I'm a fan.

Connor: I pretended you were there.

Ava: :(I wish I were.

Connor: You kind of were.

Ava: How?

Connor: I popped that balloon and shoved it down my shorts.

Ava: Gross.

Connor: Yet endearing, right?

Rhys says, "Hey, the team's going to the diner to celebrate. You're coming, right?" at the same time a message comes through from Ava.

Ava: Mom's already asleep. I can probably come outside for a little bit if you want to tell me all about it…

I look up at Rhys, the way his eyes shift from my phone to me. He sighs. "Do your thing, Ledger. But at some point, you're going to have to act like you're a part of the team, too. It's a two-way street, and I can only hold the guys off for so long."

I slam my locker shut, thank Rhys, and text Ava on my way out.

Connor: I'm leaving now.

⋄⋄⋄⋄⋄

Ava rushes down her porch steps, her arms outstretched as she pounces on me. I catch her just in time, falling back a step while she laughs quietly in my ear. "Superstar!" she whispers. There's something to be said about being able to literally sweep a girl off her feet. I spin her around, refusing to let her go. She doesn't seem to want that, either, because even when her feet are planted on the ground, she's still holding on, her arms around my neck. On her toes, she looks up at me, her eyes lit up by the streetlamp. "Tell me everything," she says, her smile contagious. "From the second you walked out until the final buzzer. And don't skimp on the details. I want a play-by-play so I can feel like I was there."

I laugh at her rambling, then say, "It was... was..." I pause, trying to remember the way I felt less than an hour ago, but the details are blurred, the moments insignificant. Because *this*... being with her and seeing her like this, seeing the pride in her eyes, the excitement in her voice—it outweighs everything else. And knowing that all of her, right now, is all for me... I pull her closer. "It was just a game, Ava." And as the words slip from my lips, I feel the heaviness of their truth dig deeper inside me.

"It wasn't just *a game*. It's, like, you're coming out, you know? Your world's about to change, Connor. I hope you're ready for it." She pulls away from me, releasing me completely. Then she smiles, but it's not the same smile she greeted me with. "Don't forget the little people who got you here," she says, only half in jest. "And by that, I mean *me*. Promise you won't forget me?"

With a heavy sigh, I take a step forward, ridding us of the space she so strongly believes she needs. "It's kind of hard for me to forget the one person I can't stop thinking about."

Her eyes lock on mine, her lips parted, and I wonder if she can hear the magic beating wildly inside me. She sucks in a breath, then seems to refocus. A smile plays on her lips as she looks down at her phone and mumbles, "I wonder if they have any game video yet."

She's tapping away at her phone, and I'm tapping away at my mind, my bravado. "Ava?"

"Yeah?"

"You're so fucking beautiful."

And it's killing me.

◇◇◇◇◇

Connor: You asked me yesterday if it would be enough; meeting you and getting to know you, and I cracked a stupid joke when I should have told you the truth. And the truth is this: yes. In the simplest of terms and the most complicated of circumstances, yes. You are enough. I wake up every single morning looking forward to the couple of hours I get to spend with you, to the few minutes I get to see you smile and hear your voice and feel you next to me. Even on the days when our time is limited, just knowing you're there and you exist is worth it. And even if I have to spend the rest of my life wondering what it would be like to kiss you just once… these moments with you… they're worth everything. YOU are worth everything.

CHAPTER 25
CONNOR

THE ENTIRE SCHOOL IS ABUZZ, hallways are filled with orange and black streamers, and everywhere I go, I get swarmed. Pats on the back from the boys, flirtatious compliments from the girls. Even the teachers are pulling me aside to talk about the game. Or more specifically, my performance. Coach has already had me in his office, along with the school paper's sports reporter. The headline for the next issue: "Ledger: The Powerhouse Import." Even the principal wants to meet so we can set up a media schedule for all the local papers wanting to do a story on me. And then there's the team. It's as if I had to prove beyond all our practices that I was actually good enough to garner their respect. Which I get, but at the same time, fuck you.

"You have to eat lunch in the cafeteria today," Rhys says, catching me in between classes.

"What? No. I have lunch with—"

"Ava, I know. But it's kind of a tradition the day after a game. Win, lose or

"But—"

"It's five minutes, Connor; it's not going to kill you. Besides, the cheerleaders do a *thing* for new players."

"What *thing*?"

He shrugs. "I'll catch you at lunch, okay? Don't be late!"

◇◇◇◇◇

I don't think I've ever cringed as hard as I am right now, watching the cheerleaders chant my name only a few feet in front of me. Next to me, Mitch keeps backhanding my shoulder, his eyebrows raised, like "How good is this?" And maybe to other guys this is a wet dream come true, but to me… I just want to be with Ava. And Rhys—fuck Rhys—because the five minutes he said it would take has turned into twenty, and I need to go. As soon as the cheerleaders have finished their routine, I thank them and start to leave. Rhys pulls me down by my arm. "Stay."

"Did you like it?" Karen asks, shooing Mitch out of his seat so she can sit next to me.

Not wanting to be rude, I plaster on the most genuine smile I can muster. "Yeah, it was great."

She nods, takes a bite out of Mitch's leftover apple. "We worked on it all morning."

"Cool." I stand again, and again, Rhys pulls me to sit back down. "I have to piss. You want me to do it right here?"

"Oh. Why didn't you say so?"

This time, I'm allowed to leave, and I practically sprint over to the football field. Ava is waiting in her usual spot, and I race up the steps two at a time. "I had to sit with the stupid team in the cafeteria and the—"

She holds out a container, cutting me off. "I *made* you lunch," she says, pouting. "But it's probably cold now."

"I'm so sorry," I rush out, sitting in front of her. "I got stuck. I had to sit through the cheerleaders—"

"The welcoming routine," she mumbles. "Shoot. I forgot about that."

I want to crack a joke about how she used to be one of them, but she wasn't the one to tell me, and I don't know if she wants me knowing. "It was horrible," I assure.

She rolls her eyes. "Yeah. It's such a *travesty* that you had to watch a bunch of hot girls in super short skirts screaming your name over and over." She mocks fanning herself. "Oh, Connor, Connor, Connor," she moans.

The sound replays in my head for longer than it should, and I stare, unabashed. Her lips are red, wet, and I can't help but lick my own, wonder for the umpteenth time what those lips would feel like against mine, what she'd taste like. I realize she's watching me, too, her focus on my mouth. She's the first to break our trance, looking away and down at her hands. "Are you still okay to give me a ride home later?"

"Of course."

"And um… what you said last night, in your text, did you mean it?"

I swallow, nervous. "Which part?"

"Did you lie about any of it?"

"No."

She nods, slowly, but still doesn't make eye contact. And before I even get a chance to open the lunch she made me, the warning bell goes off. I curse at the same time Ava drops to her knees beside me. She settles her hands on my chest, her gaze intense and locked on mine. Her lips part, her tongue darting out, spreading moisture on the parts of her I've been fixated on for days. Her touch drifts up to my shoulders, my nape, and I'm frozen with fear but melting with desire, and then she moves an inch closer and closer and closer, her eyes drifting shut and mine doing the same, my own hands blindly finding the small bit of skin between her knees and her skirt. She whispers my name, and I groan in response, and then her mouth's on mine, so fucking soft—a complete contrast to the instant reaction in my pants—and my lips part to take hers in. Her hands are in my hair, fingers laced through the strands, and mine are on her thighs, under her skirt, and she's warm… warm enough to light a fire inside me. I need air, but I need her more, and when the tip of my tongue searches for hers, finds it, I squeeze her legs—an impulse—and she tugs at my hair, pulls me closer again. My head tilts one way, hers the other, and we're two jagged pieces of two different puzzles that somehow fit perfectly when we're connected. Her breaths are sharp, short, and I hear every single one through the loud thump, thump, thumping in my chest. She's sitting higher on her knees, and my hands move behind her, to the spot right beneath her ass. She moans out my name, and all I can do is open my mouth wider, kiss her harder. So many fucking hours of fantasizing about this moment, and never—not once—did it ever feel like this. This… this…

The air hits my mouth where she should be, and I open my eyes to see her watching me, her lips red and raw from my assault. "Holy shit," she whispers, and I use her legs to bring her back to me. She falls, almost on top of me now, and I continue where we left off. This time, I go for her neck, her jaw. She holds me to her, her fingers running through my hair and I'm so fucking turned on, I can't see straight. In the distance, the bell rings again, and Ava pulls away, her eyes glazed. "We should go," she says, but I don't want to. I don't want to stop, and I don't want to leave her, and I don't want this moment to end.

She giggles, pulling away completely. She adjusts her clothes, and I adjust the bulge in my pants. She gives me one final kiss. Chaste. Then she smiles. "Now you no longer have to wonder," she says.

"Wonder what?" I breathe out, confused.

"What it would be like to kiss me… *just once.*"

CHAPTER 26
Ava

HOW MUCH DAMAGE can *one* kiss possibly do?

A lot, apparently, because it's all I can think about for the rest of the day. His lips, his hands, all the ways he touched me, the ways he made me feel… I can't focus on anything else. Not the classwork in biology. Not a phone ringing somewhere in the distance. Not Rhys hissing my name.

Something nudges my elbow, pulling me from my daydream. I turn to Rhys sitting next to me, my eyes narrowed in annoyance. "What?"

"Your phone's going off," he says, and I look up and around me, and everyone is staring. Then reality hits and hits hard. I reach for my pocket, see Krystal's name on the screen. I answer it without any regard for where I am or what I'm doing.

"Your mom's having an episode, Ava. You should come home right now. Trevor's on his way." I don't even respond before I'm on my feet and heading toward the door.

No one asks what I'm doing or where I'm going; they already know.

The two minutes waiting for Trevor in the school parking lot feels like hours.

I send a quick text to Connor to let him know I had to bail and practically jump into Trevor's moving truck when he arrives.

Dread.

Dread replaces all other emotions, all other thoughts, and my blood heats, rushes through my entire body. I can't sit still, can't stop the worst possible scenarios from circling my mind.

"It's okay," Trevor says, hand on my knee to stop the bouncing. "Everything's going to be okay."

"How do you know?" I whisper.

He doesn't have an answer, so he doesn't respond.

I burst through the front door and can hardly set foot inside. Magazines and broken glass are scattered throughout; picture frames hang crooked on the walls. Krystal is in the middle of the living room, her hands on her hips, and Mom—Mom is sitting in the corner, head in her knees, an arm covering her face. She's rocking back and forth, whispering words too unintelligible, even for my ears.

Krystal inhales a long, sharp breath before turning to me. "She's okay now," she breathes out. "She's in the—"

"Aftermath," I finish for her, taking the steps to get to my mother. Slowly, quietly, I squat down, ignoring the shattering of glass beneath my shoes. I fight back the tears, hold back my cries. "Mama?" *I am a conqueror. I am. I am.* "It's Ava. Remember me?"

Mom stills, looks up at me with eyes glazed, fighting a battle between chaos and calm. "Of course, I remember you," she says, her voice low. Her warm, wet hand settles on my jaw, taps gently. I fight back the urge to recoil. But then she breaks, a single tear falling from her eyes. "My Ava, Ava, Ava." She starts rocking again. "Ava, Ava, Ava."

I take her in my arms, hold her to me, and sway with her motions.

"I'm sorry, Ava, Ava, Ava."

"It's okay, Mama," I assure, looking up at Trevor. The sadness in his smile creates an ache in my chest.

Mom's shoulders start to shake, and I bring her closer, hold her tighter. "They came for me, Ava. They came for me and they found me… and it was so dark and so…"

"Shh," I hush, letting her bury her face in my neck. "It's okay. It's all over now. You're home, Mama. And you're *safe*."

◇◇◇◇◇

Mom has "episodes" and with them comes "aftermaths."

We've experienced more than a few of them since she's returned, and even a couple between deployments. When Krystal writes up her report about this particular episode, she'll call it a "mild" one. Most of the time I'm with Mom, or at the least, I'm near enough that I can be there to help her through it. When the aftermaths are harder to reach, Trevor has to step in, physically. Emotionally, it's all on me.

It took a half hour to get my mom to calm down enough so I could get her into bed. She was asleep within minutes. The episodes take a lot out of her.

"Ava?" Trevor says, standing in my doorway, his shoulder leaning against the frame. "You okay?"

"Yeah." I nod, saving the final changes to Trevor's calendar. Having him leave work for an emergency like today means having to reschedule his appointments. I always offer to make the calls so he doesn't have to. It's one less thing he has to worry about, and the very least I can do.

"Krystal just left," he says, entering my room. He sits on the edge of the bed, his arms outstretched behind him. "But I gotta be honest, Ava. Things aren't the greatest right now, and I really don't think I should be leaving you alone this—"

"Stop it," I cut in, already knowing this was coming. "I'll be fine." *I hope.*

"Besides, you *need* to be there. You're the best man." At his old man's wedding. The same man I used to call my stepdad. The same man who split when things got too hard for him and left all the burden on his son because apparently there's no such thing as *too hard* for Trevor.

He sighs, the sound filling the entire room. "I knew you'd say that, which is why I called in a favor…"

I spin in my desk chair and face him completely. "What do you mean?"

"Peter's flying in tonight," Trevor says, and my stomach turns, remembering what it was like the last time he was here. "He'll be over first thing tomorrow morning."

I go to tell him *no*, that I'll be okay and that Peter doesn't need to come, that I don't *want* him here… but then I look at Trevor, see the strain in his shoulders and the torment in his eyes, and my guilt… my guilt forces me to smile, to say, "I can't wait."

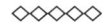

◇◇◇◇◇

Connor: You ruined me with a single kiss, Ava Elizabeth Diana.

My lips twitch, but I fight back a smile. After the day I've had, the last thing I need is to be reminded of the one thing I want, the one thing I *can't* have. No matter how desperately I yearn for it.

I squash my selfish desires and reply.

Ava: You said you were curious. Don't you know that curiosity killed the cat?

Connor: And a cat has 9 lives, so does that mean you owe me 8 more kisses?

I stare at the text, ignore the slow breaking of my heart. What I'd give for eight more greedy moments with him.

"Ava?" Mom calls from her bedroom and I drop my phone, along with all my delusions, and I go to her.

I'll *always* go to her.

Because she'll always come first.

First and forever.

CHAPTER 27
CONNOR

I'M LEANING up against my car the day after the Just Once Kiss, looking down at my phone, rereading the past few days' worth of text conversations between Ava and me. And without fail, I keep trying to scroll for more after the last one I sent. She didn't reply, and I can't help but overthink all the possible reasons. Maybe she's playing games, or maybe she got distracted or maybe—and this is the conclusion of my own mind games—maybe she doesn't *want* a repeat.

Maybe I'm a shit kisser.

A complete disappointment.

Sighing, I start writing a message to let her know I'm outside, but their front door opens, stopping me.

I wish for Ava.

I get Trevor instead.

He makes his way down the driveway and stops a few feet away. "You okay?" he asks, eyeing me dubiously.

I run my hand over my clothes, try to straighten out my thoughts. "Yeah, why?"

His eyebrows lower, his lips turned up in disgust. "Were you looking at porn?"

"No. What the fuck?" I mumble. "I was just studying some game tape," I lie.

"I heard about your game. Congrats, man."

I stand taller. "Thanks."

"So, listen, my old man's getting remarried…" he says, pausing when my eyes narrow. I remember what Rhys said about him walking out on them, and a flicker of anger fills my thoughts. "I know…" Trevor shrugs. "He's not the greatest man out there, but he's my dad, so I kind of have to be there."

"I get it."

"Anyway," he says, shoving his hands in his pockets, "I'm going to be away for a few days…"

Hope replaces my anger.

"…so, I'm having a friend come stay with Ava while I'm gone."

And hope dies in my chest. I point to myself. "I could stay with her."

He chuckles, pats my shoulder and squeezes. Tight. "You *could*," he replies. Then his eyes harden when they glare into mine, making sure I'm focused on his next words. "But you *won't*."

My lips purse. "Got it."

A car drives past us, turning at the end of the cul-de-sac, and parks behind mine.

"That's him now," Trevor states, already making his way toward it.

I can't ignore the inkling of jealousy when I see the car—a Mercedes G-Wagon—or the guy. He's around Trevor's age with surfer boy good looks that would be there even if money wasn't. And the jealousy turns into animosity at the thought that *this* is the guy who'll be spending the next few days with Ava, seeing her when I can't, talking to her face-to-face and not through a fucking phone screen. He'll see her just woken up, or just before bed. Hell, he'll probably even see her *in* bed. Bile rises to my throat, but I push it away the moment Ava appears on her porch.

"Ava, Peter's here!" Trevor calls out, looking right at her.

Ava's smile seems unrestrained as she rushes down the steps and greets the guy, completely ignoring the fact that I'm here.

My nemesis—aka Peter—wraps his arms around her the moment she's close enough. The hug lasts too long, and I want to clear my throat and yell, *hello, I'm here, too*. But that would be pathetic. More pathetic than me just standing here watching them. Peter pulls back an inch, takes her in from head to breasts and back again.

Yeah, I already don't like this guy, and I know nothing about him.

He holds her face in both his hands, and I want to rip off those hands and beat him to death with them. "Bad night, huh?" he asks, and there's no possible way he would know that just from looking at her.

Ava finally, *finally*, notices me standing on the sidewalk like a lost fucking puppy and releases her embrace. She tells him, "Just give me a second."

I stand, my hands in my pockets and my pride in her grasp. "I'm going to be late this morning."

That's *it*?

Where's my fucking hug?

I know I shouldn't be this upset, so I do my best to hide it. "Everything okay?"

"Yeah," she says, tugging on the lapels of my blazer. "I should be there by lunch."

Nodding, I glance up to see Peter on their porch watching our every move. Ava asks, "I'll meet you at our usual spot?"

Peter crosses his arms, his eyes narrowed.

Ava tugs on my blazer again. "Okay?"

My eyes drift back to the girl in front of me, the morning sun hitting her eyes, turning them orange. I smile when she does. "Yeah. I'll be waiting."

On her toes, she reaches up, plants a kiss on my cheek. It's not the kiss I wanted, the kiss I thought I *needed*, but it's something. And *something* sure beats all the uncertainty I'd been drowning in.

◇◇◇◇◇

Lunch comes around, and I skip the cafeteria just so I can get those few minutes more with her. I'm at our spot before she is, so I wait and wait and wait. My excitement turns to confusion, and then confusion turns to worry. I send her a text, ask if everything's okay. Then I wait some more. By the time the warning bell sounds and there's still no reply, that worry turns to envy, to jealousy.

And I hate that it does. Because I realize that this reaction burning a hole inside me isn't because of this guy's car or his looks or even the fact that he gets to spend time with Ava. It's because whoever the hell he is, Trevor trusts him enough to be around her, and more? Ava trusts him enough to be around her mom… something I haven't earned.

And something I'll probably never get a chance to.

CHAPTER 28
CONNOR

It's nearly midday Saturday, and the only communication I've had with Ava was a text last night with a simple "sorry."

There was nothing else to accompany it, and I don't even know if she's sorry she stood me up yesterday or sorry she didn't let me know or sorry because she's giving one or all of my eight kisses to a guy sleeping in her house.

My brain is broken. Obviously.

Which is probably why I'm sitting on the front porch with my phone in my hand, staring at the unsent message that's been flashing on my screen for the last half hour.

It says:

Hi

Because I don't know what else to say without sounding as desperate as I feel.

I delete the text and pocket my phone, then just stare out into the street as if it's my only care in the world. The guy opposite us is mowing his lawn;

a few houses over, someone is painting their porch. A woman is out walking a dog past a guy washing his car. And then some kids show up on their bikes, backpacks on. It's the same punk kids from before who TP'd Ava's house. I sit higher, watch closer. They ride in circles at the end of the road, their voices low. One of them gets off his bike, the biggest of them all, and removes his backpack. Crouched down and staring at Ava's place, he pulls out a water bomb.

I'm on my feet, walking down my steps before he even raises his arm. "You should probably think twice before throwing that!"

All four boys glare at me. The one with the water bomb yells, "Fuck you!"

Fuck me?

No.

I yell, "You suck your paci with that mouth, you little bitch!" Not my greatest moment, but it's all I could come up with. I'm barefoot, but it doesn't stop me from attempting to chase after them. The minute they see me at full height, they're on their bikes, water bombs discarded. Their laughing grates on my nerves, and they don't leave immediately. Instead, they circle the road, waiting for me to make my next move.

I pick up a stick.

The smallest of the rat-pack yells, mocking, "You should probably think twice before throwing that!"

Then from behind me, water flies over my shoulder, just missing me. I turn to see Peter with a power hose, his eyes narrowed. "Get the hell outta here, you shitheads."

The kids start to bail, and Peter follows them with the hose, attacking their backs. They get too far for the water to reach, so they stop, turn to us. One of them shouts, "Oh, look! Your boyfriend came to save you."

"Fuck these kids," Peter mumbles, standing next to me. "How fast can you run with no shoes?"

"Fast," I respond.

"Ready?"

We jet, my feet hitting the pavement hard. The kids take off, one of them shouting, "You need to get your wisdom teeth removed!"

And another adds, "Yeah. So you can fit more dicks in your mouth!"

Peter busts out a laugh, slowing to a stop. I do the same.

"Jesus Christ," he says, watching them turn the corner. "Insults sure have amped up since I was a kid." He offers me his fist for a bump when we turn back toward my house. "I'm Peter, by the way."

For a second, I'd forgotten that he was my enemy. I bump his fist anyway. "Connor."

"I know who you are," he says in a non-threatening tone.

My chest swells at the idea that Ava mentioned me.

"Trevor told me about you. Or *warned* me actually."

"Warned you?" I ask incredulously.

He shakes his head. "Not like that, just that you and Ava have a thing going on."

A Thing. That's what we're calling it? Cool.

"He said to make sure you weren't creeping into her bedroom at night."

I wish. "Nah," I say. "It's not like that." We stop in front of Ava's house, and I help him wind up the hose. I ask, as nonchalant as I can, "How is she anyway? I haven't heard from her for a couple days."

Peter shrugs. "She's been busy with her mom and all. I think she has a harder time when Trevor's gone, and I'm no back-up Trevor. I'm just here for the muscle."

Nodding, I pretend to understand what he's saying, but the truth is, besides the basics of what Ava's told me, I have no idea what she goes through on the daily.

A car I recognize as Rhys's drives past us, turns, and parks in front of my house. There are a couple guys from the team with him. And Karen. The others stay in the car while he gets out and approaches, his gaze on Peter. To me, he says, "What's up, dipshit?" And to Peter, he says, "Hey, man. Home for a break?" They shake hands as if they've known each other their entire lives.

Peter answers, "Just staying with Ava while Trevor's gone."

"Oh yeah. His dad's wedding, right?"

Peter nods. And my stomach drops. It's like I'm right here but in another dimension. Clueless to the real world. I don't know how Rhys knows Peter or how he knows what goes on in Ava's life, if it's small-town gossip or if Ava's talking to Rhys the same way she talks to me.

But *more*.

More unreserved and open, and I feel… I feel so fucking *insignificant*.

Rhys says, pointing to me, "Get your ass dressed. We're going to the sports park."

"Don't we have that showcase today?"

After a scoff, Rhys mumbles, "Yeah, in like four hours. Let's go."

I sigh, not really in the mood to socialize. "Is Mitch going?"

"Nah, he can't make it."

Good.

Then Peter says, "Maybe he's getting his wisdom teeth removed."

I can't help but chuckle.

"What?" asks Rhys, confused.

And I say, "You know, so he can fit more dicks in his mouth."

Peter laughs, and Rhys glances between us. Then Karen appears from thin air and sidles up next to me. "You coming?" she asks.

"Yes," Rhys answers for me. "Hurry your ass up. I'm hungry as shit."

"I'll go get dressed," I say at the same time Peter tells Karen, "Hi, I'm Peter."

Karen giggles. "I know who you are. You and Trevor used to chase Ava and me around the backyard with piss-filled water pistols."

His eyes widen. "You're that girl?" Then he eyes her up and down. "Damn, talk about a glow up."

"Get dressed already!" Rhys yells, shoving me toward my front door.

I throw my hands up in surrender. "I'm going." I glance toward Ava's house, shocked to see her standing in her doorway watching us all. I lift my hand in a wave. She shuts the door between us.

Ava

"What's going on outside?" Mom asks, agitated.

I close the door, jealousy and resentment forming an ache in my chest too large to ignore. I plaster on a smile and sit back down at the table, moving Mom's speech therapy flashcards around aimlessly. "It's just some kids from school," I mumble.

"Are they messing with the house again?" she asks, her eyes narrowed, fist balled on the table.

"No, Mama. They're just out there talking to Connor."

She snorts. "Who the hell is Connor?"

"He's…" He's a boy who deserves to have the life being offered to him. "He's no one."

CONNOR

In my room, between getting dressed, I text Ava.

> **Connor:** Rhys is forcing me out of the house, then I have the showcase this afternoon, but I'm free after if you want me to come by.
>
> **Connor:** We can sit on your front porch for all of twenty seconds and watch the grass grow. I don't really care. I just want to see you.

I wait a good five minutes for her to respond, ignoring Rhys on my doorstep telling me to hurry the fuck up. I send a text to Dad sleeping in the next room and tell him where I'll be.

Then I send another message to Ava.

Connor: I just really miss you is all. If you never want to talk about what happened—the kiss thing—that's cool. Just don't shut me out, Ava. Please.

Ava

"So, I met Connor," Peter says, sitting on the couch next to me while Mom sits in her room, alone, staring at the wall because she'd rather be doing that than be around me right now.

Today is a negative day. I just haven't worked out how bad it is yet.

"And?" I ask, reading back the stream of texts Connor had just sent me.

"And he seems like a decent kid."

I think about Connor and how much things will change for him now that he's in the spotlight. He'll have more friends than he knows what to do with, and girls like Karen... and then there's me. And right now, he thinks that I'll be enough, but that won't last forever, and even after an incredible life-changing kiss, nothing's changed. I'll still be me, always, and he'll get sick of the wanting and waiting, and he'll move on. I reread the message: *Just don't shut me out, Ava.* "He's a dreamer," I mumble. *A disbeliever.*

Peter asks, "What do you mean?"

"Nothing." I shake my head, rid the fog. "I don't know what I'm saying."

Connor

Sitting in the front seat of Rhys's car, Oscar moans, rests his head on the window. Next to me, Chad, another senior on the team, does the same. "What's up with you guys?" I ask.

"Not so loud," Chad groans.

Karen looks past Chad in the middle of the back seat and tells me, "They're hung-over."

"Oh man," I laugh out. "Big night?"

Karen's lips purse. "Uh-huh. My birthday party last night. I invited you but…"

Shit. I'd completely forgotten. "I had a ton of homework," I lie.

"Sure," she says, offering a painstakingly fake smile.

We get to the sports park and hit the food trucks first. Rhys seems to get one of everything while the other two guys pick at their food. Karen's sitting next to me, and I don't really know why she's here, but the other guys don't seem to mind it so it must be a regular thing. Rhys lets out an ear-piercing belch when he's done, gets up, and smacks the other two guys upside their heads. "Let's hit the cages," he orders, and the two get up groaning, but follow him anyway. I'm still eating my food and so is Karen, so we awkwardly sit in silence. I don't know what to say, and she doesn't speak. I check my phone. Still no Ava.

"Look at those dumbasses," Karen says, pointing to the cages. Oscar's in the cage, his helmet on backward, balls flying at his head. "You know what they say is the best thing to do when balls are coming at your face?"

"What?" I ask.

She faces me and says, smirking, "Don't open your mouth."

A chuckle erupts from deep in my throat. "Hey, how come you don't seem as hung-over as them?"

She shrugs. "I don't drink."

"Serious?" I ask, unable to hide my shock.

She laughs at my response. "We have the same trick, you and me. Walk around with a full cup and no one bothers you…" she says knowingly.

"I drink sometimes," I explain. "I just have to be in the right mood. What's your reason?"

"I don't really know. I tried it once, but it wasn't really enjoyable, and I'm not one to give in to peer pressure and do something just because everyone else does."

"That's… smart. I would've never thought that about you."

She shrugs. "People tend to judge me based on my looks or the way I carry myself. I'm confident, sure, and I like to look nice, but that doesn't mean I don't have brains. I have the third highest GPA in our class." There's a hint of disdain in her tone, and I wonder if she's talking about people in general, or me specifically. Because I sure as shit judged her based on everything she just said, and in this setting, outside of school, she seems like a decent person to be around. She starts packing up both our empty plates. "You ready?"

"Yeah." We stand together, and I follow her to the trash, then to the cages. I say, making sure she can hear me, "Hey, I'm sorry I missed your party. Happy birthday, by the way."

Her smile is as genuine as her response. "Thanks, Connor. I appreciate it."

◇◇◇◇◇

"Jesus. She's got a reasonable swing on her," I remark, watching Karen swing a bat as if it came with years of practice.

Rhys fingers the cage, then starts to climb it. "She ain't bad."

"Does she hang around you guys often?" I ask, pulling him down when I see one of the attendants start making his way over to us.

"Karen? Yeah. She's one of the boys. Has been for years."

"Huh."

"Don't let those legs and that pretty smile fool you," he tells me, leaping off the cage and landing in a squat. To be honest, I hadn't noticed either of those things. "She's competitive as hell. That's why she and Ava got along so well. Put those two in a room together, and they could take down the Chinese wall."

"The Great Wall of China?"

"Same thing." He shrugs. Then adds, "So Peter's home?"

"I guess. How do you know him?"

He scoffs. "Everyone knows Peter Parker."

"That *can't* be his real name," I mumble, bewildered.

Chuckling, he says, "Oh, but it is."

In the cage, Oscar asks for the bat, and Karen tosses it toward him, but he's too slow, and it hits him right in the nuts. Oscar howls in pain, folds over himself. I turn to Rhys, ask him something that's been consuming my mind all afternoon. "Hey, do you and Ava talk a lot?"

He faces me, expressionless. "Define *a lot*."

I shrug, look through the cage again. "Just seems like you know a lot about what's going on in her life." *More than I do,* I want to add, but don't.

"I told you it wasn't like that," he says, clearly irked by my question.

"No, I know," I assure. "I'm just… I'm trying to work out what we are exactly—Ava and me—and I can't seem to get it out of her, so… I don't know. I'm just looking for validation, I guess."

Rhys sighs. "My sister graduated two years ago. She took most of the same classes that Ava's taking now, and she kept most of her notes because she's a giant fucking nerd, I guess. She lets me give them to Ava for the classes she misses because that girl misses *a lot* of classes. We talk about that stuff mainly, but yeah, sometimes I'll ask how she's doing, and she'll tell me."

"She must be telling you more than she tells me. I can barely get her on the phone."

"She has a lot going on," he tries to convince. "And it's got to be hard for her."

"Hard how?"

"I don't know, dude." He rubs the back of his neck, frustrated. "I guess, trying to juggle and prioritize school while having to be a parent to your own parent, add to that the normal teenage anxiety and emotions and trying not to get too attached to people." He backhands my chest. "People like you."

"She can attach herself to me," I say. "I won't mind it."

Shaking his head, he laughs under his breath. "You say that now, but it's harder than you think. Trust me, man. You think I don't know your situation, but I do. I *was* you."

◇◇◇◇◇

I get home just in time to shower, change and get ready for the showcase—a "fun" afternoon for the fans where the team plays three-on-three, and we do nothing but show off our skills. I'm one foot out the door when I stop in my tracks. It's a different balloon, but the same writing, same number, same insult.

My stupid grin matches my foolish glee.

I bet Rhys never got balloons.

CHAPTER 29
Ava

I STARTLE when my alarm goes off, even though I'm wide awake. The biology paper I'm working on has kept me up the entire night—the only time the house has been peaceful enough to work. I set the phone down. I need the A. Not for me, but for Trevor. He works too damn hard to pay for this education, no matter how hard I'd fought him on it. "When it's over," he'd told me—whatever *over* means—"your high school education is going to be important." And then came the argument about college that ended with me promising I'd apply to some even if I had absolutely zero intentions of going. "You can defer," he'd said. "And we'll work out the rest when the time comes."

I'm typing and typing and typing, rushing through the final two paragraphs when I hear Mom's bedroom door open. *Shit.* I look at the time. 5:05. *Shit. Shit. Shit.* I shut the screen, get to my feet. "Sorry, Mama. I lost track of time. I'll get your breakfast going."

Mom's eyes are dead as she stares at me, and I can't stand to see it. I look away, start on her food. Flames heat my face when I turn on the stove. I quickly set the pan on top, drop in some oil. Then I go to the fridge, pull out the bacon and eggs. I rush around the kitchen, dropping bread in the toaster, and she stands at the doorway watching me. "Five a.m., Ava," she says, her voice as chilling as her presence. "I have breakfast at 5 a.m. every goddamn morning."

"I know, I'm sorry." I turn my back to her so I can work over the stove, my heart beating out of my chest. My hands shake as I try to pick up an egg, and then she's beside me, looming over and around me.

"Move!" she orders. "I can make my own damn breakfast."

"No, Mama," I say, trying to keep as calm as possible, but I can feel the darkness wavering above us, the doom and gloom like a ticking time bomb just waiting to explode. I inhale deeply, exhale the same way. "I got it. Please sit down. I'll only—"

"*Move!*" she shouts, grabbing at the pan handle.

I fight to get it back, even though I know I shouldn't. She's too strong, too wired, and I'm weak… God, I'm so fucking weak. Tears spring in my eyes, and I say, refusing to let go, "I'll make it! I'm sorry."

"Goddammit, Ava! I said MOVE!" she screams, pulling at the pan until I finally release it, but she wasn't expecting it, and neither was I, because the pan flips up and burning hot oil catches on my neck, my chest. I shriek, the pain unbearable, and run to the tap. Tears fall from my eyes, mixing with the oil, burning through my flesh.

"What the hell happened?" Peter exclaims, appearing in the kitchen.

I try to splash water on myself, but it's useless.

"Jesus Christ, Ava," Peter says, grabbing me by my shoulders and turning me to him. His eyes widen when he takes me in, and he's quick to grab a dish towel and soak it with cold water. He wraps it around my neck, then runs to the fridge and pulls out the ice tray. He plugs up the sink, fills it with water and ice.

"What the hell did you do, Jo?" he asks my mom.

Mom doesn't respond.

I'm on the floor now, my cries so strong they're silent. My body convulses, the burning flesh heating my insides. Tears. So many tears. Peter finds all the dish towels in the kitchen and dumps them in the filling sink. He grabs a handful and places them wherever he can see the damage. My neck. My shoulders. My chest. "Keep them there," he tells me. Then he leaves, only to return with his phone to his ear.

"Who are you calling?" I manage to get out.

"The crisis team. We can't do this alone, Ava. We need help."

"No, we can't afford—"

"Quit it. You need to go to the hospital."

"I'm fine," I cry out.

"I swear to God—" he starts, but the call must connect. He gives the person on the other end all our details, Mom's case number, and as much information as he knows about what just happened. When he hangs up, he says, "They're sending over two people. They'll be here soon."

He squats down in front of me, wincing when he pulls back a dish towel. "I'm going to call an ambulance."

I want to say no, but the pain is too much, and so I nod, let him gently wipe my tears. He exhales harshly, his breath hitting my face. Then he shakes his head, his eyes on mine. I know what he's saying without saying a word. *The offer still stands.* And I look away, unable to give him what he needs. Then I glance up, find my mother in front of the stove, a spatula in her hand. The smell of bacon fills the room, then the sound of her singing, humming. She stares out the window. "It looks like the sun's going to grace us today."

◇◇◇◇◇

Mom sits at the kitchen table, a plate of bacon, eggs, and toast in front of her. Peter stands in the doorway between the kitchen and living room while the paramedics make their way inside. I sit on the couch, covered in wet dish towels to alleviate the pain and any blistering.

The house is silent bar Mom's continuous, joyous singing.

I feel dead inside.

Dead, dead, dead.

One of the paramedics crouches down in front of me, offers me a smile that does nothing for me. "Hi," he says, his voice soft. He glances behind him at Peter and his partner while Peter explains what he thinks happened. I still haven't found my voice or my courage to tell him.

The man in front of me says, "My name's Corey. And you're Ava, right?"

I nod, even though I don't recall Peter mentioning my name, but most people around here know who I am, or at least know of us and where we live. It's a stigma we carry that I wish would just fuck the hell off.

The man—Corey—smiles again. "I uh… I actually live next door," he tells me. "I'm Connor's dad."

"Oh."

Oh, God, no.

"I'm just going to peel these off and see what we're working with, okay?"

I nod, lift my chin for him to gain better access, and wince when he starts to remove the towel. "I know it hurts, and I'm sorry. I'm going to try to make this as painless as possible for you, okay, Ava?" He has the same gentle tone as Connor, the same blue-blue eyes, too.

"You have his eyes," I murmur.

"What's that?"

"Connor. You have his eyes."

His lips form a line. "I think Connor got them from me if we're being technical…"

I stare at my mom, who's still blissfully unaware.

"Do you want to tell me what happened here, Ava?" Corey asks.

A single tear rolls down my cheek. My heart beats, but there's no life inside me. "I like them," I whisper.

"Like what?"

"His eyes. Connor's. And his heart."

Corey's hands freeze mid-movement. "His *heart*?"

My eyes drift shut, melancholy melting inside me. "His heart is full of magic."

◇◇◇◇◇

"If you need to sedate her, do it," I hear Peter tell the crisis workers. They're from the same agency as Krystal, but they're better trained for moments like these. They arrived a few minutes before the paramedics left, but I was already in my room with liquid sorrow staining my pillows.

A knock on my door and Peter appears, not waiting for a response. He sits on the edge of my bed, his shoulders hunched. He lets his face fall into his hands, a quiet moan escaping him. It's not the first time he's experienced Mom on a negative day but never this extreme and never directed at me. He looks over at me, his eyes filled with pity. "How are you feeling?"

I blink. I don't know how to respond, what answer to give him that'll alleviate his concern.

Peter sighs. "You look tired, Ava."

I swallow, my eyelids heavy, the painkillers forcing their way through my bloodline. "I haven't slept."

"All night?" he asks, eyebrows raised in disbelief.

"Mmm."

He settles his hand on my hip. "Sleep, baby girl. I'll stay up and take care of things, okay?"

I nod, my entire body too heavy to move. Eyes closed, I feel the bed dip, then his warm lips settle on my temple. "I'll take care of you, Ava. Always."

◇◇◇◇◇

I'm in and out of sleep all day, but always in a daze. Even when I feel alert enough to get up, I stay in bed. Peter checks in on me often, and I keep my eyes closed, not wanting to hear what he has to say.

When the world is at its darkest, that's when the magic appears.

It's not magic that enters my room when the stillness of the night creates a silence around us. It's Peter. My eyes squint at the stream of light filtering in from the hallway, and Peter notices because he walks in and switches on my lamp. He settles on the edge of my bed again, his hand on my leg. "Your mom's asleep, the crisis workers are going to take shifts overnight, and they'll be here all of tomorrow."

"Okay," I whisper, not looking at him.

"Have you reapplied your cream?"

I force my body to half sit up. "No, I forgot."

"Well, we better do that. We don't want that flawless skin of yours scarring." He grabs the cream the paramedics left for me and gets more comfortable on the bed. Then he reaches up, pulls the covers down until they're resting at my waist. He removes the dressing, slowly, carefully, and starts applying the cream where needed. Starting at my neck, he moves to my shoulders, taking his time, and then lower, lower, to my chest revealed by the tank top I've been wearing all day. He spends the most time there, just above my breasts. His touch is soft, heated, nurturing.

I can take care of you, Ava. But it's our little secret.

"Your mom's getting worse, Ava," he murmurs.

"Stop it."

"I know you don't want to hear this, but she needs help."

"I just need to get through this year. For Trevor. And then... then..."

He sighs. "Then what?"

I don't know. My shoulders fall with the first sob that consumes me. I keep my cries quiet, but he's there to hold me. To wipe the tears from my eyes. To assure me that everything will be okay, even when he doesn't believe it himself.

He finishes tending to my physical wounds, then gets under the covers with me. "Come here," he whispers, helping me to lie back down. I rest my head on his chest while his fingers stroke my arm. His chest rises and falls with his steady breaths, his heartbeat forming a steady rhythm blasting in my eardrums.

Thump, thump.

Thump, thump.

I close my eyes and listen; try to find what I'm looking for.

But it's not there.

Because he's not The One.

The Holder of Hope.

The Creator of Magic.

He's not Connor.

CHAPTER 30
CONNOR

MONDAY MORNING, Ava sent me a message telling me she wasn't going to be at school, that something came up with her mom. I offered to help however I could, but she didn't reply to my messages. Tuesday morning, same damn thing.

Finally, on Wednesday, she tells me she's going, but she doesn't need a ride. Peter will take her. Whatever. At least she's going, and I'll get to see her. Five days of no-Ava is too damn long. But when psych class begins and she's not sitting next to me, I start to worry, and that worry starts burning a hole in my gut. Something's... *off*. And I don't know what to do about it. Finally, about twenty minutes into class, the door opens and she appears. That first breath I inhale when I see her, God, it's like I'd been holding on to it for all five days. She hands Mr. McCallister a note and then makes her way over to me, a slight smile on her lips that has me goddamn giddy with excitement. I've missed her. In all the possible ways you can miss someone, I've *craved* her.

Just her presence alone seems to settle my anxiety, and I haven't even spoken to her yet. She sits down next to me, her leg tapping mine beneath the table.

I pull out a notepad as inconspicuously as possible and scribble down: *You're a sight for sore eyes, Ava.*

With a smile, she reads what I wrote and writes back: *It's good to see you, too, I suppose.* Then crosses it out completely and writes: *I've missed you.*

My heart does a stupid flip, and I settle my hand on her knee, praying she won't push me away. As soon as the teacher's turned his back to the class, I face her.

My eyes thirst for her, as lame as that sounds. But it's true. Five fucking days and I'd forgotten how hot she was. I'm staring, breathing her in, and I don't even care. I've missed her hair, a mess of a thing that seems to have a life of its own. And her eyes surrounded by thick, long lashes. She has freckles on her cheeks, right below her eyes, but just a few. And those lips, goddamn those lips. And her jaw… I've thought too long and too hard about that jaw, what it would be like to kiss her there, and then lower, down her neck and to her collarbone… which I can't see because she's wearing a turtleneck beneath her school shirt and it's strange because it's warm out and she's never worn… my thought trails off when I see it. I know exactly what it is because our medicine cabinet's filled with all the ones Dad takes home from work. Sterile dressing to cover a wound.

Ava catches me staring and lifts her shoulder, adjusts her clothes. She's trying to hide whatever is there, and there's only one reason why she'd do that. She doesn't want me to know how it happened.

I scribble on my notepad: *What happened?*

She writes back: *Nothing.*

Bullshit.

I watch the seconds tick by, forming all the minutes until class is over and I can ask her out loud. As soon as the bell rings, she's on her feet, rushing to get out. But she's too slow, or I'm too fast, too desperate. I catch her just outside the door and grasp her arm to stop her from fleeing. "What happened?"

She inhales deeply, before stating, "Nothing. Stop worrying." She tries to pull out of my hold, but I keep her there.

"Ava, I'm not playing. What the fuck happened? You're MIA for five fucking days, and you come back hurt?"

"It's not what you think," she says.

I don't even know what I'm thinking.

"I have to get to my next class. I'll see you at lunch, okay?"

She bails, leaving me standing in the hallway with my heart pounding and my mind racing. Five days. Five fucking days and she hasn't shown up to school once, has barely answered my texts. Ever since Trevor left—

Trevor left, and Peter came….

Peter.

Ava

I'm going to tell Connor the truth.

I decided a few minutes after leaving him in the hall that I would come clean and tell him everything. I wanted to tell him then and there, but the mix of anger and concern in his eyes had me panicking for a way out. I just needed a few minutes to myself so I could collect my thoughts and explain things in a way that would make him understand. The last thing I needed was for him to misplace his emotions and blame my mom for everything. Of all the things that could possibly ruin whatever it was we had going, his misunderstanding of my mom's mental health would be the most heartbreaking.

I sit in the bleachers, our usual spot, and wait for him to show up while I make up pieces of our future conversation. I want to be ready for any questions he has, and I want the answers to be real. To be raw.

Minutes pass, and I start to get antsy. My breathing becomes shallow, my palms begin to sweat, and the burns begin to itch. I try not to think about it as I wait. Stand. Sit again. I check the school website for the basketball roster, thinking maybe he forgot he had some prior engagement. Nothing comes up. I stand again, look over and out and everywhere I can for him. Then my phone rings. It's already in my hand, so I answer without looking.

"Connor?"

"It's Krystal, Ava. I think you might need to come home, honey. A boy is fighting Peter in the front lawn."

I hang up without a word, dial another number and start rushing toward the lot.

Rhys answers on the first ring. "What's up?"

"I need a ride home. It's Connor."

"Meet me at my car."

⟡⟡⟡⟡⟡

Rhys's car screeches to a halt halfway up my driveway. I have one foot on the ground before he comes to a complete stop. "Oh, my God, Connor, stop!"

The two are wrestling on the grass, Peter on top of Connor, his fist raised. He gets a shot at Connor's stomach, but it doesn't seem to faze him. Connor rolls them both over until he's on top, and his fist hitting Peter's jaw sounds like lightning, feels like thunder. There's blood pouring out of Connor's nose and Peter's mouth, splatters of crimson all over their shirts. "Stop!" I cry out, reaching for Connor's arm. He doesn't flinch. Another punch to Peter's gut.

"Enough!" Peter yells, half defending himself while trying to buck Connor off him.

He has his hand on Connor's throat now, while Connor screams, "Is that what Ava said, huh? Enough?"

"Connor stop it!" I squeal.

"I didn't fucking touch her," Peter yells, getting the strength to shove Connor away. Connor rolls to the side, but Peter won't quit. "Who the fuck do you think you are!"

Connor kicks up his legs, gets Peter in his chest with a knee. "That's enough!" Rhys shouts, trying to get between them.

"Ava!" Krystal calls out. "I'm calling the police."

I can't breathe. I can't see through my tears.

Connor pushes Rhys away, and now he and Peter are on their feet, fists raised, both on the attack. "You ever touch her again, I'll fucking kill you."

Peter lunges for him, his shoulder going straight to Connor's stomach. A guttural sound leaves Connor's lips, and he's on the ground, only for a second before he's back up.

"A little help, Ava!" Rhys hollers, struggling. He's holding Peter back, but he won't last long, and fear and frenzy shake me from the inside.

I run as fast as I can from my house to Connor's, my fists balled as I bang on the door. "Help!" I yell. I pound harder, faster, until the door finally opens. Connor's dad looks at me wide-eyed and startled. "It's Connor. You need—"

Corey's racing down the steps and toward my house, and before I even make it back, he has his arms around Connor's waist, trapping his hands to the side. "Knock it off!"

Now the two guys are restrained, and I stand between them, not knowing what to do or how to act. "I swear to God. I don't give a fuck who you are or where you're from, you so much as look at her again and I'll end you," Connor seethes, his face red. I stand in front of him, but he doesn't see me through the rage flaming inside him. He spits blood from his mouth, his chest heaving beneath his shirt.

"Connor," I cry, trying to calm him.

"Get out of my way, Ava."

His dad tightens his hold. "Connor, that's enough!"

Sirens approach, and when I look around, I see our neighbors outside their homes, all watching us, some with their phones out.

The Insane Asylum.

The Looney Bin.

Tears flow, cascade. I lower my gaze, cover my mouth to muffle my cries. "You need to leave, Connor," I beg.

His heavy breath hits the top of my head, and I look up to see him watching me. Beaten and bruised, his eyes hold mine. "Ava," he whispers, shaking his head.

"Please," I urge. "Just go home."

CHAPTER 31
CONNOR

'M LOCKED. Trapped in my own fucking home—my own nightmare—while outside, Ava and Dad speak to the police as if I don't have a voice of my own. An hour passes, and Dad still hasn't returned, and I'm losing my damn mind. I pace. Three steps one way, then three steps the other because it's all the room this shitty house has to offer.

I'm pissed.

Beyond it.

Because she didn't ask *him* to leave. She asked *me*.

Finally, Dad enters, and I stop pacing. Arms down, chest out, I'm ready for it. "I convinced them not to press any charges against you," he says.

"Me?" I shout. "What about that fucker?!"

"Watch your goddamn mouth, Connor!"

I draw back. "You're kidding, right? He's the one hurting her, and you're in here blasting me?"

"He didn't touch her!"

"How do you know?"

"Because I was there, okay! I'm the one who treated her!" he yells. My stomach drops, and everything inside me stills. I take a breath. And then another. I start to speak, but he beats me to it. "Whatever it is that's going on with you and that girl, it ends *now*."

I shake my head, defiant. "No."

"You think this is up for discussion?"

I start to walk away.

"I'm serious, Connor. I *forbid* you from spending time with her."

I turn on my heels, an incredulous laugh bubbling out of me. "You *forbid* me?"

"Yes." He stands in front of me, arms crossed, standing his ground.

I try to calm my thoughts, try to settle my breathing. "You *forbid* me?" I repeat, then take a step forward, tower over him. "For seventeen years I've done nothing, not one damn thing, to ever disobey you. You've never had to punish me or set rules for me. I've always tried so fucking hard to be the perfect kid because I was so afraid you'd abandon me, too—"

"Connor—"

"No!" I scream. "This is the first time in my entire life that I've ever needed your help, and this is what you do? You take away the one good thing I have in my life and—"

His sneer cuts me off. "You're acting like an ungrateful brat. You have plenty of good things in your life!"

"Like what?" I shout. "Basketball?"

"Yes!"

"It's just a game! It's not—"

"It's more than a game! It's a ticket out!"

"For you, Dad! It's a ticket out *for you!*"

His arms unfold, anger pulling at his brow. "What the hell is that supposed to mean?"

I open my mouth but stop myself from saying something I'll regret, something I've held on to for years. It means that he wants me gone, to a college far, far away, so he doesn't have to deal with me anymore. So he can get rid of the unwanted burden that was left to him. "Nothing."

"If you have something to say, say it!"

"I don't," I mumble, looking down at the floor. "But you can't stop me from seeing her."

"Bullshit, I can't," he says, his voice raised again. "She—that family of hers—they're bad news, Connor. And you don't need them in your life. Not now. Not ever!"

"I need to get out of here." I step into my room and grab my ball, then shoulder past him to get to the door.

The moment my hand's on the knob, Dad yells, "That girl is nothing but a bad distraction! She's got problems, problems too big for you to shoulder, and she's tearing you down with her! Look at you! Look at what she's made you do! She has nothing good to offer you, Connor! Not one damn thing!"

I open the door.

Freeze.

Solid.

Ava's standing on my porch, her fist raised, ready to knock. I slam the door shut behind me, my anger deflating. "How much did you hear?"

Eyes glazed, she slowly looks up at me. "All of it."

I sigh. "If you're here to tell me how much of a fuck-up I am, you can save it." I drop the ball, lean against the porch railing. "I've heard it all already."

Ava stands in front of me, her arms shielding her stomach. "Your dad's right, you know?"

"No, he's not," I breathe out, wiping the dried blood from under my nose. I inspect my hand, then wipe it on my pants. "He's right about a lot of things, Ava, but he's wrong about you."

I wince when she reaches up, touches a particularly sore spot on my jaw. I have no idea what I look like. I haven't checked. "How hurt are you?"

"How hurt are *you*?" I retort.

She doesn't respond.

"Come here," I say, my fingertips making contact with hers. I gently tug, hoping she does the rest.

She takes a step toward me, and then another. I close the distance, wrap my arm around her waist and pull her into me, ignoring the pain in my ribs when she leans against me. She settles her cheek on my chest, while I hold her to me completely, not wanting to let her go. My lips pressed to the top of her head, I whisper, "I need to know what happened, Ava."

She nuzzles closer to me, her arms going around me. "My mom happened."

I swallow the truth I knew was coming. "I'm sorry," I tell her. "And I'll go over tomorrow morning and apologize to Peter, too. I fucked up. I don't—just the thought of someone hurting you… I… I lost it. I don't even know what got into me, but…"

"It's okay," she says, looking up at me. Darkness looms in her stare, while sadness falls from her lashes. "I should've told you the truth from the beginning. It's just—"

"Hard," I finish for her. "God, Ava, I can't even imagine how hard things are for you. But I'm here, whatever you need, whenever you need me. I'm *here*."

"I can't," she says, slowly releasing me.

I grasp her hand. "Why?"

"Because—" Her phone rings, cutting her off. She looks at the screen, but I don't want my question to go unanswered.

"Why?"

She ends the call, looks up at me. "Because your dad's right, Connor." Then she jerks out of my hold. "And I have to go."

CHAPTER 32
Ava

THEY LOOK LIKE FIREFLIES. The way the water falls from the sky, illuminated only by the streetlamps. I stand in the middle of the road, barefoot and barely breathing, my arms out, face to the sky.

I don't know how I got here.

When I climbed out of my window, the sun was just setting and now… now I'm surrounded by dark skies and false hope.

I had to get out of the house. Krystal had left and Peter had called the crisis team to stay overnight again, and there were too many people under one roof. Too much pain and anguish. I couldn't breathe, and yet, I didn't want to. And even though there was so much going on, it felt…*lifeless*.

I messaged Peter once I was far enough away and told him not to look for me, that I was fine and just needed space and time to piece myself back together and prepare for another day.

I know I should go home.

That I should face my fears and tackle them head-on.

My mind travels the right roads at the right time to get me there, but my heart...

My heart takes me to Connor.

Outside his bedroom window, mud seeps between my toes, and the frigid air creates goosebumps along my skin. I raise my fist and tap, tap, tap on the glass.

A moment later, a light turns on. And then nothing. I tap again, my heart racing. The blind lifts and Connor appears, his eyes squinting. It's clear he'd been asleep, or close to it. Hair a mess, he's shirtless, the obvious beginnings of bruises mar parts of his torso, and I look down, shame filling every part of me. I bite down on my lip as he slides the window up. "Jesus Christ, Ava. What the hell are you doing?"

His warm palms meet my soaking wet elbows, and then his entire body is cocooning mine, lifting me off my feet and into his bedroom. My feet land on his soft carpet, and I look down at the mess I've made. "I'm dirty," I tell him.

Inside and out.

Dirty, dazed and damaged.

"You're soaked," he murmurs. "Just wait, okay? Don't go anywhere."

I stand in the middle of his room surrounded by blue walls and basketballs, raindrops dripping from my hair, my fingers. He returns with a towel and a first-aid box, his movements swift. His towel-covered hands start at my hair, and then down my arms. He squats when he gets to my legs, does each one in turn, and then he stands up again, his touch gentle as he leads me to his desk chair, encourages me to sit. "Your dressing's ruined," he informs. He sits on the edge of his bed and reaches across, rolling me toward him. "I have to change them, or you won't heal properly." Concerned eyes look up at mine, keep them there. His chest rises with his long inhale as if it's the first breath he's taken since he's seen me. He asks, "Can I do that for you, Ava?"

Slowly, I nod, my gaze moving from his eyes to the bruise beneath it, the cut on his nose and the corner of his lips, then down to his collarbone, another bruise, two more on his torso, and I fucking hate myself.

He starts at my neck, slowly peeling off the gauze, his eyes focused, hands steady. "Does it hurt?" he asks, his voice quiet.

I shake my head.

Breaths staggered, his gaze flicks to mine, then back down again. He moves forward, just an inch, his heated breath hitting my jaw. I hear the moment his lips part, and my eyes drift shut when his mouth finds the burn. A moan escapes from deep in my throat.

He repeats the process again and again, each kiss lighting a spark inside me, warming me from the inside out. He pulls back, his eyelids heavy, then he blinks. Once, twice. And his bright blue eyes are focused again. He grabs a tube of cream and starts applying it to the burns, gently, then replaces each of the gauzes he'd removed. When he's done, he exhales loudly, his fingers reaching up to move the hair away from my eyes. He stares at me, eyes flicking between each of mine. "What were you thinking being out in the cold like that?" His fingers trace my arms, up and down, up and down.

"I wasn't," I admit. "But I needed to see you."

His forehead rests against mine when he says, "I'm glad you're here."

I rear back, run my thumb below his eye. "Does this hurt?" I ask.

He nods, his hand circling my wrist and pulling my hand down so he can link our fingers together. "A little."

I lick my lips, kiss away his pain the way he did mine. His palm cups my jaw, his fingertips laced through my hair while his lips find mine, skimming, but not kissing. We exhale at the same time, our breaths merging. I run my hands along his arms, feeling his muscles tense beneath the contact. Then over his bare shoulders, down his chest. I pause just over his heart, wait until I feel his life beating beneath my touch. "Magic," I whisper, my lips still on his. He sucks in a sharp breath, holds it there. I run my hand to his collarbone. "Does this hurt?" I ask, finger tracing the reddish-purple mark.

I pull back so I can look into his eyes—eyes glued to mine. With his bottom lip caught between his teeth, he nods, his head falling back when I lean forward, press my lips to the exact spot. His throat bobs with his heavy swallow, and I kiss him there, smiling at the sound he makes.

I feel… *free.*

Powerful.

For the first time in a long time, I feel like I'm in control of what happens next. I push on his shoulder until he's on his back, his body held up by his elbows, his eyes watching me through his thick lashes. I kiss between his collarbone and down his chest, my tongue darting out, leaving a trail behind me. His hand claims the back of my head, fingers curling as I move lower, lower. I get to my knees, eyes closed, and lick the line between his perfect abs. I find the top of his boxers, fingers playing with the waistband. I start to pull down, but his hand tightens, tugs gently on my hair. "Ava, stop. *Fuck.*"

He sits up, his hand still on my nape, keeping me in place. He buries his face in my neck, his shallow breaths heating me. "Fuck," he says again.

"What's wrong? Do you not want—"

"No, Ava. Jesus Christ, of course I want that. It's just… I don't want *this.*"

"You don't want *what?*"

He settles his forehead against mine, his eyes shut. He takes a few calming breaths, his shoulders heaving. Then he says, "I keep telling myself that I can do this—whatever *this* is. But we keep straddling the line between friendship and *more…* and sure, I can keep doing this with you. I can keep waking up every morning wondering whether that day will be a day I get to hold your hand or kiss you or touch you or just speak to you. I *can* do that every day for the rest of my life, and you'll be worth it, but… but I don't *want* to, Ava. I don't fucking *want* to."

"I can't give you what you want," I whisper, tears pricking behind my eyes.

His forehead drops to my shoulder, his single sigh the sound of defeat. He murmurs, "You keep saying that like you know what I want."

"Then what do you want?"

He looks up now, his eyes locked on mine. "You, Ava. I want you. On your good days and your bad days—*especially* your bad days. I want you to let me in. I want you to come to me and look at me the way you're looking at me now, and know that I'm *all in*. I just want *you*." His voice cracks. "God, Ava. I want you so fucking bad, it's killing me."

"I don't… I don't know what to say."

"Say yes."

My mind tells me that it'll never work, that our paths lead to different roads and the only possible outcome is heartbreak, but my heart…

My heart says, "Yes."

His mouth is on mine before I can take a breath, his strong arms lifting me off my knees and on top of him. Then he rolls us over until he's over me, his weight held up by his elbows. Every inch of him covers every inch of me, and he's so warm. So solid. So *safe*. There's no pain, physical or otherwise, when his hands drift up my side, along my breast, until he's palming my neck. Careful of my burns, he places his mouth on my collarbone, licking, tasting, and I can't breathe, but the good type. The type that comes with excitement and joy and anticipation for what's to come. My foot makes contact with something on his bed, and I lift my head, look at the source. And then I laugh. I shouldn't, but I do. It starts as a giggle and turns into an all-out grandpa wheeze laugh. Connor looks up, his eyebrows drawn. "What's so funny?"

"There's a basketball in your bed," I laugh out.

He gets on his knees between my legs, the bulge in his boxers prominent. I try not to stare. I fail. He says, "I told you I sleep with a basketball."

"I thought you were joking!"

He shakes his head.

My laughter simmers down enough to say, "Show me how you sleep with it."

"Right now?" he asks, and I nod. He adjusts himself, his hand going in his boxers, and I let out a groan as I watch every one of his muscles shift. Disbelief laced in his tone, he adds, "You'd rather watch me pretend to sleep with a ball than continue what we're doing?"

I nod again, unable to hide my grin.

"Fine," he says, standing. He taps my leg. "Get off the bed."

"Sheesh, you're my boyfriend for all of a minute, and you think you can boss me around?"

"Boyfriend?" he asks, smirking. "I like that. A lot. You must refer to me as that for all of eternity."

I push him toward the bed. "Show me how you sleep with the ball, you fucking weirdo."

Chuckling, he fixes the covers, then gets underneath. On his side, one leg bent, he cuddles the ball to his chest and closes his eyes. "Nigh nighs, *girlfriend*," he whispers, then sucks his thumb.

With a short laugh, I ask, "Is it normal to be jealous of a basketball?"

He throws the ball across the room, then lifts the covers. All humor gone, he says, "I'll let you in if you do the same for me."

I don't miss the double meaning in his words, and so I bite my lip, hesitant. "I can't stay."

He smiles. "I'm not asking you to." Because he doesn't want anything more from me than what I have to offer. He wants me. Just me. Exactly as I am.

I get into bed with him and settle in the crook of his arm, my head against his chest. And if magic didn't exist *within* Connor, then it exists all around him. Because moments ago, I was dirty, dazed and damaged, and now…

Now I was falling asleep under a starlit sky, surrounded by tiny glimmers of hope.

CHAPTER 33
CONNOR

Ava: Good morning, boyfriend. My alarm went off at 4:30 and I had to get home. I didn't want to. I could've stayed in your arms forever.

Connor: New phone. Who dis?

Ava: Sorry. Wrong number. I meant to send that to my other boyfriend.

Connor: I'll beat his ass.

Ava: Before or after you get done sucking your thumb, you giant baby.

Connor: Listen here, you little shit.

Ava: I miss you.

Connor: Me too. I'll be around earlier to take you to school. I have a lot of apologizing to do today, remember?

Ava: Oh yeah. Sucks to be you.

Connor: Not really. Last night I had a girl sleep in my bed for the first time ever, so that was kind of cool.

Ava: Yeah? Was she hot?

Connor: *Eh.*

Ava: Listen here, you little shit.

Connor: I can't wait, Ava.

Ava: For what?

Connor: Everything.

◇◇◇◇◇

"Damn, I did a number on you," Peter says, coming down Ava's porch steps.

"Yeah, you got me pretty good," I admit, rubbing the back of my neck. I'm feeling a little ashamed, to say the least, and even though my anxiety had me practicing my apology speech before I got here, I'm stuck on how to start.

He backhands my stomach, and I wince at the sudden pain. "If it makes you feel any better, you got in a few good shots, too."

"I wish it did, but no." Groaning, I look at him but keep my head down. "Look, I'm sorry, man. I wish I had more to say than that, but…" I trail off.

He lets out a heavy sigh, then motions for me to follow him. He walks down the driveway and onto the sidewalk, far enough that Ava can't hear us from the house. Leaning against his car, he shoves his hands in his pockets. "I'm not going to lie; I spent most of yesterday pissed. But I think it was more that you messed up my pretty face than the fact that you did it at all."

"So, you're not pissed at *me*, specifically?" I ask.

"No."

I exhale, relieved.

"Why?"

"I don't know. I feel like that would be worse. You're obviously important to

Ava, and she's important to me, so the last thing I want is to jeopardize that by becoming your enemy."

"You're not my enemy," he laughs out. "And even though you were dead wrong about what happened, your intentions were in the right place. And I can't be mad at you for thinking you were protecting Ava. That's..." He looks toward the house. "That's kind of why we're all here, right?"

I nod, though my gut tells me there's an underlying meaning to his words that has me questioning *his* intentions.

"Look," he starts, standing taller. "Ava's had it rough, and she might come across as tough, as though she's *fine*, and sure there are days when she might be, but those days, Connor, those days are rare. And if you want her in your life the way I know you do, you have to prepare yourself to care about her during all the times in between. Because you don't get to pick and choose."

"I know," I reply, my voice hoarse. "I'm aware of all of this."

Nodding, he asks, "She stay with you last night?"

I return his nod.

He smirks. "Five hundred bucks and I won't tell Trevor."

"Dude, I don't have five hundred." I don't even have *five*.

He chuckles. "I'm kidding, man."

Ava opens the door, saying bye to Krystal and her mom over her shoulder. Then she turns to us, her eyebrows raised. Her grin warns me of what's to come. "You guys are so cute," she hollers. "Now kiss!"

Peter shakes his head. "It's good to have you back, Ava," he says, widening his arms for her to embrace him, which she does. "I'll be gone when you get back from school, so this is goodbye."

Ava pouts, looks up at him. "I'll see you soon, though, right?"

"I'm a phone call away if you need anything." He kisses the top of her head, but his eyes are on me. "Anything, Ava. I mean it."

◇◇◇◇◇

"What's with you?" Ava asks, squeezing my hand that's settled on her lap as we ride to school.

I ask, distracted, "What do you mean?"

"You're being weird. Distant." She starts to release my hand, but I hold hers tighter.

"Sorry. It's just…" I struggle with my phrasing, then just come out and say it. "Peter gives me the creeps."

She giggles. "Maybe you should go beat him up."

"Maybe," I say, pushing away those thoughts. "Hey, just curious. If you had to score that fight, who do you think came out on top?"

She doesn't skip a beat. "Me."

"You?"

She shrugs. "I got the guy."

◇◇◇◇◇

I barely sit my ass down for first period when the teacher calls my name. "You're needed in the principal's office. Now."

Rhys is already in the office, along with Coach Sykes, and there's a sinking in my gut because I know where this is going.

Principal Brown says, "Due to your lack of class attendance yesterday, I'm suspending you both for tomorrow's game."

Coach swears under his breath, throws his hat across the room. "Dagnammit, gentlemen!"

"Ooh, he maaaad," Rhys sings, and I can't stifle my chuckle in time.

"You think this is a joke, Ledger?" Coach says, getting in my face.

I flatten my features. "No, sir."

"It's probably for the best," Coach retorts. "We don't need a face like yours representing the team."

I flinch and turn to Rhys. "How bad do I look?"

He shrugs. "Nothing a little trip to Sephora can't fix."

"I'm glad you gentlemen are finding this amusing," says Brown. "But I'll have you know that a scout from Duke is attending the next game, and while he'll be looking for boys to hand acceptance letters to, you two will be riding the bench."

◇◇◇◇◇

When you think college ball, you think Duke. For so long, the idea of going to Duke had been exactly that: an idea. A pipe dream, really. But now… now I was here and *fuck*.

Rhys doesn't care as much as I do. Sure, he's the team captain, but college ball is as far as he wants to go with it. Plus, he has the finances to get into most places. And yeah, I'm sure more opportunities will present themselves, but they won't be Duke.

I try to push all those thoughts aside as I make my way up the bleacher steps, toward a waiting Ava.

"Is it true?" she asks the second I'm in earshot. "That you were suspended for a game and Duke is going to be there?"

"How do you know?"

"Rhys."

"Rhys has a big mouth."

"Connor, I'm serious," she whines, tugging on my arm so I sit down next to her. "Maybe I can talk to Principal Brown. It's the least I could do considering it was my fault you both—"

I grab her legs, cutting her off, and settle them over mine. I place my hand on her thigh, just below her skirt. "You didn't force me to skip class and act like a Neanderthal. It's on me, and I'll bear the consequences."

"But—"

"Ava, *please*, let it go. I get this half hour with you, and I don't want to waste it arguing about dumb shit. Now kiss me already."

"Okay," she says, kissing me once. Her lips lift at the corners, and my eyes drift shut when she runs her fingers through my hair.

"Ava?"

"Yeah?" she murmurs, her mouth pressed to my neck.

I pull her closer. "Promise not to tell anyone about the whole sleeping with a basketball thing?"

She laughs but doesn't pull away. Her lips skim along my jaw, stop just below my ear. "But then the whole flashing my boobs to the AV guys so they'd broadcast it at the next game would be for nothing."

I grunt when she bites down on my earlobe and bring my hand higher up her leg. "Don't fucking joke." Then I pull away, capture her mouth with mine, kissing her with a possessiveness I didn't know was in me.

She giggles into my mouth.

"I'm not playing, Ava."

She just laughs harder.

◇◇◇◇◇

Trevor hisses the moment I open my front door. "Damn, kid. You took a beating."

I step onto my porch and close the door behind me. "You should see the other guy."

"I did, dude, and he doesn't look anywhere near as bad as you."

I shrug. "What's up?"

"Can we maybe walk, talk about what happened?"

"There's not much to say. I thought Peter was the reason Ava got hurt and I wanted to kill him."

Trevor's lips thin to a line, and he jerks his head toward the road. "Let's walk anyway." It's not a question this time, so I reopen the door, tell Dad I'm heading out for a bit. We haven't said much to each other since yesterday's blow up, and I don't plan on being the first to break. I have nothing to add to the conversation, and if he genuinely thinks he can stop me from seeing Ava, he obviously doesn't know me as well as he thought he did.

Trevor walks beside me with his hands in his pockets. I do the same. We're two blocks away from our houses, and he hasn't said a word. I've got shit to do, so I say, "So... how was your trip?"

"You know it's not the first time this has happened," he says.

"What?" I ask, turning to him. "That one of Ava's friends has started a fight with your friend on your front lawn?"

It's supposed to be a joke, but Trevor shakes his head, his eyes on mine, not even a hint of humor in them. "That Ava's mom has hurt her." Oh, so we're *not* here to talk about Peter and me. *Noted*. "It's not the first time," he repeats. "And it won't be the last."

Oh. "Right." I didn't know, and the way Ava explained it, she made it sound like an accident. Or maybe I chose to hear it that way.

I follow behind him as he walks up a steep hill. At the top is a little playground. One set of swings and a single slide.

He sits down on a swing, the entire frame bending with his weight. I stay standing... because I'm pretty sure the entire thing would collapse with both our loads. Trevor's legs bend, then outstretch. He's not really going for air; he's just kind of... swaying. He exhales a sharp breath, his eyes to the ground. It's clear that whatever he plans on saying next is hard for him, and so I focus, give him all my attention. "What's going on?"

He scratches at his jaw, his brow furrowed. "Ava's mom..."

"Yeah?"

"She's been through a lot."

"I mean, that's pretty obvious, right?"

"No, Connor." He shakes his head, his shoulders slumped. "You don't even know the half of it." He pauses a beat, and I let him gather his words. "She's a POW. Do you know what that means?"

Swallowing, I nod. "Prisoner of war, right?"

"Yeah," he says, his voice cracking. He clears his throat, looks up at me, his eyes clouded. "I don't want to get into too much detail, but her unit was under fire and uh… they caught her. They caught her and they…" He takes a breath, and then another, and I can see the struggle in his eyes, hear the weakness in his voice. "Jesus, Connor, do you know what they do to *women*—"

He can't finish and I don't want him to.

"They kept her for months, and when she finally managed to escape—that's when the grenade…" A single tear falls from his eye, and he swipes at it quickly, sniffing back his emotions.

My legs give out beneath me, and so I sit on the stupid swing next to him, my stomach in knots. There's an ache in my chest, a burn so intense it has me groaning. Tears prick behind my eyes, and I rub at them, sniff once to keep my rage in check.

"I'm sorry," I manage to say through the lump in my throat.

Trevor shakes his head. "Ava doesn't know any of this. My dad told me, and I made the decision not to tell her. So this is between us. Man to man. Okay?"

"Of course."

"Look," he says, a sigh escaping him. "There are going to be times when you'll hate her for the way she treats Ava, and for the way she acts and the way she feels, but you have to keep perspective, Connor. You *have to*. For Ava. Because you only know her now, but you didn't know her as Ava's mom, back when she was able to *be* Ava's mom."

"I got it," I assure.

Two little kids approach the swings, toy trucks in their hands. They stop when they see us and run back to their parents. I can only imagine what we look like: two big-ass dudes on tiny swings, trying to hold back tears.

"I'm just letting you know," Trevor informs, "because Ava's flitting around the house with a stupid smile on her face that she can't seem to wipe off, and I'm assuming maybe *you're* the reason for it."

I think about the strength Ava must possess, far greater than I had initially assumed, and I say, "I guess."

"So, you guys are a *thing* now."

"Yeah."

"Good," Trevor acknowledges, standing. "I mean, it's good for her to have something in her life that brings her happiness." Pride fills me, but there's a nagging in my gut that tells me I'm not worthy. "But you can't go beating people up every time Ava gets hurt, especially when there's no source to that pain."

"Yeah," I say, because it's all I *can* say.

"Okay," he declares, eyes on mine, cheesy smile in place. Back to the old Trevor, he squeezes my shoulder, his thumb digging into the bruise on my collarbone. "You get her pregnant, and I'll fucking kill you."

CHAPTER 34
CONNOR

"I LOOK like I'm going to a funeral," I say, glaring at myself in the mirror. I'm wearing the school-issued suit that the team has to wear when we're attending the games but are ineligible to play.

Dad sighs, watching me from my bedroom doorway. "I can't believe you got suspended. And tonight, of all nights, Connor. What the hell—"

"Stop," I tell him. "Just stop, okay? I *know*."

"Well, you have to show up, right? Maybe you can catch the scout before he leaves."

"Okay," I say, my eyes drifting shut, shoulders tense, hands balled in frustration.

My phone dings with a text, and I pick it up off my desk.

Ava: BOYS!!

> *Rhys:* A little early in your relationship for a three-way, but I'm down.
>
> *Connor:* Gross.
>
> Ava: ***Hot.***
>
> *Connor:* What's up?
>
> *Ava:* Suit up, boys!
>
> *Rhys:* Huh?
>
> *Connor:* What?
>
> *Ava:* Suit up! Or whatever the term is. Get in your uniforms. You guys are playing tonight.
>
> *Connor:* No fucking way.

I rip off my tie and slip out of my shoes, my grin unconfined.

> *Rhys:* Are you serious?
>
> *Connor*: How?
>
> *Rhys:* ^^ what he said.

"What's going on?" Dad asks.

"Ava got me back in."

"Good. It's the least she could do," he murmurs.

I ignore him. Read the next message.

> *Ava:* I just had to show Brown my boobs. He was very appreciative.
>
> *Connor:* Dammit, Ava!!!
>
> *Rhys:* Noice!
>
> *Ava:* Does it matter how? Just go!!! Get ready!!! You'll be late.
>
> *Rhys*: Thanks, A.

Another message shows up in a different box, just mine and Ava's.

> *Ava:* So… is this what they call coming in clutch?
>
> *Connor:* It is! You're amazing. I don't know what you did, but thank you, Ava. THANK YOU.
>
> *Ava:* You're welcome, baby.

Ava: Now go!!

Connor: I'm going!

I change as quickly as I can and rush Dad out the door so I can make it for pregame and warm-ups. I practically sprint to Dad's car, and with my fingers on the door handle, I stop when I hear Ava call my name. I turn to see her running toward me, barefoot and beautiful. Her hair's wet and free of its usually messy knot. It's the first time I've seen it like that. The curls flow behind her as she races toward me. She's holding a bright orange balloon and the marker used to write her usual words. She stops when she gets to me, her breathing heavy. "Boo!" she jeers, handing me the balloon.

I take it from her grasp, my cheeks aching with the force of my smile. One hand on her waist, the other shifting her hair. "I like your hair down."

"You do? I just got out of the shower to answer Brown's call and messaged you as soon as I could." She glances over my shoulder to my dad, who no doubt watches us. Her smile falls, and she takes a step back. "Good luck, okay?"

I pull her back to me, not caring who's watching, and plant a kiss on her lips, passionate and painfully perfect.

Just like her.

◇◇◇◇◇

Sweat drips down my forehead and into my eyes, and I blink it back, pour water over my face. It's our last timeout of the game, and I've given it everything I have. Our score reflects that, and so does the burn in every one of my muscles. My chest heaves, my shoulders, too. Flames fire in my lungs, and Coach looks at me. "You want out?"

"No, sir."

"You haven't had a minute off, Ledger. It won't break you."

I swallow between shallow breaths. "I'm good." Then I look up at Dad watching from the stands, his arms crossed. He nods, a show of encouragement. And then he smiles at me, and I'm reminded of all the times he's been there, all the times he's done exactly this—even before the end game. "You got it, son!" he shouts loud enough to hear over the chanting of the crowd.

"You okay, man?" Rhys asks.

"Yeah." I shake off all other thoughts. "I'm good. Let's do this."

We're only on the court for another two minutes before the final buzzer sounds. I shake hands with the other team and then rush to the bench so I can sit down, give my body time to recover. Elbows on my knees, I hunch over myself and towel the sweat off my face. "Good job, Ledger," Coach says. "You really turned it on tonight."

"Thanks, Coach."

I stay on the bench longer than the rest of the team. While they leave to hit the showers and the crowd starts to depart, I let my muscles start to solidify again. I'd been weak, weaker than I should be, and I make a promise to start hitting the gym more and working on my stamina. I should be focusing on sprint sets rather than long distance.

"Connor?"

I look up to see Principal Brown and a man I've never met before standing over me. I get to my feet. "Yes, sir?"

Brown smiles, waving a hand to the man next to him. "This is Tony Parsons. From Duke. He wanted a word with you."

My pulse picks up pace, as if I'm on the court again, overtime, two points down and I'm at the three-point line, ball in my hand. "It's good to meet you, sir," I say, shaking his hand.

"Likewise," he responds. "That's quite a shiner you've got there."

"Yeah, it's…"

"It's one of the hazards of basketball, right, son?" Brown says.

I nod, grateful for his response.

Parsons continues, "Well, Connor, have you ever thought about playing for Duke?"

"Only when I'm breathing."

He smiles, then opens his mouth, but I interrupt, my finger up between us. "Sorry, just one second."

I look up at the stands, at one of the only people left—my dad. His eyes are wide, clear. "Dad!" I wave him over and watch as he makes his way toward us. Then I turn back to the scout. "This is my dad," I tell him. "I uh…" I give him the truth that, lately, I'd been too stubborn to realize. "I just like to have him around."

◇◇◇◇◇

"It's not like I'm going to get my hopes up or anything," I say into the phone, pacing my room, the adrenaline inside me still pulsing.

"You should totally get your hopes up," Ava encourages. "I mean, it's *Duke*."

"Yeah, but do you know how many scouts they have looking for high school ballers? I'm, like, one in hundreds these scouts would be talking to."

"Connor," she laughs out. "You're looking at it wrong. You're one in *only* hundreds that they're talking to. That's a big deal no matter how much you try to downplay it."

I hold the phone to my ear, and pick up a ball, then spin it on the tip of my finger. "I guess."

"I'm proud of you," she says, and I can hear the genuine honesty in her voice.

I drop the ball to the floor and sit on the edge of the bed. "It wouldn't have happened without you."

"Well, technically, if you think about it…" she trails off.

"How did you get us back in, anyway?"

"I told you."

"Ava…"

She giggles into the phone, causing my chest to ache in longing. I wish she were here. In my bed. So I could see her. So I could run my hands through her curls and kiss her and hold her and maybe fool around a little. "I just wrote him a heartfelt letter about what had been going on and how you and Rhys were my saviors, and that you didn't deserve to be punished for it. Vincit qui se vincit."

"What does that mean? The last part?"

"It's the school motto. It means *He conquers who conquers himself.*"

"What does that have to do with anything?"

"Well," she says, mocking. "How the hell is Brown supposed to let you conquer the world if you're on the sidelines for being chivalrous?"

"I can't believe you managed to work that in there."

"Your girl can be quite convincing, Connor."

I smile into the phone, let the silence fill the space between us.

"I wish I were there," she says quietly, reading my mind.

"I know. Me too."

Dad knocks on my door, enters.

I lower the phone to my lap.

"I'm heading off," he says, smiling. "You did real good tonight, Connor. I'm proud of you. You're one step closer."

"Thanks, Dad," I reply, genuine. "And thanks for being there. I would've been a nervous wreck if you weren't."

His smile widens. "Anytime, son. We'll call Ross tomorrow and fill him in on what happened."

"Okay."

"Don't stay up too late, all right? You've had a long day."

"Yes, sir."

I wait until he's out of my room and out of the house before lifting the phone to my ear again. "Hey, sorry."

"You and your dad are talking again?" Ava asks.

"Yeah, I guess."

"That's good," she says, but I can hear the uncertainty in her voice.

"Look, about what my dad said about you…" I sigh. "It's not as if he has something personal against you. It's just, he's being protective, you know? And it's not like he *knows* you, because if he did…" I trail off, not knowing what to say.

"You don't need to explain," she assures. "It's okay. I know what we are—my family—and I know how it seems from the outside looking in. But just… if it ever gets too much for you—being with me—just say so."

"Ava, stop." I flop down on the bed, cover my eyes with my forearm. "We don't need to be having this conversation."

She's silent a beat too long.

"Ava?" I sit up.

"Sorry," she says. "Someone's just uploaded the game, and I'm trying to download it as fast as I can. Oh, my God, I'm so giddy. *Hurry up!*"

"I can probably get you a copy tomorrow."

"Guh! Tomorrow's too late. I need it *now!*"

"You're not—"

"It's here," she cuts in. "Blah blah blah, people I don't care about! Hey, it's you! Okay, I'm going to watch it. Bye!"

She hangs up before I get a chance to respond. But no more than five minutes later, she sends me a text.

> *Ava:* Damn, Connor. You look good on camera.
>
> *Connor:* Stop it.
>
> *Ava:* You think I'm joking? *unzips*
>
> *Connor:* Hey. No unzipping unless I'm with you.
>
> *Ava:* Hmm. The thought of you unzipping me… *unzips twice*
>
> *Connor:* You could come here… if you want to. I can leave my window open. Dad doesn't get back until morning.
>
> *Ava:* I wish I could, but the doctors came by today and changed Mom's meds. I have to be here in case she has a reaction.
>
> *Connor:* How is she?
>
> *Ava:* She's doing much better. She just had a few bad days,

that's all. Thanks for asking.

Connor: Of course.

Ava: Okay, I'm going to go watch now. Bye, boy, bye!

An hour passes, and I'm already in bed when the next message comes through.

Ava: Welp. It's decided. Sorry to tell you, but you kind of suck, #3.

Connor: I know.

Ava: Feel like giving me a goodnight kiss?

Connor: …

Ava: ?

Connor: Sorry, I didn't realize that was a question. How? When? Where?

Ava: Now. Left side of the house. Second window.

I'm out of bed and into sweats and out the door in less than ten seconds. I smile when I see Ava waiting for me, half leaning out her window. She brings her finger to her lips in a shushing motion, and I slow my steps, go lighter on my bare feet.

"You're crazy fast," she whispers.

"I wasn't sure how long the offer would stand."

She rolls her eyes, leaning farther forward to grasp my shoulders. Pulling me as close as I can get, she kisses my forehead. "Goodnight, boyfriend."

"That's it?" I deadpan. "You made me come over—"

Her lips meet mine, soft and warm, while her arms wrap around my neck. I reach up, fingers threading through her curls, and hold her to me. She tilts her head, her tongue swiping against mine, and I let out a guttural moan. Then she gently bites down on my bottom lip, and no joke, my knees give out beneath me. I catch myself, one hand on her window ledge, the other grasping her hair, tugging with enough force that her head rolls back, giving me access to her jaw, her neck. I release the window ledge and bring my hand to her shoulder, down her chest, the backs of my fingers skimming a part of her I've fantasized about for so long. *Too* long. She moans, taking my mouth again. Then my jaw. My throat. God, I love her there. She nuzzles into my neck, her breaths heavy. My heart races, blood rushing to an organ I'll no doubt be paying attention to as soon as I'm back in bed. "I could do this all night," she whispers.

I grunt. Because I'm incapable of forming words, apparently.

"But we can't," she says, laughing silently. "Another minute, and what we're doing will be illegal."

I take a few calming breaths, let my pulse settle. "Yeah, you're probably right."

She rears back, my hand still in her hair. Then she offers one last kiss. Chaste. Her eyes lock on mine, a smile playing on her lips. "Goodnight, boyfriend."

CHAPTER 35
CONNOR

WITH MY BASKETBALL schedule and school and Ava's *life*, we don't get anywhere near as much time together as I want. And with the team doing as well as it has been, there are more commitments I have to deal with. Pep rallies, meetings, and media interviews. It's not a *bad* thing. It means more chances of being noticed, but it sucks that I barely get to even speak to my girlfriend. And we're only ten days into the relationship.

Ava: Hey, can you ask your dad when my dressing is supposed to come off? I can't remember whether he said ten or fourteen days.

I peel myself off the couch and go to the kitchen, where Dad's starting on dinner. "Hey, Ava wants to know when she should take the dressing off her burns."

Dad looks up from whatever he's doing. "It depends on how well it's healed."

"Okay, I'll tell her," I say, starting to type out a text.

"She can come around if she wants me to have a look at it."

I pause, my thumbs hovering over the screen. I look at Dad again, my eyebrows raised. "Yeah?"

He nods.

"Are you sure?"

"I'm sure."

Connor: Dad says it depends on how it's healed, but you can come over, and he can take a look at it.

Ava: …

Connor: ?

Ava: Are you sure?

Connor: That's what he said.

Ava: Okay, I'll be over in a bit.

"She says she'll be around soon," I tell Dad.

"Good."

Something's off with Dad's reaction, but I can't quite put my finger on it. Regardless, I find my home back on the couch and wait. Fifteen minutes later, there's a knock on the door, and I'm on my feet and swinging that bitch open. The door. Not Ava. She's not a bitch. She's The Best. I lean down to kiss her, but she presses her hands to my chest, stopping me. She shakes her head, and I smell… perfume? Ava never wears perfume, at least not that I know of. I take a step back to let her in. She's dressed *nice*, but like, if she were going-to-church type nice. I like Ava in tank tops and sweats, and yeah, her school uniform, but that's a *whole* other conversation. "Why are you dressed like that?" I whisper.

She elbows my gut. "Shut up."

"Hi, Ava," Dad calls from the kitchen. He points a knife at the couch. "Just take a seat, and I'll be with you in a moment." He's all sweetness and smiles, and I'm suspect.

My eyes narrow at him and then Ava when she says, "Thank you, sir. I appreciate this a lot."

I flop down next to her, throw my arm over her shoulders. She pushes my hand away. "What's *with* you?"

"Not now," she hisses without moving her lips.

Dad comes into the living room drying his hands on a dish towel. He sits on the coffee table, dish towel beside him, and asks, "Can I take a look?"

Ava cranes her neck. "Sure."

While Dad's focused on peeling off the dressing, I put my hand on Ava's knee. She pushes it away again.

"It looks like it's healed just fine," Dad says. "No more dressing, but be sure to use the cream I gave you until it's all gone, okay?"

Ava nods. "Thanks again, Mr. Ledger."

He gathers all the dressing and stands. "No problem."

Ava stands, too, and I take her hand. This time, she lets me. "I'll walk you back."

I open the door at the same time Dad calls Ava's name. Ava turns to him, her eyes wide, shoulders rigid. Dad stands between the kitchen and the living room. "I'm just starting on dinner. You're welcome to stay if you'd like."

Ava does her best not to let her shock show, but I see it even if Dad doesn't. "I appreciate the invitation, but I have to get back home."

"Oh." Dad drops his gaze, his shoulders. "Okay, sure."

"It's just..." Ava starts, sensing Dad's disappointment. "I can't really leave my mom, so..."

Dad tilts his head. "Isn't your stepbrother home with her?"

Ava nods, her grip on my hand tightening. "Yeah, he is, but he's really only there for when things with her get uh..." She glances up at me, and I try to offer an encouraging smile. If this is Dad's attempt at getting to know her, then we *have* to try. "Sometimes she gets physical and he—he has to restrain her." I can hear her voice weaken with every word, so I release her hand, place mine on the back of her head and bring her to my chest, her ear to my heart. Ava exhales slowly, her eyes drifting shut. When she opens them again, she says, "I have to be there, because I'm the only one who can really *talk* her through whatever she's experiencing."

It takes a moment for Dad to respond. "Right. And… Trevor's father? Where is he?"

I speak up. "Dad, what's with the twenty questions?"

Dad shakes his head as if clearing the fog. "You're right. I'm sorry."

"No, it's okay," Ava says. "He left a while back."

"So, it's just you kids taking care of her and the house and all the bills?"

Ava nods, then shakes her head. "No, we have a caregiver stay with her when Trevor's at work and I'm at school. But yeah, on the evenings and weekends it's just us."

"Oh, good," Dad says. "I assume that's all done through your health insurance?"

"I wish, but no. Insurance doesn't cover nearly enough of it. The military only really covered her physical injuries, and even though we still get her full benefits it's not even close to…" Ava pulls away. Just a tad. "I sound like I'm complaining, but I'm not. I promise. Things could be a lot worse," she says, looking up at me. She faces my dad again, a frown on her lips. "At least she's alive, and we can be a family. And I'm sure you and I can both agree that there's nothing more important in this world than family. That's why we sacrifice the things we do and protect the people we love."

Dad sucks in a sharp breath, exhales slowly. "You're absolutely right, Ava."

Ava smiles at him, then, on her toes, she kisses me once. "Stay," she tells me. "Have dinner with your dad. I'll call you later."

"Ava," Dad calls again. "If you or your brother or your mom… if you need anything that I can help with, please…" he trails off, nodding, before disappearing into the kitchen.

◇◇◇◇◇

"Jeez, Connor. I had no idea how bad things were for her," Dad says, setting the table for us. "I feel horrible for the things—"

"I appreciate it," I tell him. "But I'm not the one you should be saying this to."

With a nod, he sits opposite me at the table, his hands clasped under his chin. "I'm going to make a few calls in the morning, see what I can find out about getting her some financial help for her mother's care."

My brow lifts. "Yeah?"

"It's the least I can do."

I sit back in my chair, watching him closely. "What's with you?"

"What do you mean?"

"It's like you've done a complete 180. Your attitude's changed, and now you're acting... I don't know."

Dad's chest lifts with his inhale. "I reconnected with an old friend today, and they gave me a little perspective. That's all."

"Anyone I know?" I ask.

He shakes his head. "No."

CHAPTER 36
Ava

CONNOR SAYS, downing last night's pasta as he sits on the bench in front of me, "It sucks that our paper's done. Now we don't have an excuse to whisper dirty things in each other's ears during class."

My eyes narrow. "You've never whispered dirty things in my ear."

He chuckles while chewing. "Shit. Different class. Different girl."

"Hmm. Now I'm *really* glad I put cyanide in your food."

He eyes me a moment, then slowly lowers the container next to him.

"I'm kidding," I laugh out.

Shaking his head, he says, "I'm not willing to risk it."

"Speaking of murders…"

"It's such a turn-on when your girlfriend talks about killing people." I push on his shoulder with my foot and regret it the moment he grabs hold of my ankle and then my waist, effortlessly lowering me until I'm sitting across his thighs. "Go on."

I get comfortable in my new position and throw my arm around his neck, fingernails scratching the back of his head. He moans, drops his head between his shoulders. I say, "So I read a story this morning about this twenty-nine-year-old man who saw his dad kill his mom and bury her in their yard when he was three years old. Apparently, when she 'disappeared,' he told the cops his dad hurt his mom, but the cops didn't believe him. Because, like, he's *three*, right?"

He's quiet a moment, then, "Huh."

"And who remembers stuff like that when they're *three*."

His eyes are on mine, searching.

"Anyway," I continue, "he moved back to that same home twenty years later and dug up the spot where he remembers seeing it and guess what?"

"They found her remains."

I nod, lips pressed tight.

"That's crazy."

"I know! Imagine carrying around those memories for so many years, from when he was *three*."

He swallows, looks away. "That'd be pretty horrible."

"Right?" I exhale harshly. "Thank God you don't remember anything from when your mom—" I cut myself off, because *shit*. "Sorry," I say, my voice quiet. "I wasn't thinking."

He shrugs. "It's okay."

"No, it was insensitive," I admit. "I just had a brain fart moment."

"Speaking of brain farts," he says, "what the hell were you wearing when you came over last night?"

My eyes go huge, my breath catching. I pull on his hair, ignore his screech of pain. "I was trying to make a good impression. The first time I met your dad wasn't exactly under the best circumstances!"

"You looked like my grandma."

I laugh. I can't help it. "You make out with your grandma?"

"I barely make out with you," he mumbles.

"Aww." I settle my hands on the sides of his head and make him face me. "You want to make out with me?"

"I'd like to do more than make out with you, but..." He looks around us. "Here?"

I quirk an eyebrow. "You got your car keys?"

He nods, biting down on his lip. Then he's practically throwing me off of him and taking my hand, dragging me down the steps. I giggle the entire way to the parking lot.

Five minutes later and he has my back pressed to the inside of his car door. His mouth is on my neck, lips warm, tongue wet. His hands are everywhere, all at once. I untuck his shirt from his pants and feel the muscles on his stomach, then bring my hands to his back, clawing him closer to me. I can't get enough, and neither can he because he whispers my name as if it's air in his lungs. He covers my mouth again, his tongue sliding against mine, and I wish he had a bigger car, or I had a car *at all* because he's too large for such a small space and I want to feel him all over me and around me, and God... *inside* me. My legs part when his hand slides up from my knee to my bare thigh. He pauses an inch below where I want him the most, his forehead going to my shoulder. He curses, and I look at the roof of his car, my breaths shallow. And then he covers that inch, his thumb stroking. Just once. I buck beneath his touch, and he curses again. And then he's pulling away completely, his eyes glazed, hooded, leaving me cold and confused. He settles back in his seat, adjusting himself, his chest rising and falling. "We can't do it like this..." he murmurs, looking at me. I adjust my clothes and sit up. "In my car? At school?" He sighs heavily.

"I know," I whisper.

"But I want to, Ava. God, I want to do everything with you."

"I know," I say again.

And then we let the silence linger between us because we both know what the next question will be. *How?*

◇◇◇◇◇

Connor: Send me a picture of you.

Ava: Are you… are you asking for nudes? Because you can fuck right off, please and thank you.

Connor: Lol. No. I just don't have any pics of you that aren't taken from outside your bedroom window while you're sleeping.

Ava: *Dude…*

Connor: Hi, I'm Connor. Pleased to creep you.

Connor: But seriously send me a pic. I don't have any of you, and I want it as my home screen.

I bite down on my lip, scandalous thoughts running through my mind. In the month we've been together, we've not shared anything more than a slight touch to the wrong—or *right*—places. I switch off my bedroom light and turn on the lamp, then I get into bed, lower the thin strap of my tank top to reveal my bare shoulder. Eyes on the lens, I lick my lips, take a snapshot. I send it to him without a second thought.

Connor: Jesus Christ, Ava. That's not home screen material, that's…

Ava: You want another one?

Connor: Maybe move your top down a little more? Just an inch.

I comply, shifting until the neckline barely covers the top of my breasts. I take another photo, send it to him.

Minutes pass with no response.

Ava: Are you there?

Connor: Can I call you?

Ava: Yeah.

My phone vibrates in my hand, and I quickly answer. "Give me a sec. I'll just plug in my headphones."

"Mmm."

After grabbing my headphones from my nightstand, I connect them wirelessly and put one in my ear, needing the other free so I can hear the rest of the house. "What's up?" I ask.

"Ava," he says, his voice low. Rough. "I need you to send me another one."

I swallow, knowing what he's asking for. "You first."

My phone vibrates almost instantly. He's lying on his back, his hair a mess, eyes half-hooded. And he's shirtless, his collarbone and muscled chest on full display.

"Your turn," he insists, his voice barely audible.

I hesitate a beat, before lifting my shirt and angling the camera so my stomach and the underside of my breasts are in view. I quickly hit send, my body heating, pulse throbbing between my legs.

"Fuck, Ava," he groans, his voice muffled by what I assume is his pillow. "You're killing me."

"Send me another one," I whisper, gasping for air.

I hear him shift, and a moment later, his picture comes through. This one's similar to the one I sent, an image of his perfect six-pack, each one defined by deep dips. There's a scattering of dark hair between that V that drives women wild. It leads to a spot covered by the waistband of his boxers, an inch above his basketball shorts.

My mouth is dry. So dry. And I squeeze my legs together to try to increase the sensation there. I'm breathing heavy, so heavy I'm sure he can hear it. I force a swallow, try to regain some composure, but I can't. My entire body is on fire, and I'm squirming, trying to find some form of reprieve from the powerful ache building inside me.

"Babe," he says, but it comes out a moan. I can hear him shifting, moving, and I imagine him in his bed, eyes closed, chest rising and falling, his hand in his shorts… thinking of me. "Your turn."

I shove my hand beneath my underwear, the tip of my finger pressing down on my nub. I let out a moan before picking up my phone and hitting the button.

I check the picture, just enough for him to know what I'm doing without revealing too much.

I hit send.

"Fuck, Ava."

I close my eyes, listen to the sounds of our breaths. Short. Sharp. Shallow. Amplified by the silence around us. I move my hand faster, faster, my back arching off the bed as I climb, climb, climb.

The phone vibrates again, and I open his next picture. A whimper escapes when I see it. His hand's in his boxers, the outline of his knuckles clear, his hand circling his rock-hard—

Connor grunts, and I close my eyes again, my pleasure soaking my fingers. We don't say another word. We're nothing but heavy breaths and grunts and whimpers. I listen intently. Every sound, every movement. Every rapid, rhythmic shift. I know he's doing the same as what I'm doing, and I imagine that we're doing it to each other. The vision pushes me over the edge, a muted scream bursting from my throat. I bite down on my lip, my entire body convulsing as he moans with each of his breaths, louder and louder until one last, long grunt.

I listen to his breathing settle while mine does the same. An entire minute passes before I hear him chuckle. "Holy shit, Ava."

I sigh, long and loud. "Teenage hormones are one hell of a drug."

CHAPTER 37
CONNOR

"So... last night was..." I say, looking down at Ava's legs. Her skirt seems higher today, or maybe it's the way she's sitting, or maybe she's doing it just to mess with me.

"Intense?" she asks and lifts her skirt another inch. Yeah. She's definitely messing with me. I grip the steering wheel tighter, and she giggles when I moan and adds, "Keep your eyes on the road, stud."

"Fine." I do as she says and tell her, "You know I have that pep rally in the cafeteria today, so I can't meet you at lunch."

"Oh really? I must've missed the six hundred posters plastered all over school."

"Funny. Maybe you should get your eyes checked."

"Eh," she says, shrugging. "I think my eyes are just fine. I mean, I *do* have the hottest boyfriend in school."

I can't help but smile. "You think I'm hot?"

She scoffs. "As if you don't know."

I shrug.

"Connor! Have your exes never told you?"

Another shrug. "I don't have any exes."

"Shut up!"

"I don't," I laugh out. "You're my first, Ava."

"First girlfriend?"

"Uh huh."

"But you've, like, kissed girls before?"

"Yeah," I nod. "I touched the side of a boob once, too."

"Connor!" she squeals, laughing. She pushes my side, and I straighten the steering wheel. "Ew. I don't want to know that!"

I settle my hand on her leg and gather the courage to ease into the next question. "So, I was thinking… maybe… if you wanted to… you could come to the pep rally today."

She tenses beneath my touch, then whispers my name.

"I know it's not really your thing," I tell her, doing my best to mask my disappointment. "But I just thought I'd ask. It'd be nice if you were there to support me, but it's cool."

"I would if I could," she says quietly.

I glance at her. "So why can't you?"

She sucks in a breath and then exhales slowly. But she doesn't answer my question. In fact, she doesn't say anything else for the rest of the drive.

◇◇◇◇◇

I stand between Coach Sykes and Rhys while the school band plays, and the rest of the students are chanting *Wildcats! Wildcats! Wildcats!* The team has been doing well, amping up the school spirit, and I wish I could join them in their hysteria, but I'm too busy looking at the entrance, my hopes rising and dying every time the sliding doors open and it isn't Ava. Don't get me wrong. I appreciate the amount of support she's shown, and I understand why she can't go to the games, but this—this is *in* school—the few hours a day when we actually exist in the same space.

The band finishes their performance, and one of the AV guys appears out of nowhere to hand Coach a microphone. "Thanks for that. What a great intro!" There's a sarcasm in his tone that's readily forgiven because he's old and cantankerous, but he's a staple in the school and the reason why the program runs so well.

He starts going through the team's roster for tonight's game, calling names one after the other, waiting a few seconds for the cheers after each one. Then he gets to my name, and the screams are loud, louder than with Rhys, but beneath all those screams I hear a single sound that has my heart racing, my lips lifting. "Boo!"

My eyes dart everywhere, looking for the sound, and then I spot her. She's standing in front of the students milling by the entrance, and she must've forced her way through because she wasn't there only seconds ago. I thought it would be impossible for my grin to widen, but here I am. I raise my hand, a small wave, and she does the same, a proud smile playing on her lips.

The rally's over as soon as Coach is done talking. I start to make my way over to her, but Coach stops me with his hand on my chest. "One minute, Ledger," he says, and I look at Ava and mouth, "Hang on." She nods, points to the cafeteria line. She gets to the end of the line and picks up a tray. I don't know how long it's been since she's had cafeteria food, but boy, is she in for a treat.

"Ledger," Coach says again, and I turn away, give him all my attention.

"Yeah, Coach?"

Rhys is next to him, wearing a shit-eating grin.

I start to panic.

"Rhys and I got to talking," Coach starts. "And we were wondering if you'd be interested in co-captaining for the rest of the season?"

My jaw drops as I look between them. "Are you serious?"

Rhys shrugs. "It'll look good on your college applications."

"Yeah." I nod incessantly. "Hell, yeah. Thank you."

Coach offers me his hand, and I shake it, unable to hide my elation. The cafeteria breaks out into small giggles, and then all-out laughter. I'm still holding his hand when I turn around to see Ava at the start of the line, her tray of food held at her waist. In front of her, a punk kid has his arm pulled out of the sleeve, his long hair flipped to one side, covering half his face. He's talking to her—no, he's *shouting noises* at her, and then he's swaying his body, using his armless sleeve to knock the food off her tray, his shouts getting louder, and I see red.

Red.

Hot.

Rage.

I release Coach's hand and start toward him, but Coach and Rhys are both holding me back. "I'll take care of him," Coach says.

"Calm down," Rhys tells me, as if I can. As if it's possible. And then I look at Ava. At the way her lips part, the way her eyes are wide open but filled with tears, as if she refuses to blink because if she does, her tears will fall and she doesn't want to give this asshole the satisfaction. Slowly, she places the tray back on the rail and turns, the crowd around her parting as she walks away. People are still laughing and my heart… my heart is sinking.

And then I blink.

Come to.

I chase after her, calling her name. Her steps are fast, but mine are faster. I try to grasp her arm, but she shrugs me off. Within seconds, we're at her locker, and she's stuffing books into her bag, refusing to speak, refusing to look at me.

"Ava!"

She slams her locker shut, and then she runs… a slow run, but still a run. The first sound of her cry comes just as we pass the office. I manage to get her around the waist, force her to stop and face me. "I'm sorry," I say, "I'm sorry." It's all my brain can come up with.

She squeezes her arms between us, her hands on my chest, and then she pushes. She pushes me away, swiping at her tear-stained cheeks. Her cries echo through the empty halls as she holds her bag to her chest and takes the few steps to the psych office. I follow after her, but I don't touch her, too afraid of her reaction.

She opens the door without knocking, and I'm right behind, stopping just inside. Miss Turner stands as soon as she sees Ava, dropping her sandwich on her desk. "Ava?" she whispers, then looks at me. "What happened?"

Ava's cries are louder now, uncontrollable, and there's an ache in my chest that prevents me from answering.

"Ava?" Miss Turner says again, moving around the desk to get to her. "Sweetheart?"

"You said!" Ava cries, the loudness of her voice shaking me to my core. I pull out of my daze, only to realize she's talking to me. "You said, Connor! You said you didn't want anything more from me!"

My heart squeezes, flatlines. A lump forms in my throat. "I didn't…" I look between Ava and Miss Turner. "I didn't know."

"Of course you didn't know!" she screams. "They don't do it in front of you or Rhys, but they do it. And they do it to me. And to *her!*" She takes a breath. "You said…" she repeats, quieter this time. She leans against the wall and then slides down until her ass hits the floor. "You pressured me to be there, to face *that*… You said you just wanted *me*, but you lied!" She lifts her knees to her chest, her face going between them, arms covering her head, shielding her from… from *me*. "You lied, Connor."

She's rocking now, back and forth, and I haven't taken a breath. Haven't felt a single beat in the place I keep just for her. "Ava, I don't—" I choke on my words. "I don't know what to say."

Her cries are silent, the sound replaced by hiccups, and she won't look up, won't stop rocking. And then her breaths get louder, faster, escalating to a point harsh enough that Miss Turner curses, grabs a paper bag from her desk drawer.

She drops to her knees in front of Ava and strokes her hair, imploring her to look up.

Tears fill my eyes while the knot in my stomach grows and grows and grows some more. Ava takes the bag from Miss Turner and breathes into it, her breaths slowing, but her cries still steady. Her shoulders shake with every one of her hiccups, and all I can do is stand.

Watch.

Wait.

Worry.

The bell rings, and Miss Turner looks up at me. "Go to class, Connor."

I widen my stance, my arms at my sides. "I'm not leaving her."

Ava's single whimper shatters every living cell inside of me.

Miss Turner's voice hardens. "That wasn't a suggestion, Mr. Ledger. Get to class. *Now!*"

⋄⋄⋄⋄⋄

I don't know how I make it through the rest of the afternoon, but as soon as the bell rings, I go searching for Ava. First her locker, then my car, then Miss Turner's office. She's nowhere to be found, and so I call her. Again and again and each time there's no answer. I try messaging her:

Connor: Where are you?

And then Rhys:

Connor: Do you know where she is?

And then I go to send one to Trevor, but I realize I don't even have his number. Hands pulling at my hair, I look up at the sky for answers—answers that aren't there. I check the basketball court, the locker rooms, and then Miss Turner's office again. It's locked.

I knock. "Ava?"

There's no response, so I go to the office and ask where Miss Turner is. Apparently, she's clocked out for the day. I give up on school and am almost home, my phone continually dialing Ava's number as I drive. And then a text comes through:

Rhys: She's here.

I pull over.

Connor: With you?

Rhys: Yeah.

Jealousy burns a hole in my chest.

Connor: At your house?

Rhys: No, but yeah. Just drive to my house. You'll see us.

Rhys rushes to my open window the second he sees my car. I spot Ava sitting on the sidewalk, her legs crossed, staring up at her old house. "She won't talk," Rhys says, his voice low as he pulls on the car door to get me out faster. "I tried, man, but… I don't know. I don't know what to do."

"All right," I tell him, calm. As if I have all the answers. I'm as lost as he is, if not worse, because I *should* know what to say. Or do. But I don't. And maybe it's worse that I'm here, because maybe I'm the one who caused all of this, but I'm not willing to walk away like I did before. "Just go home; I'll take care of her."

He leaves without another word, and I gather what little strength I have left and slowly go to her. Her cheeks are wet, but there are no tears in her eyes. At least not yet. "Ava?" I whisper, and she blinks, looks down at her hands. "Can I sit with you?"

She nods slowly but refuses to meet my gaze.

My heart races as I sit behind her, my legs on either side. I wait a moment, pray she doesn't push me away. When enough time passes, I scoot forward until my chest is pressed to her back and wrap my arms around her waist. A single sob escapes her, and she drops her face in her hands. "What's this for?" she whispers.

"I don't know," I say, remembering the first time she'd been there for me. "It just looked like you needed it."

Another whimper, and I'm moving to the side so I can see her. I reach up, hesitant, and cup her jaw. I wait for her response, because if she's done with me, with *us*—if I fucked up beyond forgiveness, I'll hate myself, but I'll have no choice but to wear it.

Right now, the most important thing is her… and I need to make sure she's okay.

Her eyes finally lift to mine, holding more pain than I know what to do with. And then her head tilts, her cheek pressing to my palm. She reaches up, holds my wrist in both her hands to keep me there.

Air fills my lungs, and I exhale, relieved.

I finger the strands of loose hair away from her eyes and bring her face closer to mine. "I'm sorry, baby. I shouldn't have asked you to—"

My hands move with her head shake. "No, I'm sorry, Connor." She releases a staggered breath. "I didn't mean to say all those things to you. I needed someone to blame, and you were there. I'm *so* sorry. And I'm so fucking embarrassed."

"Why? Because of what that asshole—"

"No, because of the way I was." She cries harder, her tears falling fast and free. I swipe them away with my thumbs, kiss them off her lips. "Connor, I never wanted you to see me like that, to see me break and fall apart and… God, why are you here? Why do you still care about me?"

"Ava," I breathe out. "You had every right to feel the way you did… Jesus, I had no idea it was like that for you at school, and I'm sorry. I'm sorry for asking you to do something I knew you weren't comfortable doing. I'm sorry that shit happens to you and to your mom. I'm sorry it happens *period*. But you have to believe me; nothing you said or did today changes the way I feel about you."

She grips my forearms, a single sob falling from her lips.

"Babe, look at me."

Tear-soaked eyes lock on mine.

I kiss her once. "Promise you believe me."

She shakes her head. "You can't possibly tell me that you still look at me the same."

My response is there, on the tip of my tongue, but it's not enough. And even though I want to tell her how I truly feel, that I've fallen so hard and so fast and so deep… that my every thought, every action is consumed by *her*, this isn't the right time or place, and so I take her hand in mine. "Let's get you home. Your mom will be worried."

◇◇◇◇◇

I get ready for the game, but my heart's not in it like it's always been. There are too many thoughts flying through my mind, and every single one of them begins and ends with Ava. I peek out the living room window through the gaps of the blinds and wait.

"What are you doing?" Dad asks, slipping on his shoes.

"Waiting for Ava."

"Is she coming to the game?" he asks, a hopeful lilt in his tone.

I shake my head. "No, but she always…" I trail off when I see her on the sidewalk, her steps slow, a single balloon on a string flopping down by her legs. "I'm going to need five minutes," I tell Dad, now waiting by the door.

I wait a few seconds, my ear to the door, listening for the sound of her footsteps on our rickety porch. I count to three, then open the door, and sweep her into my arms from behind. She squeals, and a tiny bubble of laughter comes next, eliminating all prior worries about how she'd be feeling.

"Jeez, Connor, give the girl some room to breathe," Dad jokes.

I close the door between us while I allow Ava to turn into me, her hands pressed to my chest. "Hi," I say.

She bites down on her bottom lip. "Hi, boyfriend."

I exhale, her words giving me the courage to say the words I'd been planning all night. "I need to tell you something, and I need you to listen to me, okay?"

She nods, eyes on mine.

I take one more deep breath before saying, "You told me before that it wasn't possible for me to look at you the same. And you're right. I don't. And I *can't*."

Her gaze drops.

"Because when I look at you now, I see these curls," I say, tugging on a loose strand, "and I picture you when you were little, and I imagine your mom getting frustrated with you because you won't sit still so she can brush it. I bet you were stubborn, even back then."

She exhales a staggered breath, her gaze lifting to mine again.

"And your hands…" I link my fingers with hers. "I used to look at them and just want to hold them, but now… now I see them, I touch them, and I realize how much weight these small hands can hold." I grasp her face, swipe my thumb along her lips. "And these lips… I mean, yeah, sometimes I used to kiss them just to shut you up, but now… now I'll kiss them and wonder what it'll be like to kiss them ten, twenty years from now… And your eyes, I used to look at them, and they'd remind me of the hardwood of the courts, but now… now I look at them, and I see your strength and your courage and your fight to keep them clear. To keep them dry." Liquid hope pools in her eyes, her chest rising with her intake of breath. And when she blinks, I catch the tears with my thumbs and kiss each of her cheeks. "But you never have to hide who you are with me. Because I'm here. And I'll wear your pain as if it were mine. I promise."

"Connor," she whispers. Her entire body envelopes mine, her arms tight around my waist, ear pressed to my chest. Listening to the magic she creates within me.

"But, Ava," I start. "I think what's changed the most is the way I see your *heart*. I used to just feel lucky that you've given me a piece of it. But now… now I know what that heart is capable of. I know the strength and the perseverance and love it carries because I see it in the way you care about your family, the way you protect them. And I'm not just lucky, Ava. I'm…" I pause, take a breath. "I moved here with one thing on my mind. Work hard enough to get noticed so I move one step closer toward the *end game*. But… but maybe fate had other plans for me. *Bigger* ones. Because you're here, with me, and you *noticed* me, Ava, so maybe… maybe the end game was never about basketball. Maybe my end game is *you*."

CHAPTER 38
Ava

Ava: Good game, #3.
Connor: Thanks, #1 goat.
Ava: #1 goat?
Connor: #1 Girlfriend of All Time.
Ava: I… *rolls eyes* Dammit, that made me all gooey inside.
Connor: he shoots, he scooooores.
Ava: Hey… I've been wondering. Why #3?
Connor: I don't know. It was the first number given to me. I've just kept it ever since.
Ava: Did you know that in every story, act three is the most important chapter?
Connor: How so?
Ava: Well, it delivers the story's lowest point (me today) and then how the characters cope with that (you today) and then the climax and resolutions.

Ava: I think maybe you're my resolution, Connor.

Ava: So #3 suits you.

Connor: *Unzips*

Ava: *what??*

Connor: Sorry, I read climax and then… what? Let me go back and read the rest.

Ava: OMG! I hate you.

Connor: Wait. That was actually really sweet. Thank you.

Ava: No, I take it back.

Connor: How far back?

Ava: What?

Connor: Are we still ending on the climax part because if so… *unzips*

Ava: Goodnight, boyfriend.

Connor: Goodnight, goat.

CHAPTER 39
Ava

THE KID who messed with me in the cafeteria got a two-day suspension. The first day of his return, he had a little "accident" during gym class and decided to take the rest of the week off. Funny what a handful of laxatives, an underpaid cafeteria worker and two basketball co-captains can achieve. At first, I was mad that Connor and Rhys stooped to that level, but then… fuck that guy.

That was a few weeks ago, and since then, Connor hasn't asked me to do anything besides let him kiss me goodnight every night, to which I comply. And, if anything, what that kid did to cause my little breakdown just brought Connor and me closer together. Made us stronger. So… thanks, shit-stained-ball-sack kid!

◇◇◇◇◇

Connor looks up from his phone when he hears my front door open. I should smile or wave or do something, but I'm too busy arguing with Trevor to do anything else.

"You're doing it, Ava," Trevor says, his voice firm, as he opens his truck door. "It's not an option."

I shake my head, my jaw tense, nostrils flaring. "Fine!"

"Fine!"

I stomp my foot. "I said fine!"

"Fine!"

I grunt, "Go to work!"

Trevor scoffs. "Go to school!"

"I am!"

"Good!" he shouts, but there's no malice left in his tone. Instead, he's holding back a smile.

My defenses crack, just a tad, because we're arguing over something so important to him because he thinks it should be important to me. This morning, he handed me a piece of paper with a dollar amount on it, and when I asked him what it was, he told me it was my budget for college applications. I reminded him that it was useless, and he reminded me that I already promised him I'd do it... hence the pointless argument that in the end, I know I'll lose. Because just like everything else Trevor does, he only does it *for me*. "I love you, you idiot."

Trevor laughs and says, before closing his door, "I love you, too, you brat."

Connor's wide-eyed by the time I get to him. "Man, if that's what having a sibling is like... I'm kind of glad I'm an only child."

I mumble, my brow furrowed, "Good morning, boyfriend."

And he responds, "Hmm. Neither your face nor your voice leads me to believe there's anything *good* about this morning."

I kiss him quickly and make my way to the passenger's side of his car, where

I get in, slam the door, and *pout*, my arms crossed, nose in the air.

Connor gets in after me. "You know, if you weren't so damn cute, I'd agree with Trevor. You *are* a brat."

"Shut up," I say, but I'm half laughing because I'm so fucking tired, I'm delusional. "I've had, like, an hour's sleep," I say through a sigh. I grab his hand, settle it on my thigh where he usually keeps it. "Sorry, I'm grumpy."

"It's okay," he assures, starting the drive to school.

"My mom kept waking from these horrible nightmares." Or flashbacks, going by how badly she reacted to them. I add, yawning, "I ended up falling asleep on her floor at around three."

"I'm sorry, babe. I can drive you back. You shouldn't be at school."

"No," I whine, pout some more. "It's the only time I get to see you."

"Yeah, but—"

"Shh," I whisper, holding his entire arm to me. "Just let me cuddle your arm and close my eyes. I'll be fine." I let his warmth settle over me and give in to the heaviness of my eyelids. Just a few minutes, I promise myself, and I can get through the rest of the day.

My own snoring wakes me from my sleep. There's a heat pack against my chest and a wetness on my chin. I try to force my eyes open, but I'm too damn exhausted. Then I try to remember how I got into bed… One minute I was getting into Connor's car, and the next… My eyes snap open, and I cower when the bright sunlight hits my eyes.

That heat pack? It's Connor's arm.

And that wetness on my chin? Fucking drool!

I pull away, mortified, only to see my spit all over Connor's arm. "Oh, my God!" I use my sleeve to wipe his arm. "I can't believe I drooled all over your—"

"Weenus," he interrupts.

I'm too humiliated to look at him as I scrub, scrub, scrub. "What?"

"Weenus," he repeats. "That bit of loose skin on an elbow is called a weenus."

"It is not!" I tell him, inspecting his elbow closer, making sure I got everything.

"It is. It's called a weenus."

"Stop saying weenus."

He laughs. "Can I have my weenus back now?"

I release his arm and wipe my chin, then finally look over at him. He's rotating his shoulder as if he'd been in the same position for hours. I look at my watch. "Oh, my God, Connor!" I practically squeal. "You let me drool all over your weenus for three hours?!"

He busts out a laugh. "Say it again but whisper it seductively."

"Shut up!" I laugh out, then look out his window. It's nothing but trees. "Where the hell are we?"

"I don't know," he says, looking around.

"Wait. Did you bring me here to murder me?"

He smacks his lips together. "You know, I left my shovel at home, so no, at least not today."

I take a calming breath, try to regroup. "What the hell happened?"

"I don't know," he says with a shrug. "You were fast asleep by the time we got to school, I didn't have it in me to wake you, so I just drove and found this turnoff and… yeah, I'm going to have to use the navigator to get home."

I take a better look around us. We're in an empty parking lot with only a few spots, surrounded by trees. And because my window doesn't work, I open my door and listen. The sun's out, the birds are chirping, and somewhere in the distance, there's a stream of water. It's kind of beautiful. I look back at Connor, who's focused on a book between the steering wheel and his lap.

"What are you reading?" I ask.

"College essay prep," he sighs out, closing it and tossing it in the makeshift backseat. "It's so overwhelming."

I nod. "I know. Trevor's forcing me to apply."

He smiles, but there's a hint of sadness in his eyes, and I know where it's coming from. We try not to talk about anything beyond *now*, but we both know what's ahead. At some point, we'll have to deal with it.

I ask, "Have you or Coach Sykes or your agent heard any more?"

He shakes his head. "No. Besides that one guy from Duke, nothing. Ross, my agent, thinks I might need more time. He says it's not because I don't have the skill, it's just… I haven't had the exposure."

"So, what does that mean?"

Connor shrugs. "I'll probably get a walk-on at a decent college, but it won't be a D1. At least not yet. He's hoping if I work hard enough freshman year, more options will open up for me." He adjusts so he's on his side, facing me completely. "What about you? Where are you thinking of applying?"

"I don't really know," I murmur. "And I don't even know what Trevor's game plan is. Like, yeah, I get accepted somewhere and then what? I move Mom into the dorms with me? Or I *leave* her?" I shake my head, my cheeks puffing with my exhale. "It doesn't make sense."

"Maybe he's just giving you options," he suggests.

I sigh. "There *are* no options for me, Connor. As soon as I graduate, I become my mother's keeper."

"Is that what you want?"

I stare out through the windshield, then suck in a breath. "It's what she needs," I whisper. And it's true. Because as much as I try to ignore it, she's getting worse, and I don't know how to fix it.

"That's not what I asked, Ava."

I straighten my features and turn to him, my hand going to his hair. "Are you going back to school?"

"Are you going to answer my question?"

"No."

"Then no."

A grin tugs at my lips. "You want to go for a walk?"

We walk through the thick brush, listening for the sounds of the water stream. "Is it weird that I always look around for dead bodies when I'm walking through bushes and trails?" I ask.

"Not weird at all," he says sarcastically.

We walk for a good fifteen minutes before we reach a clearing, and the sight that greets us is nothing less than spectacular. The clear skies reflect off the clear blue water of the calm lake, not a wave in sight.

"You think it'll be cold?" I ask, standing on the water's edge with him.

Connor squats down and runs his hand through the water, then comes up shaking his head. "It's surprisingly warm," he says, then looks up at me, his eyebrows raised. "You want to go for a swim?"

"In what?"

"The water, dummy."

Smartass. "I mean, *wearing* what?"

"I vote nothing."

"I veto your nothing vote."

He laughs, eyeing me. "Well, isn't your underwear the same as a bikini?"

I chew on my lip, nervous. Technically yes, but even if I were standing in a bikini in front of him, I'd still feel self-conscious. "Turn around."

His eyebrows lift. "Why?"

"Because I said so."

He sighs but complies.

I take a moment to breathe, gather my courage. I slip off my shoes and socks first, and then my blouse and skirt. Then I throw them to the side of him, so he's sure of what I'm doing. As soon as he sees the pile of my clothes, he starts stripping out of his own. With my thumb between my teeth, I watch his every move, entranced. It's as if he was born to remove his shirt the way he does, his back muscles flexing, and then he unbuckles his belt, and my mouth goes dry. He drops his pants to his ankles and then kicks his feet to remove them altogether. "Can I turn around now?"

"No."

I take a few steps forward until I'm right behind him. Reaching up, both hands start at his shoulders, then down his back. I marvel at the way his head droops forward, the way his muscles ripple beneath my palms. I kiss the spot between his shoulder blades, his whisper of my name doing nothing to deter me from closing the gap between us, my front to his back. I reach around, my hands on his bare chest, and then down, down, down, to each dip of his abs. I close my eyes, trace each one, and then move lower and lower. "Ava…" He spins in my arms, so quick I shriek a little. "You're so fucking bad," he whispers in my ear, his arousal pressed against my stomach. I bite down on my lip, crane my neck to allow him to kiss me there, his heated hands on my bare back. He moves up with one hand, fingers curling in my hair, gently pulling, forcing me to throw my head back. His mouth is on my collarbone and then on my chest, my breast. He bites down on the top of my bra, tugging just enough that I feel the air against my nipple. He makes a sound from deep in his throat before capturing my mouth with his, warm and wet and open—just for me. With one hand in my hair, the other lowers, curls against the curve of my ass. "So fucking bad," he murmurs. And then he's lifting me off the ground, my legs instinctively going around his waist. Our most intimate parts connect in the most painstakingly perfect way. He grips my thighs as our kiss deepens, our desperation revealed in the sounds we make, the heat emitting between us.

Charged.

Electric.

Magic.

I writhe against him, searching for more.

"Ava," he groans, pulling back.

I suck in breath after breath, needing the oxygen, but needing him more.

His gaze drops to my breasts, rising and falling, frantic and frenzied. "I'm about to…" He clears his throat, then nuzzles my neck. "I'm so fucking close to…" Then he laughs. "We need to cool the fuck down."

I nod, eyelids heavy, hands going to the back of his head.

"You ready to go in?"

"Carry me?"

He rears back, his eyes holding mine. "Always, Ava." And I know what he's saying without saying it—he'll not just carry me physically, but metaphorically, too. He'll carry the heavy weight that comes with all my burdens. *Always.*

◇◇◇◇◇

The water is cooler on our bodies than we expected, but we adjust quickly. "If you could be anything in the world, what would it be?" he asks, circling me while I wade around the shallow water.

"Easy. True crime fact checker. No, wait! I'd host my own podcast. Or, like, make YouTube videos, but without me in them. Maybe just my voice. I like my voice."

"You do have a nice voice," he says, stopping in front of me to hold me to him. I instinctively wrap myself around him. He adds, "But you'd definitely get more views if you showed your face."

"You think?"

"Ava, I'm a guy with working eyes. Yes."

"Do you think guys would—*you know*—over me?" I joke.

He laughs. "Also, yes. But I don't like to think about that."

"If I get enough views, I could possibly make an income from it."

"Possibly," he says, amusing my random thoughts.

"Maybe I should get a boob job," I murmur, looking down at my breasts.

He rolls his eyes. "Your boobs are fine, Ava."

"Just fine?" I pout.

He kisses the top of each breast. "They're perfect."

◇◇◇◇◇

"Tell me when you fell in love with basketball," I ask him, my chest to his back while he piggybacks me through the water so we can explore what looks like a cave.

He shakes out his hair, flicking droplets all around him. "I don't really know. There wasn't a specific defining moment. I remember being around twelve and... I mean, I didn't really know how well I'd played, but apparently one of the recruits from FSU was there, and he spoke to Dad after the game, told him that I had 'real potential.'" He turns us around so I can climb onto the rocky embankment covered by a low cliff edge. I sit on the edge, listen to him speak. "I swear to God, Dad told everyone about that conversation, even the lady at the gas station on the way home. He was so damn proud." He pulls himself up to sit next to me, his knees bent, elbows resting on them. The sun beats down, making his eyes as blue as the lake in front of us. He smiles when he turns to me, his shoulders lifting. "So... I don't know. I think, for me, it was never about my love for *basketball* so much as it was about my dad's love for *me*."

I hold his arm to me, rest my head on his shoulder. "So... you do it all for your dad?"

He kisses the top of my head. "Kind of like how you do everything for your mom, right?"

◇◇◇◇◇

We're farther in the narrow cave, still exposed to anyone in the lake, but hidden away enough that we'd see them first. We spent the first few minutes exploring, finding rocks strong enough to carve our names on the underside of the cliff. I glance at him, at the way his brow dips in concentration as he works on the middle stroke of the letter A. So far, he's written *Connor 4 A*, and it's so sweet and innocent and brings to mind my own innocent insecurities. "Connor?"

"Ava?" he responds, not looking away from his task.

"Why don't you want to have sex with me?"

He drops the rock he'd been using, then curses and picks it back up. He continues the middle stroke, digging deeper and deeper.

"It's just, you've had the chance. You've had me in your bed, and me here, now, and you don't really… touch me… like *that*, I guess…" I mumble, tripping over my words. I sit down, my back against the stone wall.

He rubs the heel of his palm against his eye, groaning.

"You don't need to answer; it's okay. I was just wondering, is all."

He's on the final *A* when he says, his voice low, "I'm scared."

"Scared?" I repeat. "Of me?"

"No," he shakes his head. "I'm just worried that I won't *perform*, I guess. And you're a lot more experienced than I am."

"Not *a lot*," I rush out.

He shrugs. "You've done more than I have. Hell, you've done *all* of it."

I'm quiet a moment, wondering how he knows, but then… "Rhys told you?"

He nods, still refusing to look at me. "He wasn't bragging or anything. I asked him why he cared about you so much and… yeah."

I blow out a breath. "It didn't mean anything. With him, I mean. It would mean something—*everything*—with you."

He finishes our names, then runs a hand over it, blowing the loose dust off, his cheeks puffing with the force. Then he takes a step back, admiring his work. He looks over at what I'd written, a simple *#3*. His smile widens. After a moment, he slowly sits down next to me, his hand on my thigh. "I want to," he says. "You have no idea how badly I want to. I think about it all the time."

"Do you…" I smirk, do the hand signal for jerking off. "Like my future YouTube viewers?"

He chuckles. "I'm pretty sure you were partially present for one of the hundred times I've done exactly that thinking about you."

I go back to that moment, to the bliss that followed. "What exactly do you think about?"

"You."

"But what about me? Like, where am I? What am I doing?"

His eyes drift shut, his breaths coming out shorter, sharper. He adjusts himself quickly, licking his lips. "You're on top," he whispers.

I get on my knees, carefully, while his eyes stay closed. Then I straddle his lap, whimper when I feel him pressed against my center. His hands find my waist while mine settle on his shoulders. "Like this?" I ask, and he nods, licks his lips again. "And what else?" I ask, breathless as I shift, back and forth, slow, slow, slow.

He grasps my ass, hard, and I moan, feel the throb build in my core. Opening his eyes, his teeth clamp down on my shoulder, then bite down on my bra strap. "And this is gone."

I swallow, reach behind me and unclasp my bra. "Like this?" I ask, releasing the straps and letting them fall to my elbows. He rears back, his lip caught between his teeth. His fingers stroke up my arms, and then down again, taking the straps with them. I'm exposed, in public, but right now, it's just him and me and all the scandalous thoughts racing through my head.

His eyes are fixated on my breasts, first one, then the other. My chest heaves, lifting them, and his mouth opens, so close.

"Connor," I whisper, and he glances up, his eyes hooded. "Please?"

He keeps his eyes on mine when his tongue darts out, flicks at my pointed flesh. I instinctively push my hips down, wanting more, needing all of him. "Shit," I moan when he goes for the other nipple, this time taking the entire thing in his mouth.

"Is this okay?" he asks.

"Please don't stop," I sigh, scooting back an inch. I run my hands down his chest, his stomach, fingers playing with the band of his shorts. I hesitate a beat, not knowing if he wants to go this far...

He makes the choice for me, his hand taking mine, guiding me beneath his shorts until my hand circles his cock. So smooth, so hard, so—

"Move," he says.

"What?" I breathe out.

"Your hand, move it up and down." Every word is a plea, and so I do as he asks, swallow the groan that bursts from within him. He kisses me, his hands tightening on my backside as I stroke him, long and slow. I break the kiss so I can fill my lungs, but he doesn't stop. He goes straight to my breasts again, and my back arches, inviting him, while I try to stay focused on his pleasure. And then I feel him, his fingers at the place I crave him the most. He shifts my underwear to the side, a single finger exploring the evidence of my pleasure. He doesn't stop with my breasts, teasing me, tasting me. I pull on his hair when a single finger slides inside me, again and again, and I can't breathe, can't... the world is a blur, our heavy breaths the only sounds filling my ears.

"Fuck, Ava, I'm so close. And you—you're so fucking perfect."

At his words, I feel the throbbing escalate, two fingers inside me now. I ride his fingers, fucking them without shame, and continue to stroke him. His cock hardens even more, and I build, build, build, until I fly, soar over the edge.

His groan comes at the same time *he* does, his pleasure covering my fist.

My eyes snap open to see him watching me, his mouth wide, breaths harsh, chest rising, falling. "Mmm," he murmurs, then swallows. "Well, that sucked."

I laugh into his neck. "It was horrible."

"The worst."

◇◇◇◇◇

Connor lies on his back post-bliss cleanup, stroking the loose strands of my hair while I listen to his heartbeat thump against my cheek. He asks, "Did you and Trevor have a hard time getting along at the beginning?"

"We *still* have a hard time," I joke.

He chuckles.

"Why do you ask?"

"I don't know," he says through a sigh. "Every now and then I get this random thought in my head that my mom's out there, you know? And she has this new family... and that new family is everything she ever wanted. Everything

I wasn't." His voice cracks, and I lean up on my elbow so I can look down at him, at his distant eyes and the slight frown pulling on his lips.

I run my mouth along his, but I don't kiss him. "I hope one day you wake up and realize that the mistakes she made are her burdens, not yours. I hope that you'll eventually understand that what she did isn't a reflection of you—of your *three-year-old* self." I'm getting worked up, so I try to take a calming breath, but I fail. "And if she is out there, I hope that one day she'll find you, and she'll see the same man I do. The strong, empathetic, courageous, protective man who cares so much about so many things, who wears other people's pain as if it were his... I hope she sees you and she fucking *hates* herself for not being the one to raise you, to guide you into becoming that person." My nostrils flare with my exhale. "I hope she *hates* herself as much as I hate her." I grind out the last few words, my anger getting the best of me. I sob. I don't mean to, but I do, and as promised, Connor wipes the tears away, his heavy sigh hitting my cheeks.

"It's okay, Ava."

"It's not," I cry out. "It's not okay, Connor. How dare she... how dare she leave you like that—to fucking die—and leave you with these questions and these... these doubts about yourself! God, I hate her so much!"

He leans up a little, lifts his hand to my jaw, his eyes taking me in for a long moment. Then he says, "Do you know the name of that movie with Omar Epps? It's like this guy and girl who live next door to each other, and they're both trying to pursue basketball careers..."

"*Love and Basketball?*" *I ask.*

He smiles, settles his head back down. "That's pretty much what my life is at the moment." I try to hide my stupid grin on his neck while he brings me closer, my heart racing, flying. Kissing my forehead, he murmurs, "Love and basketball."

We hold on to each other for the rest of the afternoon, talking about everything but tomorrow. We fight, we float, we laugh, and we *fall*. God, do we fall. Deeper and deeper into these reckless emotions.

CHAPTER 40
Ava

THE MOMENT CONNOR pulls up in front of our houses, my heart begins to sink. I know it's not reasonable to feel this way, to fear the idea of missing someone so achingly even though it's just one night.

Connor sighs, his head rolling to face me. "I wish today lasted forever," he murmurs.

I take his hand, kiss the inside of his wrist. "Me, too."

A short, sharp whistle has both of us looking up. Trevor's fists are balled, his shoulders squared as he comes down the porch steps. Only they're not my steps… they're Connor's.

◇◇◇◇◇

Connor's dad sits on the couch opposite us while Trevor paces the living room, back and forth, back and forth, and I wish he'd stop because it's not *that* big of a deal. "What the hell were you thinking?" Trevor all but shouts. "Ava, I've been calling you nonstop. Where the hell is your phone?"

I try to remember… I'd left it in the car. All day. My pulse spikes. "Oh, my God, is Mom—"

"She's fine, Ava, but that's not the point! Do you know how worried I was? Do you know how many times I tried calling you? And you think you can just cut school for no reason? Do you know how expensive that school is? How hard I work to—"

"I'm sorry!" I cry out, tears welling. "I won't do it again."

"Sorry's not really good enough—"

"What do you want me to say?"

"It's my fault," Connor speaks up. "She fell asleep on the way to school, and I didn't want to wake her so—"

Corey interrupts him. "So you just didn't bother going to school at all? Or not tell anyone where you were or what you were doing?"

"Jesus, Ava!" Trevor yells. "Goddammit, you have that phone glued to your hand twenty-four-seven and all of a sudden it's not—"

"Stop!" I yell back. "Don't take this away from me!" I swipe at the tears refusing to stop and look up at him. "Please," I beg, my voice cracking, my heart breaking. "Today was the best day I've had since Mom got back, and I don't want you or anyone else taking that away from me, okay? I said I was sorry. But I just wanted *one* day, Trevor. Just one day when I could act my age, when I could be careless and reckless and… God, I just wanted to be a seventeen-year-old girl spending time with a boy I love—"

"You *love* me?" Connor cuts in.

I drop my head in my hands, humiliated. I glare at Trevor, imploring him. "Can we just go? *Please!*"

"Ava," Trevor sighs out. "There has to be consequences…"

"I know." I stand and head for the front door. "And I'll deal with them like I *always* do, but please… just enough, okay? I just…"

"Hey," Connor coos, wrapping me in his arms. "It's okay."

Tears blur my vision when I look up at him. "I just..." *I don't want to go home,* I admit only to myself. I don't want to go home and live in the darkness now that I know what it's like to breathe in the light. "I just have to go home."

Connor

Dad waits until Trevor and Ava are out of the house and for sure out of earshot before speaking, his tone a lot calmer than Trevor's. "Your coach called. You're suspended for a game, and they assured me that no matter what Ava says or does, this time it has to stick. They're using you to set an example."

I nod, keep my gaze lowered. "That's fair."

Dad sighs. "Connor, if you want to tell me what happened, I'm happy to listen."

"Nothing," I say, looking at him for the first time since I entered the house. "I picked her up this morning, and she mentioned she hadn't slept well because of her mom..."

Dad nods, urging me to continue.

"And by the time I got to school she was fast asleep, and I... I don't know, I felt bad waking her, so I just kept driving."

"What did you guys do all day?"

Shrugging, I give him the truth. "I ended up parking near a lake, I guess, and we just spent the day... just..."

"Being teenagers?" Dad asks, a compassionate smile tugging on his lips.

"Yeah," I confirm through an exhale.

"Well, I'm sure Ava needed that," he says, sympathetic.

"She did. She *does.*"

Dad stands, stretches, then starts pacing the living room like Trevor did. I'd ask if we're done here, but I know him... there's more. I just don't know which way he's going to flip it. He sits back down at the spot he left only seconds ago, his elbows on his knees. "You have to start thinking long term here, Connor."

I *almost* fail at hiding my eye-roll. "I know. The end game. I get it, Dad."

He shakes his head, rubs his chin. "It's more than that now," he explains. "If you care about Ava like you seem to and you want a future with her, you need to think about more than just *now*. And while *now* is good for you guys, *great* even, you need to think about the future. Because if you want her in your life for more than *now*, you have to find a way to take care of not only her but her mother… because that girl—she's never going to leave her mom. And as much as she loves you, she loves her mom more, which she should." He pauses a moment, before asking, "So how are you planning on doing that, Connor? Taking care of both of them emotionally and *financially*?"

My head spins while I replay every one of his words, over and over. I think about what I want in my life, in my future, and the only thing I see is Ava. "I go pro," I declare. "I *have* to."

He nods. "So, what you do *now* is going to determine what happens tomorrow. You got that?"

"Yes, sir."

He stands. "Right now, your focus is what?"

I release the only truth that makes sense. "Basketball."

Ava

Krystal offers to stay so Trevor and I can "chat." Luckily, he's calmed down enough to have an *actual* conversation with me. In my room, he sits on my desk chair while I sit on the bed, my fingers gripping the edge of the mattress.

"I understand why you did what you did today, Ava. And I'm sorry I blew up on you like that. I was worried, but I get it. You deserve that time… but you can't be bringing Connor down with you."

"Down *with* me?" I ask, looking him right in the eyes. "I didn't put a gun to his head—"

"That's not what I meant," he sighs out. "What I mean is I know that school. I know the athletic program. He skips class, and it's an automatic one-game suspension."

"I'll write another letter."

"Ava, you're missing the point," he pushes. "Look, that school is lenient with you because of your circumstances. You skip a class here and there, and they allow it. You fall asleep in class, and they send you to the nurse's office so you can sleep some more, but… Ava, it's such a pivotal time in Connor's life right now. He has college scouts and coaches watching his every move on and off the court. What he does off the court is a representation of his character, not his skill, and his character is just as important to them as his contribution to the scoreboard or whatever—" Trevor shakes his head. "Basketball is dumb, but you understand, right?"

"Yeah, I get it," I say, and I do. Truly. I should've made him go back. I should have explained to his coach what happened and fought for him instead of being selfish and only thinking about what I wanted. What I needed. *Him*.

Trevor scratches his cheek, then his head, then his chest, his tell-tale sign of nerves. "So… you… you *love* him, huh?"

"I don't know," I whisper, watching my legs kick back and forth. "I think so."

"You *think* so, or you know so?"

"I don't know, Trevor," I whine. "I have all these thoughts and emotions, and I don't know what to do with them, and I have no one to talk to about them."

He nods, his chest heaving with his heavy breaths. Then he swallows. "Like… like… *sex* thoughts and emotions?" he asks, his voice wavering at the end.

I look to the side. "Maybe."

He's silent a beat, and then another beat, and a whole damn song could play in the time it takes him to react. "Right." I watch him press his lips together, then get to his feet. He jumps up and down on the spot, rolling his shoulders and tilting his head side to side as if he's gearing up for something. "I got this," he whispers… to himself.

My eyes narrow as I watch him, confusion clouding my brain.

"I got this," he says again and then flops back down on the chair.

"Ava," he deadpans.

I eye him sideways. "Trevor?"

"When a man ejaculates—"

"Oh, my God, *NO!*" I throw my pillow at his head. "Get out!"

CHAPTER 41
Ava

> "I'M NOT HUNGRY," Mom says, her tone flat as she stares at the wall. It's the fifth day in a row she's refusing to eat breakfast, and I really don't know why I bother getting up when I do.

I cower when I drop the spatula and pan in the sink louder than expected. The last thing I want is to wake Trevor. "You have to eat, Mama," I say, turning to her. "Krystal says you haven't been eating much throughout the day." And she's losing weight, fast. I can see it in the hollow of her cheeks and the way her clothes seem to droop against her body. There are dark circles around her eyes from her lack of decent sleep. The doctors had prescribed some sleep meds for her, but she wakes up foggy and out of sorts and her reaction to that is far worse than the constant waking throughout the night. I try to assure myself that it's just a phase and that as soon as they work out the right cocktail of medications to help her both physically and emotionally, we'll be able to move on. I might even get a positive day out of her at some point.

Mom sighs heavily, pushing away the plate I'd just made up for her. "Where are my cigarettes?"

"You don't smoke, Mama."

Her gaze flits to mine before going back to the wall. "Buy me cigarettes on your way home from school, okay?"

"I can't," I tell her, trying to keep my composure. But inside me, something is ticking, ticking, ticking. "I'm not old enough."

She blinks. Slowly. "Then I'll have William get them."

"William—" I exhale, my hands at my sides. I need to calm down. My getting frustrated will just set her off. "William doesn't live with us anymore."

Another slow blink, and then the tiniest hint of a smile. "He'll be back."

I should tell her that he won't. That he's remarried. That he has a new wife and new stepkids and that all of this was too much for him. That it might be too much for me, too. "Can I make you something else to eat?"

"I'm not hungry."

"But you should at least try to get something in your stomach, Mama."

"Where are my cigarettes?"

My head drops forward, my shoulders lifting with the force of my inhale. I squat down beside her, hold her hand in mine. And then I push down the knot in my throat, kiss the scars that created this stranger. "I'll get them on the way home from school, okay?"

CONNOR

I knock on the door of Coach's office and wait for him to look up from whatever he's reading. When he does, his eyes widen, and he looks at his watch. "You're going to be late to first period."

"I know," I say. "I was hoping to talk to you in private."

He settles back in his chair, his arms crossed. "If it's about the suspension—"

"It's not," I interrupt. "I know what I did, and the punishment stands."

Nodding, he motions to a seat on the other side of the desk. "Let's talk."

Nervous energy swarms through my bloodline as I take a seat, my knees bouncing.

"What's got you on edge?" he asks, eyeing me.

"Nothing." I lie. "Well, yeah. *Something*."

"Spit it out, kid."

"I need your help," I rush out. "I mean, I'd like some *extra* help. Please. Whatever you can offer me. I need to start focusing more on basketball, or else…" I take a breath. "I'm not getting any offers, Coach, and I need to do something about it."

He laughs once, closing the newspaper in front of him. He trashes it under his desk, then opens his drawer, pulling out a pile of envelopes three inches thick. "These are letters of interest," he deadpans.

My eyes widen. "For me?"

He chuckles, killing any form of hope I'd momentarily allowed. "You heard of Graham Sears?"

I nod. "Spurs, right?"

"Yep. He was one of mine junior and senior year. An import, like you. These are the letters he garnered during those two years. You want to see yours?"

I nod.

He reaches into his drawer and pulls out *air*. He pretends to drop it on the desk. "That's your pile."

Discouraged, I look down at my hands.

"Sears was taken third to last in the NBA draft, Connor, and that's the amount of interest he had. So, if you want just a taste of what he had, you better get ready to work."

I look up at him. "I'm here for it, Coach."

"Good," he says, leaning back in his chair. "You know what the main difference is between you and Sears?"

"He was better than me?"

"No," Coach says, adamant. "That's the thing, Connor. He wasn't. But off the court, he was with his team, building relationships and team camaraderie. He treated his teammates like they were his brothers, and in turn, those men made him *look* better, made him stand out. So, if I were you, I'd start there."

I lift my chin. "Okay."

He picks up his phone, calls the office to excuse me from first period. Then he makes another call, and a moment later, his office is occupied by the entire coaching staff and a few trainers.

All eyes are on me when Coach says, "Son, if we do this, we *do this*, you understand?"

I nod, puff out my chest. "Yes, sir."

Ava

Connor said he had to get to school extra early this morning, so Trevor ended up giving me a ride. I sit in my usual spot first period, my eyes glued to the door, my heart waiting for just a glimpse of what she desires the most. When the bell rings and he still hasn't shown up, I send him a text.

Ava: Where are you?

"Psst," Rhys hisses from behind me. "Connor said he was meeting with Coach after practice so he might be late, or not show up at all. He said he'll see you at lunch."

Oh. I nod, put my phone away. "Is he in trouble?" I ask.

Mr. McCallister calls out, "Connor's not, but you two might be if you don't stop talking."

CONNOR

We spend all of first period going through a game plan that includes extra practices, one-on-one coaching with all the coaches. More gym time. More studying. More of everything. Coach even puts in a call to an old friend about getting me into a four-day invitational held by some big name pros around Thanksgiving. It would be a dream, but I'm not holding my breath.

At the end of the period, Coach says, "Today, you have lunch with your *team*."

"I spend time with my girlfriend at lunch," I tell him.

He eyes me over the rim of his glasses. "Do you now?"

I shake my head, my heart heavy. "I guess not."

Ava

Lunch comes around, and I spend the first half sitting in the bleachers without my partner in crime. When he does appear, he's grinning from ear-to-ear. "Hey, girlfriend," he says, kissing my cheek. He sits opposite me with the lunch he acquired from the cafeteria. "Sorry I'm late. I had a thing I had to do."

"A *thing*?"

He shrugs. "Just a basketball thing. It's not important."

"It sounds important," I murmur, shoving his knee gently with my foot. "Tell me."

He holds on to my ankle, tugging gently. With a smile, I get down to his level, sit sideways on his lap. He nuzzles my neck. "I missed you," he says, kissing me there.

"I missed you, too."

He exhales, slowly. "Sorry about first period and being late. I know our time together is so limited, but…" he trails off.

I lift his head in my hands, look in his eyes. "It's okay; I know you're busy. What's going on?"

"Nothing." He shakes his head. "Nothing," he repeats. His eyes search mine, his features falling with every second that passes. "I just miss you is all." But that's *not* all, and I can see it in the way he looks at me, the way his lips tremble.

I hold his face in my hands and release the words I've held on to all night. Words I've been looking forward to saying to *him*. "I love you, Connor," I tell him. "God, I love you so much."

CONNOR

I swallow down the pressure that had been building inside me and stare at the soul that causes my heart to beat. Where my world begins and ends. I hold her to me, afraid to let go. "I love you, Ava… with everything I have."

I keep my eyes closed, hiding the fear in my heart.

What if I do all this?

Risk it all.

And still fail?

What happens to Ava?

To her mom?

What happens to *us*?

CHAPTER 42
Ava

"We need to do something," Trevor whispers.

I look down at the floor. "I know."

"So… what are we going to do?"

Lifting my gaze, I look at my mother sitting on the couch in the same clothes she's been in for over a week. She's been refusing to shower, and no amount of convincing seems to work. "I don't know."

"It's getting bad, Ava."

"The smell?"

He shakes his head. "That, too, but just… her. She's getting worse," he says, his voice hushed as we stand in the doorway between the kitchen and living room. On the kitchen table behind me, another dinner is left untouched.

"It's fine," I argue, trying to convince myself more than anyone else. "She'll be okay; it's just… a phase."

My phone dings with a text.

> **Connor:** That game just about killed me. About to hop in an ice bath if you want to join me?

"Shit," I hiss.

"What?" Trevor asks.

"I forgot Connor's game." *And the balloon.* "Dammit."

"He'll understand," Trevor assures. "You've been dealing with a lot."

I read over his text again, trying to find a way to respond. And then: "Hey, Mama? What if I run you a bath instead of a shower?"

Her expression doesn't change, neither does the direction of her stare. "A bath sounds nice."

"Thank God," Trevor breathes out.

I rush to the bathroom and start running the water.

> **Ava:** As bad as that sounds, I wish I could, just to be near you. I'm sorry there was no balloon. Give me five, I'll check the school website and get a rundown of the game.

He doesn't respond, probably in the bath, and so I focus on getting the water to the perfect temperature, filling it with as many scented bath products as I can find. I call her when it's ready, and she comes willingly, stripping out of her clothes without care. "Will you stay with me?" she murmurs.

"Of course, Mama."

I close the door behind us and help her get in. She sits with the water to her neck, her eyes open, staring at the ceiling. She doesn't speak, our breaths the only sound in the small room. I push away all other thoughts—thoughts that seem to invade my mind and ruin me from the inside out.

"Do you…" I start, careful. "Do you want me to wash you?"

Nodding, she sits up and bends over, allowing me to have access. I pour body wash on a loofa and start at her back, ignoring the ailing paleness of her skin, the way her spine sticks out far more than it should. I hear her sniff but stay silent. And then her shoulders… her shoulders start to shake. A single whimper fills the cold, dead air, and I reach up to her shoulder, move her hair to the side. "It's okay, Mama," I say through the knot in my throat. "Sometimes we all need a little help."

She reaches up with her good arm, takes my hand in hers. "Thank you," she whispers, and it's all I need. All I want. For her to know that I'm here for her. Always.

She doesn't say anything more, and neither do I. We finish in the bath, and I help her into fresh clothes and into her bed, pull the covers over her chest. She stares up at the ceiling, and I get on my knees beside her bed, put my hands on her upper arm. "Are you not tired?" I whisper.

Her head lolls to the side, her eyes welling with tears. "I'm scared," she admits.

I sit taller. "Of what?"

She lets out a sob. "To close my eyes."

"Oh, Mama." I settle my head on her chest, my eyes drifting shut when she holds me to her.

"Stay with me, Ava? Just until I fall asleep?"

I wipe my tears on her covers, then suck in a breath, attempt to keep my broken heart bound. "Of course." I get into her bed and try to be her courage while hiding my weakness. She holds me close, using just a portion of the strength of the woman she used to be. The *mother* she used to be.

I lie awake, listening to her breaths settle until I know she's asleep. Then I get out, careful and quiet. I wipe the wetness off my cheeks before opening the door and facing Trevor.

"Is she down?"

I offer the most genuine smile I can come up with. "Yeah, she's sleeping like a baby."

Trevor nods, goes back to watching whatever game is playing. I go to the bathroom and retrieve my phone.

Connor: I figured something was up when there was no balloon.

I hope everything's okay?

Connor: Just got out of the tub. Is everything okay there?

Connor: Can you come out in five? I feel like I haven't seen you in forever.

I look at the time stamp. It was sent over a half hour ago.

Ava: Sorry, I just got the message.

Ava: I can maybe come out now if you're still up for it.

Connor: Slipping on my shoes.

I tell Trevor I'll just be five minutes, and practically run outside, my heart racing, longing for the only person in the entire world who's capable of letting me forget, even if it's just for a minute.

I wait for him on the sidewalk, smiling when I see his door open. I'm in his arms a moment later, and it should be impossible—that one person can hold so much power in just their embrace—but I physically feel the tension inside me dissolve until it's just him and me and *now*. "I miss you, Ava," he sighs out.

"I know. Me, too."

He pulls away but keeps his arms around my waist, holding me close. Looking down at me, his eyes shift, as if taking me in for the first time. "I promise, once the season's over we'll go back to normal."

Normal. As in one class every other day and lunch breaks and the occasional ride together to and from school. As opposed to what it's been like the past two weeks… when I get to see him in class but not really talk to him, and sometimes he'll show up at lunch, sometimes he doesn't. There are no more rides to and from school. The only reason he gives me is that it's basketball related, but he doesn't give me much else. Any other girl would become suspicious about who he's with and what he's doing. "I understand," I tell him. Besides, he's never once questioned my inconsistencies, and apart from that one time for the pep rally, he's never asked for more of my time than I could give him.

He leans against the chain-link fence of my front yard and pulls me between his legs. I link my fingers behind his neck and just look at him, really truly look at him. He's in dark jeans and a plain gray hoodie, and his hair's wet, or… I reach up… there's product in his hair. I sniff him. "Are you wearing cologne?"

He nods. "You like it?"

"Did you wear it for me?" I ask, half joking.

"Actually…" he starts, grimacing. "One of the guys from the team is having a party tonight, and I said I'd go."

Oh.

"Is that okay?"

"Connor, you don't need my permission to go out."

"I know." His shoulders lift with his shrug. "I just wanted to check anyway."

Well, not really. He's already dressed and ready to go, so he's beyond checking. He's just… *informing*.

"Rhys is coming to get me. He should be here any second."

I get on my toes until my mouth is level with his. "So we only have seconds to get in days' worth of making out?"

His mouth covers mine without a response, his head tilting, getting better access. He pulls me closer again until there's nothing between us. I squeal when his hand covers my ass, squeezing, and then laugh into his mouth. "A little handsy, no?"

Chuckling, he kisses me once more. "I still have a ton of adrenaline. I had a good game."

"You did?" I ask, annoyed at myself for not checking first. I drop down to the heels of my feet. "Shit, Connor, I haven't even had time to check. I'm the worst girlfriend ever."

"You are," he deadpans. But there's a gleam in his eye, a slight smile playing on his lips. "You better make it up to me."

"How?" I ask with a flirtatious lilt.

He's quiet a breath, his eyes on mine, lips parted. "I was talking about that crazy lasagna you make, but whatever you're thinking right now, I choose that."

I tug down on his hoody until his ear is to my lips and whisper, "I want to know what you feel like in my mouth."

Instantly, he has both hands on my butt, lifting, and my legs go around him, holding on to him as he starts carrying me to his house. "Fuck this party," he hisses.

I can't help but laugh. "Your dad's home, and my mom—"

"Get a fucking room," Rhys shouts, pulling up to the curb.

We've barely made it into Connor's yard when he releases me back on my feet. I push him toward Rhys's truck. "Go. Have fun."

He kisses me quickly. "Love you."

"I love you, too."

Rhys says, "I love you both; now hurry the fuck up."

Connor kisses me again. "Can I message you when I get home? Maybe get that goodnight kiss?"

I nod. "Hey. No talking to girls tonight," I joke.

"Yes, ma'am," he says, kissing me again before opening the car door.

"You're so whipped," Rhys remarks.

"I don't mind it." Connor laughs. "Besides, she knows how to dispose of a dead body with little to no evidence. And I like breathing. It's *fun*."

◇◇◇◇◇

Mom's stirred twice since I put her to bed, but she hasn't fully woken, which is an improvement from the previous nights.

It's close to midnight, and I'm working on these stupid college applications when a text comes through.

Connor: I is home, woman. Kiss me.

Ava: Are you drunk? Come to my window. BE QUIET.

I open my blinds, lift the window and rest my elbows on the frame, half out, looking for him. He appears, a silhouette lit only by the phone he's looking at. "Connor," I hiss.

"One second." His thumbs are moving, and so is he, closer and closer. When he gets to my window, he finally looks up. "God, you're beautiful," he mumbles at the same time my phone goes off.

Connor: I be there soon.

I drop the phone, reach out and pull him toward me with the ties of his hood. "How much did you have to drink?"

He shrugs, his eyes hooded. "Just a couple beers to take the edge off. I'm not drunk."

I eye him sideways. "How many girls did you talk to tonight?"

"Twelve."

"That's an oddly specific number."

"I made it up. No girls." He shakes his head. Then he reaches up, holds my entire head in his grasp. With his eyes on mine, he says, a seriousness taking over him, "You're the only girl for me, Ava Elizabeth Diana." He kisses me, soft and sweet, and then pulls away. "Can you turn your light on?"

"Why?"

"I always wonder what your room's like, and every time I come here, it's dark. I just want to see… maybe I could come in? Just for a few minutes?"

Biting down on my lip, I hesitate before nodding. "You have to be quiet, okay? My mom's asleep."

He draws a cross over his heart, and I lift my window higher so he can fit through. I step back, watch him climb in, first his arms, then his upper body, and then he's army crawling across my floor with his legs still out the window. When he's all the way in, his feet hit the floor with a thud. "Connor!" I whisper-yell, my finger to my lips as I listen for any movement. I'm not sure what would be worse, Mom waking or Trevor knowing there's a boy in my room.

"Sorry." He grimaces. "That was harder than it looked."

I switch on the light on my nightstand and watch him look around my room. There's nothing in here but my bed, desk, and bookshelf. "It's… different from what I imagined."

"What did you imagine?" I ask, sitting on the edge of my bed.

He sits down next to me, his giant frame almost comical on such a small bed. "I don't really know."

"It was supposed to be temporary," I admit, looking down at my feet, shame washing through me. "We weren't supposed to be here this long. I guess part of me was hoping for a miracle. Maybe William would come back and save us or—"

"Ava," he interrupts, nudging my side. "You forget we live next door. My dad works full-time and only has me to worry about, and that's all he can afford. There's nothing wrong with where we live, and that's not what I was getting at. I just meant that… I don't know. I thought there'd be pictures on the walls or something."

Not in here, I don't say. "Of what? All my imaginary friends?"

He sighs, rubs his eye with the heel of his palm. "Rhys is your friend."

"Rhys feels sorry for me."

"Karen misses you."

I can't help the flash of jealousy that knots my stomach. "You talk to Karen?"

"I mean, sometimes. I talked to her tonight."

My voice cracks when I ask, "About me?"

He settles his hand on my leg, and I can't help but think that his guilt put it there. "She asked about you. About *us*. And I told her how much I love you."

His answer is perfect. *Too* perfect. My old insecurities come back to me, and I swallow the lump in my throat.

"Ava," he says through a sigh. "What's wrong?"

I don't look up when I answer, "Nothing."

He sighs again, this one heavier. "Are you mad that I went out tonight?"

"No."

"Because I needed it, Ava. I need to get the guys on my side so I can… I've just been under a lot of stress, and I just wanted a night out, but the whole time I was there, all I wanted was to be with you, and now I'm here and…"

And I couldn't even be there for him if I wanted to. I'm not able to carry his stress like he carries my pain. I turn to him. "I'm sorry I haven't been there."

"I don't expect you to be, Ava." Even though he said it so matter-of-fact, so innocently… the truth behind those few words shatters any dignity I have left. He adds, "I told you I don't want anything more from you than you, and I meant it."

But it's not enough anymore.

And maybe I'm not enough.

He shifts, getting more comfortable on my bed. His back to the wall, he pats his lap. "Come here."

I ignore the blinding ache in my chest and move to him, straddling his lap.

His hands settle on my thighs while mine go to his shoulders. "I came here for my goodnight kiss, remember?"

Nodding, I close my eyes, hide my doubt, and press my lips to his. His mouth opens, wanting more, and so I give him what he wants. It doesn't take long for his hands to wander, first to my butt, then my breasts, under my top. His kisses move down, down, down, while his hands move up, up, up taking my tank with him. I do the same with him, our bare chests pressed together as he holds me to him, shifts us until I'm underneath him and he's between my legs. He starts to unbutton his jeans and then unzip his fly, and if this is what he came here for… if this is what he wants from me… I'll give it to him. It's the least he deserves, the least I can do. I roll us until he's on his back and make fast work of removing his shoes, then his jeans. I kiss his stomach and move lower to the smattering of hair just above his boxer shorts. His hands find the back of my head, fingers curled, and I pull down on the waistband and don't waste any time. I take him in my mouth, taste him, feel his thighs tense beneath my touch. He whispers my name, and I should feel *something*… aroused or dominant or desired, but I don't.

I feel like a whore.

The sudden sound of glass breaking has us pulling apart. I rush for my top at the same time he quickly covers himself. "Stay here," I tell him, throwing my top back on. I run out of the room, switching on lights, my heart thumping against my chest.

Not again.

Not again.

Not again.

I check the living room and kitchen, but they're empty. Trevor's out of his room, and his panic matches mine. I open Mom's door. She's on the floor, shards of glass around her. "Mama!" I scream, and she looks up, points to her foot.

Blood.

"What happened?" I rush out, moving in on her.

"I knocked over the glass," she deadpans. "Stepped on it." There's no life in her words or her eyes.

I glare at Trevor and shout, "Why the hell is there glass in her room?!"

He rears back. "I must've left it there when I gave her the meds earlier. Shit, Ava, I don't know."

"You know she can't be around this!" I say, dropping to my knees, ignoring the blood pooling around her. There's so much. Too much. Memories flood my brain and I try to push them away, but they're too strong. Too forceful. "How could you do that!" I scream at him.

"It was an accident!" he shouts back.

"Stop yelling!" Mom says, covering her ears. She starts to rock back and forth, and I try to settle my breathing, try to calm myself down. But I can't.

"You can't have *accidents* with her, Trevor! You know you can't!" Tears fall, fast and free, and I open her drawer, pull out whatever I can find to stop the bleeding. I press it to her foot, and she screams, kicks my hands off of her.

"Get away!" she yells, a terror in her voice that has my pulse escalating. I glance at Trevor, and he feels it, too.

"I need to check your foot. There might be glass!"

She kicks my chest and screams, "GET AWAY FROM ME!" And then she looks up, her eyes wide and focused on my doorway. "Who are you?" she breathes out, fear and horror etched on her face.

Connor's in the doorway, his eyes huge. He opens his mouth, but nothing comes out.

"Get away!" She kicks me again. "Go! Go! Go!"

Ignoring Connor, I grab at Mom's foot, blocking her kicks, and now Trevor's on the floor behind her, pinning down her arms. "Connor, a little help!"

Connor steps into the room, alarm evident in his voice. "What can I do?"

I'm still wrestling with Mom's legs when Trevor orders, "Hold her legs down."

"I don't want to hurt her," Connor says, panicked.

"Just do it, Connor!" I plead.

He drops to his knees in front of me and wraps his arms around her legs, holding them together.

Liquid crimson on my hands, I hold on to Mom's foot, but I can't see through the blood. "I can't see!" I cry out.

"Get off of me!" Mom thrashes, trying to get out of all our holds.

Distressed, Trevor says, "We need to call—"

"My dad," Connor cuts in, phone on the floor, on speaker, already dialing.

His dad answers on the first ring, and Connor says, "I need you at Ava's."

"I'll be right there."

For the few minutes it takes to hear the sirens approaching, the only one who speaks is my mom, mumbling words in a language only she understands. Trevor and Connor keep their hold on her while she thrashes around, screaming, then whispering, over and over. Outside, dogs bark, and inside… inside is the world at its darkest, and there's no magic in sight.

I look down at my hands, at the blood dripping from my fingers, and the only thing I can think is… at least she's breathing this time.

I take over holding down Mom's legs while Connor opens the door for his dad and his partner to enter. As soon as they see us, they get down on the floor. Mom screams again, "Get away from me! Don't touch me! Don't touch me! Don't touch me!" She's thrashing around again, harder this time, and I'm too weak… too fucking powerless.

"I think there might be glass in her foot, but I can't... I can't..." I am empty. Void. Running on hopes and dreams that are entirely unattainable.

Corey says, "We're going to have to give her a little something to calm her down so we can—"

"Ketamine?" I ask.

Corey nods. "You've been through this before, huh?" He taps Connor on the shoulder, urging him to move out of the way. Connor gets up, leaves the room completely.

He doesn't want to be here.

And neither do I.

◇◇◇◇◇

When it's over, when the glass is out, and the bandages are on and the meds have done their job and Mom's fast asleep in her bed, I stand in the middle of her room while Trevor gives a report, and Connor... Connor stands with me, holding my hand tight in his grasp. "So this is where all the pictures are," he muses.

I look up at him, my eyes dry for the first time since I heard the glass breaking, and then glance around the room. Every inch of every wall is covered in photographs—photographs I put up. From when I was a baby, through to now. Some with Trevor and William and Mom and me, as a family, and some of just us—Mom and me. I inhale a shaky breath, my voice barely a whisper, "Sometimes I hope that she'll one day wake up and see all of this, all of her life, all of *me*, and that's somehow going to be enough for her to... to miraculously snap out of it, as if it's..." I break off, my emotions getting the best of me. "It's so stupid."

"It's not," he whispers, holding my head to him. His heart beats against my cheek, and I close my eyes, listen. I try to hear the magic in there, but my thoughts are too loud, like a constant buzzing of words and memories and pain. So much pain. "It's not stupid to hope, Ava. Sometimes hope is the only thing that gets us through to the next day."

In my mind, I know he's right.

But in my heart, I know the next day will be the same as all the other days. So what difference does it make?

"I should stay," Connor says.

I shake my head, release his hand. "You should go. Try to get some rest. You have early practice tomorrow."

"She's right, Connor," his dad interrupts, standing in the doorway.

"But—"

Trevor stands next to Corey. "I'll walk you out, Connor."

Corey waits until they've left the house, along with his partner, before saying, "This is a lot to handle, Ava. Even for a girl as strong as you."

I don't respond.

He steps farther into the room, glancing at Mom, and then the pictures on the wall.

"Have you thought about putting her in a—"

"I'm not abandoning her," I cut in. Then mumble, "I'm not Connor's mom." Regret forces my eyes to shut the moment the words leave me.

"He told you about that?"

I nod, open my eyes again. "I shouldn't have said that."

Corey offers a reassuring smile, but it doesn't reach his eyes. "You know what I learned early on? Life is a series of decisions. You make them because they feel right at the time, but you're not bound to them forever. She made the decision to leave, and you're making the decision to stay. The difference is, her choices have done irreversible damage. Yours haven't. Yet."

CHAPTER 43
CONNOR

I BARELY SLEPT after what happened last night and could hardly get through the standard practice this morning. Luckily, most of the guys were hungover, so my lagging didn't seem so bad. Now I'm in the cafeteria, sitting at the "jock" table because I know Ava isn't coming.

Connor: Just checking in, babe. How is she?

Ava: She's okay now. She's on painkillers, so she's been in and out all day. Krystal's here. I'm just trying to get sleep in when I can.

Connor: Anything I can do?

"Are you in, Connor?"

Ava: No. I'm just sorry you had to witness what you did. A little embarrassed, I guess.

Connor: What I witnessed doesn't change anything.

"Connor!" Rhys nudges my side. "Earth to Connor."

I look up from my phone, see him motioning to Oscar sitting opposite me. "What?"

"Game tape after school? Our next game is Philips Academy, and they're fucking fierce."

"Yeah, sure," I mumble and look back at my phone. She hasn't responded.

Oscar says, his eyes flitting between me and my phone, "Ava wasn't in AP English this morning. Is everything okay?"

My gaze drifts to him. "She had a rough night."

He nods, and I see the genuine concern in his eyes. "Ava's a nice girl. It sucks what happened to her mom."

I look around the table, see all eyes on us, ears glued to our conversation. "Yeah, it's uh… it's tough."

"If there's anything I can do," he says, "for you or for Ava, just let me know, man."

Rhys adds, "That goes for the entire team, right, boys?"

I look around the table, at my teammates who I've gotten closer to over the past few weeks, all of them nodding, agreeing. And maybe Coach was right, and I was wrong. Maybe it wasn't the worst thing in the world to get to know these guys beyond what they had to offer on the court. Because they all seem sincere, and maybe I'd spent all this time thinking they were judging me when I'd been doing the same thing to them. "Thanks, guys. I appreciate it."

A flurry of "no worries" and "all good" sounds around the table, and then Rhys speaks up. "Here's trouble." He motions to Karen, who's walking toward us. She drops her tray on the other side of me, greets us all with a "What's up, *fuckboys*."

"Was that your mom at the game last night?" Mitch asks her.

Karen nods.

"Did she get new boobs?"

She nods again. "Provided by husband number six."

Mitch chuckles. "If they get any bigger, I might make a play. One day I could be your stepdad."

Karen throws a handful of fries at his head. "Gross, jerk."

Then Mitch waggles his eyebrows. "You can call me Daddy."

I ignore the rest of the banter and check my phone.

Still no reply.

    Connor: Ava, I love you. ALL of you.

CHAPTER 44
CONNOR

Another week goes by in a blur, and my time with Ava is limited, at best. And while we try to make the most of what we have, I can feel the distance growing between us, the disconnect. I convince myself that it's just in my head, that a lot is going on in both our lives and the last thing we need is to talk about my insecurities. Besides, it's only for a few more months. Once I get accepted somewhere, *anywhere*, and the season is over, I can focus all my time and energy on her.

On us.

On the end game.

⬦⬦⬦⬦⬦

The balloon on my porch brings a stupid smile to my face, and Dad says, "I don't get it. Why the *boo!?*"

"Because it's Ava," I tell him, following him to the car. "And it's my good luck charm." Once in the car, I pop the balloon, shove it down my boxer shorts. "And I could use all the luck in the world tonight." Tonight's opponents are currently on top of the leaderboard, a team full of all-stars. Every single person on their roster has already committed to various D1 colleges throughout the country, and *my* team is expecting me to perform, to outsmart, outrun, and outplay every one of them.

"You'll be fine, Connor," Dad says.

But I wasn't fine. Not even close. I'm double-teamed during every second I'm on the court, and I can barely get a possession, let alone score. My frustration shows in the way I yell at my team, pushing them to go harder, stronger, and then halfway through the third, I hit my fucking limit. I throw my mouthguard across the court, get a technical and hand the opposition two free throws. I ride the rest of the quarter on the bench with my head between my shoulders and my pulse racing, blood boiling.

It's our first L for the season.

My team lacks any form of responsibility for the way the game played out.

Coach is pissed at me.

Dad is disappointed in me.

And I haven't said a word to anyone since the final buzzer.

For the past few weeks, I've come just short of killing myself to play as hard as I did tonight, and it wasn't enough.

I'm not enough.

While Dad drives us home, in silence, I flip the phone in my hand, jumping every time a notification comes through. Usually there's a text waiting for me when I get to the locker room, *a good game, #3* or something similar. But there was nothing after this game or the last, and it just amplifies all the insecurities I've been trying to ignore.

When Dad stops by the gas station to buy the bags of ice I'll be soaking in later, I hit my limit of patience and send her a text.

Connor: You okay?

Ava: Can I call you later?

My eyes drift shut, my frustration growing.

Connor: Yeah

◇◇◇◇◇

I sit in the stupid bath, my teeth chattering, muscles recoiling, and my phone gripped tight in my hand, waiting for Ava.

By the time I get out, she still hasn't called, and I ignore all the other calls and texts from the guys on the team.

I don't need them.

I need her.

After checking that my phone is charging, working and the ringer is set to the loudest possible setting, I settle in my chair, college essay prep notes and applications in front of me. The screen of my laptop is bright against my eyes, the cursor flashing. I type, delete, retype, over and over, but nothing sticks because none of it matters.

An hour passes.

Then two.

Three.

I read over some past essays, make more notes.

Four.

Five.

"Connor?" A hand on my shoulder forces my eyes open. I look up to see Dad standing beside me.

I lift my head off the pile of papers on my desk and stretch my arms, my back, snapping my muscles and bones into place. With a grimace, I ask, "Aren't you supposed to be at work?"

"Son," he says, eyeing me dubiously. "It's morning. You must've fallen asleep at your desk."

"What?" I sit up straight, look at my watch. "Goddammit."

And then I check my phone.

No sign of Ava.

"Maybe you're pushing yourself too hard," Dad suggests.

Disappointed and disillusioned, I don't bother responding.

He adds, "Why don't you take the day off school? Maybe you just need a little reboot."

I nod, already getting into bed.

"You need anything?" he asks.

I stare up at the ceiling. "I'm good."

The second the door's closed, I send her a text.

Connor: Not at school today. I guess I'll catch you whenever.

And then I switch off my phone because I'm done waiting.

Done *hoping*.

◇◇◇◇◇

I wake up to the sound of Dad's voice, and when I peer through my heavy lids, I see him standing in my doorway. "You have a visitor," he tells me, stepping to the side.

In her school uniform, Ava stands just outside my room. I force my eyes to open wider so I can check the time. It's mid-morning. "Shouldn't you be at school?" I mumble.

Ava shrugs, her gaze down, her bottom lip pushed out in a pout. She glances between Dad and me as if asking us both, "Can I come in?"

She's a vision of guilt and remorse, and my chest tightens, but it doesn't give out, and I don't give in. I'm still pissed, and I don't have it in me to hide it. "If that's what you want," I breathe out.

Dad closes the door once Ava's in the room but leaves it ajar—his way of setting rules we haven't yet discussed.

Ava stands at the side of my bed, looking down at me. She's chewing her lip, her eyes on mine. Tears pool there, and I look away.

She fumbles over her words, starting and stopping, and I just want to go back to sleep where time didn't exist, and I don't have to deal with this. Not today. Not after last night. "I've been calling and messaging all morning, and when I couldn't get through, I left school and I... I caught a cab here."

I push down my anger and frustration. "You didn't need to do that. I'm fine."

She sits on the edge of my bed and is quiet a beat, then: "I told you I'd make a shitty girlfriend and you—"

"You're going to blame me?" I face her now. "Dammit, Ava. I waited all night for your call." I sit up. "I *needed* you. You're the only one who can refocus the mess in my head, the only one who can make everything inside me settle and allow me to see straight, and if you were too busy, I understand, but don't tell me you're going to do something and then just forget I exist."

"I didn't forget—" She stops there, shaking her head. Then she blows out a heavy breath. "I'm going to go," she says, standing. "I'm not making things any better by being here, so... I'm sorry, Connor. I'm sorry I disappointed you," she cries out. "And I don't know what else to say."

She starts to leave, but I grasp her hand, my heart and head pounding. I come back to reality. It was one fucking game. Just *one*. And if I want her forever, like I know I do, there are going to be other games, other moments where she can't be there, and I've been selfish. God, I've been so fucking selfish.

I won't lose her over this.

I can't.

She allows me to pull her closer, her back turned. I press my cheek into her open palm, kiss the inside of her wrist. "Don't go," I plead.

She turns to me, her tear-stained cheeks cracking open my chest. "I want so badly to be everything you need me to be."

I pull on her arm until her knees are on my bed, my hands going to her face, thumbs swiping away her sadness. "You are, Ava. And I'm so sorry I made you feel otherwise."

She nods, grasping my wrists.

"Stay?"

Another nod, and I'm shifting until my back's against the wall. She gets to her feet to slip off her shoes while I lift the covers to let her in. Her head on the crook of my shoulder and her hand on my heart, I ask, "Is everything okay with your mom?"

"I don't want to talk about it right now." She leans up to look down at me. "I'm here now. For you. I want to know everything."

I shake my head, push away the past twenty-four hours of my life, and start living for now. "You're right. You're here now. And nothing else matters."

She kisses me, her tongue swiping against my lips, and I'm suddenly awake and alive, and when she moves down to my neck, I stop her. I get out of bed, peek my head out the door to see Dad's bedroom door closed. He's asleep after his shift. I close the door. Lock it. Then strip out of my shirt and get back into bed with the girl I love.

She sits up to remove her blazer, and then she unbuttons her top, dropping them both on the floor by the bed. I hold on to her hips, guide her until she's straddling my lap. I pull at the front of her bra. "Off."

She complies and then lies on top of me, her bare breasts against my chest. I run a hand down her spine while the other settles on the back of her head.

"Thank you for coming," I tell her.

She smiles against my skin. "I haven't yet."

A chuckle erupts from deep in my chest, and she sits up again, starts removing her skirt. I place my hands on hers, stopping her. "Can this stay on?"

She eyes me, questioning.

I don't bother hiding my grin. "And the socks, too."

"Oh, God," she says through a giggle. "Do you have some weird schoolgirl kink?"

I shrug. "I didn't know I had one until you walked into class the first day of school."

"The first day?" she asks, incredulous, eyes widening.

I nod. "I've wanted you since the first time I saw you."

She leans down, bites down on my collarbone. "So now that you have me, what do you plan on doing with me?"

My hands are already under her skirt, pulling down her underwear.

We spend the rest of the afternoon in my bed, under the sheets, in a state of half-naked. We tease, and we touch, and we taste, and we go as far as we can without going all the way. We're lazy and we're carefree, taking breaks to eat or nap, to laugh and to talk and to just *be*. With each other. Within the four walls of my bedroom, we find peace in each other's arms, find solace in each other's touch, and find a *home* in each other's hearts… even if the space is limited.

CHAPTER 45
Ava

It's the most time I've been able to spend with my boyfriend in weeks, and it's in the form of a giant poster just outside the school gym. I had no idea that it was going to be there. I heard a few girls in my English class talking about it, so I had to check it out for myself.

I sit on the wall opposite with my paper bag lunch and make myself comfortable, smiling at the picture of him with a ball held at his side, standing tall. The poster takes up the entire height of the wall, and I couldn't be prouder.

I take out my phone, snap a picture of myself eating my sandwich with the poster behind me, and send it to him with the caption:

If I can't have the real you, I'll have the next best thing.

I don't expect him to respond, because I know he's spending the lunch break on a conference call with his coach and agent.

"Damn, you look good, babe!" I whisper, holding my sandwich in the air as if I'm toasting him.

"What the hell are you doing?" I recognize the voice as Rhys's and look up to see him walking toward me. His gaze shifts between fake-Connor and myself, and I say, "Talking to my boyfriend, who I miss dearly."

Rhys laughs, plants his ass down next to me. "Yeah, he's putting in the work at the moment. No off days for that kid."

I nod.

"It's nothing against you, A. You know that, right? He's just trying to get as much exposure as possible."

"I know," I tell him. "I get it."

He opens my paper bag and peers inside. Then he takes an apple and bites into it. I quirk an eyebrow. "You know I'm poor now, right? That apple was all I had for the rest of the day."

Chuckling, he reaches into his pocket and pulls out his wallet. He hands me a twenty. "I hear that's the going rate for an apple these days."

Shrugging, I shove the cash in my bra. He can spare it.

"How's your mom?" he asks.

I stare up at twelve-foot Connor. "I'm kind of getting over that question, to be honest."

"Fair," Rhys says. "Manage to get your license yet?"

"No." I haven't even gotten my permit. "I should really look into doing that with all the spare time I have."

"You're feisty right now."

"I'm feisty always."

"True. So how are you and Connor doing?"

"I don't know." I turn to him. "How are you and the rotating door of girls doing?"

He chuckles. "It's been slim pickins 'round these parts," he drawls.

"You should head over to West High. I'm sure there are plenty of girls there looking for a sugar daddy."

His nose scrunches. "I'm not that desperate yet."

I shoulder him, shoving him sideways. "You're a jerk."

He straightens up, throws his arm around my shoulders, then looks up at fake-Connor. "Hey, Ledger. I'm making moves on your girl. Whatcha gonna do about it?"

Out of nowhere, Connor appears. "Get your hands off my girl before I rip them off and glue them to your balls."

"Oooh," I tease, giggling. "You're in trouble now."

Rhys removes his arm, slides a good foot away from me. "We were just playing."

Connor sits down next to me at the same time Rhys gets to his feet. "I'd love to stay and be a third wheel and all but… no… I don't really want to. Peace out, fuckers." And then he's gone, disappearing around the same corner from which Connor appeared.

"Guess what?" Connor says, pulling his phone from his pocket. He taps a few times and then hands it to me.

I read the email on the screen:

Dear Connor Ledger,

Please consider this your official invitation to the—

I don't read the rest because I've lost my breath entirely. "Connor!" I squeal. "You got into that—that thing with all the pros and the—" I imitate shooting, even though I'm sure my form is all wrong. "And the dunk thing! *Thing*!"

Connor laughs. "The invitational, yes, I got in!"

"Oh, my God." My grin widens. "That's amazing. That's a big deal, right? What am I asking? Of course it is. It's a *huge* deal." I hug his neck, loving the chuckle that comes out of him. "I'm so proud of you."

When I release him, he says, "Coach had to pull a lot of strings to—"

"No," I cut in. "Don't you dare undervalue your worth. There are only, what, a hundred spots you told me? They wouldn't have sacrificed a single one of those spots if they didn't think you earned it."

"I guess," he mumbles, but he's not as excited as he should be. He's definitely not as excited as I am.

"What's wrong?" I ask, handing back his phone.

"It's just… it's four days over Thanksgiving break, and I was hoping to spend that time with you."

"This is a once in a lifetime opportunity, babe." I smack the back of his head playfully. "And I'll be here when you get back."

He smiles. "Promise?"

My shoulders drop. "Of course."

Smirking, he says, his tone playful, "You're not going to run off with Rhys and have all his babies?"

"Nah… Rhys's genetics are all messed up. His parents are second cousins."

"You're kidding?" he asks, wide-eyed.

"Am I?"

He glares at me a moment, contemplating. Then he gives up on my shenanigans and leans back against the wall, his chin up, looking at himself on the poster. "Damn, Ava. Your boyfriend's pretty."

I laugh, loud and free. "He's modest, too."

"Thank you," he says, sobering.

"For what?"

His head lolls to the side, his eyes on mine. "For being proud of me."

I settle my legs over his and cuddle into him. "You make it easy, Connor." I kiss his lips, and then his jaw, loving the way he brings me closer.

A deep throat clearing has me pulling away, hiding my face in his neck. Connor's shoulders shake with his silent chuckle. "Coach," he says in greeting.

"Ledger," Coach Sykes returns. "Y'all leave room for Jesus now."

CHAPTER 46
Ava

I swipe up on my phone, my hands shaking as I rush to read every word on the email Trevor has forwarded to me. It's from our health insurance company about Mom's coverage, but I don't understand what it means. There are too many technicalities, withdrawals, and limitations, and every line, every paragraph has my heart beating faster and faster, my airways tightening.

"Ava!" Connor snaps, and I come back to reality. For a second, I'd forgotten where I was, too embroiled in what the changes to the coverage mean for my mom, for our future.

Connor has one hand on the wheel, his entire body leaning to the side, facing me. "Have you been listening to a word I've been saying?"

We're on our way home from school, I remember that much, and I remember opening the email with the subject: *URGENT* and everything after that was filled with panic. "Sorry, what?" I try to focus on his words over the sound of my pulse pounding in my ears.

His brow lifts. "I was telling you about the tournament this weekend. How there are going to be twenty-five college coaches and eight NBA scouts…"

I peer down at my phone again.

"Ava?!"

"Huh?" My eyes snap to his. "Sorry."

"It's cool," he mumbles, his expression falling. He focuses on the road again. "I was just confessing all my fears and doubts to you, but it seems like you're preoccupied…" Shaking his head, he adds, barely a whisper, "Like always."

"I'm sorry," I rush out, dropping my phone in my bag. I turn to him, give him my full attention. "I'm sorry," I repeat. "Just start again."

He shakes his head. "It's fine."

I grasp his arm. "Connor, no. Just tell me everything again."

He pulls up in front of our houses, his gaze distant as he stares out through the windshield. "I have to get back to school. Coach is waiting for me."

"What?" I huff out. Then realization dawns. "Wait, did you push back practice to give me a ride?"

Connor nods but keeps his eyes trained ahead.

My stomach sinks. "You didn't have to drive me home."

He turns to me now, his movements slow, and just like he stared out the window, he stares at me. Unblinking. But his gaze looks *past* me, and I feel… exposed. I watch him closely, see the disappointment in his eyes, the frustration in his brow. And I hear the defeat in his words when he says, "I just needed to talk to you."

I exhale loudly, try to calm my thumping heart. "Connor, I'm so sorry."

He shakes his head, then reaches across me and opens my door. "I really do have to go."

My stomach is in knots, and I don't want to leave him, not like this. "How long will you be gone?"

Without looking at me, he says, "I don't know, Ava."

"Well, will you call me later?" I'm *trying*. I'm doing my best to fight for his forgiveness, but I don't know how. "You think I can get my goodnight kiss?"

"Sure," he says, but there's no inflection in his tone. No promises.

And while my mind is back on that email trying to process everything it had to say, I get out of the car without another word and leave my heart in the driver's seat, the distance between us growing with every second.

◇◇◇◇◇

I spend the rest of the night worrying about Connor, or more specifically, *Connor and me*, when I know I should be more concerned about Mom's insurance. It doesn't escape me that I seem to be focusing on Connor when I'm around my mom and then my mom when I'm around Connor, and I really wish there was a switch for my brain. I wish I could train it to stop and go at the right times. I wish my mind weren't always stuck in a fog. I wish… I wish for so many things. But right now, I wish for Connor. For him to message me and tell me he's home and that he wants his kiss.

It's eleven thirty, and I still haven't heard from him.

Dread pools in the pit of my stomach, because I know how flakey I've been lately. I can see how frustrated he's getting with me, and I want to make it up to him. I do. I just don't have the time or the resources or the… I fight back the constant thoughts attempting to ruin what we have.

That he needs more.

Deserves more.

Ava: How's that goodnight kiss coming along?

It takes him a few minutes to respond.

Connor: I'll be there in five.

I open my blinds and lift the window. And I wait. And wait. And wait. Five minutes turns to ten, and I check my phone. Nothing. I wait some more, the frigid cold air forming goosebumps along my arms as I lean halfway out, searching for him.

After fifteen minutes, he finally appears, but there's no swing in his step, no hint of a smile.

There's no boy who loves me. *All* of me.

"Hi," I whisper, waving.

He gets close enough so he can kiss me, just once. When he steps back, his eyes are on mine, tired and tortured. "Hey."

I swallow the instant lump in my throat, but it just moves lower and lower until it's wrapped around my heart, making it impossible to breathe. "What have you—" I break off when I notice him clenching his jaw.

There's no life in his eyes as he scans my face. "Goodnight, Ava." He turns on his heels and starts to leave.

"Wait," I rush out, grasping for him.

My hand catches air, but he stops anyway.

"Did you…" I want him with me. I want to show him that I care. I want him in my bed, and I want to give him everything he's wanted. And I don't care if it makes me a whore. I just want him to not look at me the way he is. I *need* him to forgive me. "Did you want to come in for a bit?" I say, my entire everything timid and submissive.

Without a second thought, he shakes his head. "I can't."

"Oh." My gaze drops, shame igniting my flesh. "Okay."

He doesn't look back when he says over his shoulder, "I'll see you whenever."

CHAPTER 47
CONNOR

Four balloons are waiting for me on the porch, one for each game if we make it through to the final of today's single-elimination tournament. Thirty of the best high school basketball teams in the region all compete for a cash prize that goes directly to the school, but that's not why we play. The arena will be filled with college coaches and NBA scouts, all of them searching for the one hidden gem. That one player who nobody knows about. And today, I'm hoping that one player is me. But so are hundreds of other kids.

I remove the balloons one by one, and I wish they gave me the same knee-jerk reaction as all the other times I'd seen them here. That feeling of elation, of pride, of wanting to do something *great* for someone else.

For Ava.

But it doesn't.

And I don't know if it's because things are rocky with us at the moment or if it's my nerves, because there sure as shit are a lot of those, too. I could barely sleep last night, my mind focused on every play, every opponent. This tournament is my chance to show up. To rise above the rest and make an impact. If this goes well, Coach assures me that colleges will have no choice but to make an offer. And I need that. God, do I *need* that.

Ava

"Trevor!" I call out, sitting on the couch with Mom in front of me while I do her hair. She's having another zero-day, and in a way, I'm glad. Lately, zero days have been the best we can get out of her.

He storms out of his room, his eyebrows drawn, focused on his phone. "What's up?"

"They're streaming today's tournament. Can you connect my laptop to the TV so I can watch it on there?"

Trevor nods, looking up and pocketing his phone. "How does Connor feel about it?"

"Connor," Mom mumbles. "Six-five but is hoping for a growth spurt."

My eyes widen. So do Trevor's. I lean over her shoulder. "You remember Connor, Mama?"

She nods once, staring into the abyss. "Handsome boy."

I can't help but smile. "Do you remember anything else about that day?"

"What day?" she asks.

"The day you met Connor."

"Connor, six-five but is hoping for a growth spurt."

Trevor chuckles, shaking his head as he goes into my room to retrieve the laptop.

"We're going to watch him play in a tournament today," I say, more to myself than anyone else. "He's going to kill it; I just know it."

"Who is?" Mom asks.

"Connor."

"Connor, six-five but is hoping for a growth spurt."

Mom and I spend most of the afternoon in front of the TV watching all the games while Trevor sleeps or works or does whatever it is in his bedroom. When Connor's not on the court, Mom and I do our usual weekend routine: flashcards, speech therapy, basic chores to remind her of daily tasks. She takes long breaks in between, her mental fatigue just as prevalent as her physical.

When Connor's playing, I try to give him my full attention so that I'm *present* when he wants to talk about it all. But sometimes it's hard. When Mom needs me, I have to stop. But it's always on in the background, and I try to retain as much of it as possible. I do my best not to squeal whenever he scores because sudden sounds and movements can set Mom off. So on the outside, I'm still, but on the inside, I'm jumping up and down and screaming and booing, and he's such a phenomenon to watch. And even though I've managed to find shitty-quality live streams on students' social media or post-game highlights online, I'll never not be amazed at his skill, at his level of dedication.

The team flies through the first two rounds, making it to the semis, where their opponents give them more of a challenge. They scrape by with a three-point win and move on to the final.

The camera zooms in on Connor at the end of the game, sitting on the bench with Rhys beside him. He's covered in sweat, his face red with exhaustion. His chest heaves as his lips part, clearing his airways for the stream of water he pours into his mouth from inches above. I stare, fixated, my heart racing, longing for the boy who carried me through the clear blue water and darkened cave. It seems so long ago; that one day of adolescent bliss, and I wish we could go back there. Both physically and metaphorically. I wish we didn't have all this burden and pressure from things outside our control that always fight to pull us apart. Sometimes I think that fight is winning. But then he'll hold me. He'll kiss me.

And he'll pull my head to his chest, my ear taking in his existence, a reminder that magic is real, and it lives within him, within *us*.

I whip up a quick dinner between games, and we sit in front of the couch to eat. I don't want to miss a single second. I've thought about messaging him between games, but I don't want to be a distraction.

The final starts and I'm on the edge of my seat, my pulse racing, nervous energy flowing through my veins. The leading score is continually changing, and by the third quarter, it's a draw.

"I think I'll try my prosthetic today," Mom says out of nowhere.

I practically sprint to her room, retrieve it, and come back out, not wanting to miss a thing. I focus mainly on the game while I fiddle with Mom's prosthetic arm, pretending to clean it and adjust it just so I can watch more of the game.

The team they're against, Philips Academy, is at the top on the school district leaderboard and the same team that gave us our one and only loss. And Connor—he's out for blood. I can see it in the way he plays. Everything is amplified. Every step, every dribble, every shot he takes. He's nothing less than perfection, and the opposing team knows that because he's double-teamed, and yet, he's still managing to carry the team. He scores two three-pointers in a row halfway through the final quarter, giving us a three-point lead, and I don't hide my squeal this time. I can't. Mom sits up with a jolt, and I apologize immediately and calm her down. Two minutes to go, and we're up by five, and I focus on the TV while trying to get Mom's prosthetic on. "Ava, you're putting it on wrong."

"Just one second, Ma."

"Ava!" She yanks the prosthetic out of my hands, and I watch, as if in slow motion, as she throws it across the room, smashing the TV square in the middle.

"Mama!"

She shakes her head. Doesn't stop.

I gawk, wide-eyed, at the TV as the picture stutters, and then fades, fades, fades until there's nothing but darkness.

Rage pulses inside me, beats strong against my flesh. "Why would you do that!" I scream, standing over her.

She keeps shaking her head, and she won't fucking quit.

"Answer me!"

"Ava!" Trevor yells, coming out of his room. "What the hell's going on?!"

Mom stands so fast I almost miss it. She pushes past me, sending me back a step, and then charges, full speed, full strength, right into the TV. It falls back, glass shattering. Mom wails, for no other reason than to wail, and I…

I yell, tears blinding my vision, "Go to your fucking room!"

Mom's laughter is hysterical in the most menacing way.

I ball my fists at my sides, my jaw clenched.

"Ava, calm down!" Trevor orders.

Pressure builds in my chest, and I can't… I can't breathe. Through clamped teeth, I seethe, trying to hide my anger, "You need to take her to her room so I can clean up the glass!"

Trevor's throat bobs with his swallow as his eyes bore into mine. He nods once. "Okay."

He helps Mom into her room, closing the door between us. I pick up my phone with only one thing on my mind. *Connor*. I need to show him that I'm here. That I care. That I'm *trying*.

Ava: Good games, #3.

Then I take a moment to put myself back together, to hide my anger and my fear and my self-loathing. I've never yelled at her like that before. Never. No matter how hard things got… I never raised my voice. At least not to her.

I get what I need to clean up the glass, careful not to cut myself. It takes an hour on my hands and knees, making sure there are absolutely no shards left so we don't have a repeat of the last two times she was around broken glass. I go outside to trash what I need to, all the while listening for signs that things will get worse. That we might need to call the crisis team… and it will all be my fault.

I have one hand back on the front doorknob when a text comes through.

Connor: Are you fucking serious?

CONNOR

I choked.

And while the winning team celebrated around me, I collapsed on the hardwood, fatigue setting every muscle ablaze. Failure blocked my airways as I stared up at the arena lights, wondering if this was it.

Some people peak in high school.

And that's as far as they'll ever go.

We were one point down with five seconds on the clock, and I choked. I had time, I had space, I had enough muscle memory to go blind into a simple lay-up. I went for the three-pointer. The rest is history.

I thought all of that was as bad as it would get, and then I opened my locker, reached for my phone, and read her message.

It's ironic, really, because while I was on that hardwood, she was the first thing that came to my mind. I thought if I could just leave, if I could go to her, if I could see her, speak to her, then everything would be better. It wouldn't be perfect, it wouldn't even be *okay*, but it would be *better*.

But I can't get to Ava, don't really want to, and so I search for what I needed from her and find it at the bottom of a bottle of beer. Or six.

Rhys's house is full of kids, and I don't think any of them care that it's a Sunday night and we have school tomorrow. Most of the team are in the pool house watching the highlights from today's games. I watch, too, my lids heavy from the booze. I listen to the guys talk about how good they look on camera and how much pussy they think it's going to get them. And then Karen enters the room, sits on the arm of the couch right next to me. "Tough break, Ledger," she says, ruffling my hair.

My head falls forward, and it's an effort to lift it again.

I focus back on the screen, and my heart drops, my stomach twisting when I see him—Tony Parsons. From Duke. And he's shaking hands with the two guys from Philips who had me covered the entire game. At no point today did he shake *my* hand or even acknowledge that we'd spoken before.

I drop my head in my hands, tug at my hair and groan the loudest groan in the history of groans. Mitch laughs. "It's just a fucking game, man."

I glance at him, my words sloppy. "Hey, guess what? Fuck you."

Karen scoffs, taps me on the shoulder.

I look up at her.

"You want to get out of here?"

Yes.

But *Ava*.

I check my phone. She hasn't replied. Hasn't called. And all it does is heighten my frustration. "Why the hell not?"

I grab another six-pack on the way out and tear into it the second I'm in Karen's coupe. Top down, I welcome the cold chill against my face.

I don't ask Karen where we're going because Karen seems to have a plan. Karen's also got good taste in music. I turn up the stereo to full volume and rest my head on the seat. I close my eyes, get comfortable, and don't bother opening them until the car's stopped. We're parked just outside the sports park gate, and Karen turns off the car, filling my ears with silence.

"Are we breaking and entering, because if so, I should call my dad and warn him about the bail money. We're poor, Karen."

"You're not poor," she tells me, her blond hair blowing in the breeze. "You're middle class. You just live in an area that has too many one-percenters."

"Perspective," I mumble.

"What?"

I heave out a breath. "It's all about perspective. You have good perspective."

"Riiiight," she drawls. "And no, we're not breaking and entering. Stepdad number five owns this place." She hops out of the car, taking her keys with her, and uses them to open the giant padlock on the gates.

"Will you get in trouble?" I ask when she's back behind the wheel.

With a shrug, she says, "He gave me a key for a reason." And then she puts the car in drive and makes her way through the park, around the batting cages, and parks right in the middle of the basketball courts.

Great.

More basketball.

Just what I need.

"Let's go, baller."

I force my body to move. Hand on the door, pulling at the handle. I use all my weight to push open the door. One leg first, then the other. Karen's at her trunk and she pulls out a basketball, and if she wants to play one-on-one, I'm noping the fuck out.

I'm done for the day.

Dee-plee-ted.

She stops a foot in front of me, slaps me across the face. *Hard.*

"What the fuck?" I cry out, hand to my cheek.

"Wake the fuck up, Connor! I'm not here to baby you." She takes the beers from my hand, dumps them in her open trunk. "Let's go."

"I don't want to play," I whine.

She eyes me, hand on her hip. "You have ten minutes to sober the fuck up and get back to reality. If this is how you're going to act after every loss—"

"It wasn't just a normal loss."

She slaps me again.

"What the fuck, woman! Knock it off."

"Ten minutes," she says, setting a timer on her watch. "I'll wait."

I sit my ass on the ground, legs bent in front of me, arms outstretched behind me. And I look up at the stars, breathe fresh air into my lungs, again and again, and I let the coolness of it wash through me, my vision slowly returning to normal.

I ask, because it's something I've often wondered, "Why did you and Ava stop being friends?"

Karen's quiet a moment, and when I glance at her, she's sitting cross-legged, staring down at her hands. "I don't think we ever really *stopped*. Things just got too hard after everything with her mom. We couldn't really hang out, and too many calls went unanswered, and after a while, I just stopped trying to reach out to her." She looks up now, her eyes on me. "I don't think it's anyone's fault. At least I hope she doesn't feel like I'm to blame. I tried, Connor. We all did, but..."

"It got too hard," I finish for her.

She nods. "How are you guys doing?"

I shrug. "I don't really want to talk about it."

"You brought it up."

"Then I'll bring it back down."

Her watch beeps, and she gets to her feet. "Time's up."

Moaning, I stand, catch the ball she throws at my chest.

"Where were you?" she asks, pointing to the three-point line.

"What do you mean?"

She stands around the area where I made my choke shot. "Was it here?"

"About, yeah."

She motions for me to join her at that spot, and so I do. I stand there while she walks off the court.

"Shoot your shot," she says.

I chuckle. "I'm still kind of drunk."

"Do it anyway."

I shoot, sink it.

She grabs the ball, throws it back. "Again."

I do it again.

She returns the ball to me. "Again."

I make the next five shots. Miss one. Then sink the next two.

When I'm done, she takes possession of the ball and holds it to her hip. "Nine out of ten and you're drunk, Connor," she states.

"So, what you're saying is that I should've made the shot, because I know this, *Karen*. But thanks for reminding me."

"No." She shakes her head. Adamant. "What I'm saying is that you miss 100% of the shots you don't take." She throws the ball back.

Dribbling lazily, I retort, "You're just quoting Wayne Gretzky, and that's hockey—"

"Shut up," she laughs out. "Now I've forgotten my point. It was going to be something amazing about 90% of the shots made or… something."

"I get your point," I say through a chuckle. "And I appreciate what you're saying, even if it doesn't really make sense."

She rolls her eyes and moves toward me, hands out asking for the ball. I throw it to her and step aside as she takes over my position. She sinks a three-pointer effortlessly. "Damn. Skills much?"

Her eyes narrow. "You know I'm captain of the girls' basketball team, right?"

"I didn't even know we had a girls' basketball team."

◇◇◇◇◇

She asked for no mercy during our one-on-one, so I beat her 21-3. I do a celebratory Steph Curry dance around her. She smirks, then says, "Hey, who am I?" She drops to the ground, on her back, and looks up at the sky. "Boo hoo. I missed a three-pointer under immense pressure, and now my life is over. Wahhh."

I stand over her, brows bunched. "You're kind of a bitch."

"I kind of know this already."

I lie down next to her, the ball between us, and stare up at the darkness above.

"What's your favorite game of all time?" she asks.

"Umm… 1980. Game 6, Lakers versus 76ers."

"Yesss. Magic came to play!" she whoops.

"You?" I ask.

"Without a doubt, 1976, Game 5, Celtics versus Suns."

I shake my head. "Such a weak answer. That's *everyone's* go-to. Do you like the actual game or the fight?"

"I mean, it went triple OT, so it was a good game, but man, I do get all tingly between the legs when I see guys beating the shit out of each other."

"You're weird."

"No, you."

Ava

"Mama, stop, please!" I cry out. "I'm sorry I yelled at you." I hold her head to my chest, try to stop her from banging it against her bedroom door like she has been for the past fifteen minutes.

I can barely see through the tears of frustration constantly filling my eyes, and now Trevor's at the front door letting the crisis workers in. More money wasted.

Mom stops with the headbanging, only to start smacking the heel of her palm against her head. She's rocking back and forth, her knees up between us, and I don't know how much longer I can take this. "Just stop, Mama!"

"I can't. I can't. I can't."

"Yes, you can! I don't understand—"

"What don't you understand?" she screams so loud I release my hold. She continues with the pounding, and I grasp her arm, try to get her to stop. "I don't want to be here, Ava!"

"Don't say that!" I cry out.

She glares up at me, eyes wide. "I. Don't. Want. To. Be. HERE!"

I cower, wiping the tears off my cheeks with the back of my hands, my breaths coming out in puffs. "I know!" I yell, exhausted. Mentally. Physically. All of it. "I know you don't want to be here, but I *need* you here! Why can't you see that?!" I break off on a sob. "Look at me!" I clutch a hand to my chest to stop the pain. So much pain. Years and years of it. "This is killing me as much as it is you!" I try to push down my hurt, but it just grows and grows and grows, every fucking day, and I'm *done*. "I can't do this anymore," I cry. "I just can't."

"I never asked you to!" she screams, her spit flying. "I *hate* you for what you did to me, Ava! I *hate* you."

Everything inside me stops.

My breaths.

My pulse.

My cries.

I look at her, try to find any semblance of the woman I love, the mother who raised me. But she's gone. She's so far gone, and there's nothing left of her. And nothing left of me. "I'm trying," I whisper, getting to my feet. My chest heaves, but I'm breathless. *Lifeless*. "I'm trying so fucking hard, and it's not enough. It never will be."

I grab my phone before storming past Trevor and the crisis workers and run outside.

I need time.

I need space.

I need air.

I need *Connor*.

I stand in front of his house with the phone in my hand, and I remember his text, barely. The phone hardly visible through my tears, I try to calm down, my thumbs searching for the last couple of minutes of his game.

I need to be prepared.

I need to be present.

For him.

I find the video, skim until the end, my heart dropping, lips parting when I watch it back.

I don't think. I just run to his window and knock, guilt building a solid fortress in my stomach. When enough time passes and there's no sign of life, I knock again. Wait. I check for his car, but it isn't there, and I knock again and again and again, getting louder each time.

My heavy breaths create a fog in front of my eyes and inside my mind, and I check the time, 2:27 a.m. I sniff back my cries, dial his number and hold the phone to my ear.

It rings on my end, but it's silent in his room, and I have no idea where he could be. My self-doubt and insecurities fight for a space in my thoughts, and I don't have the energy to push them away. The call connects to his voicemail, and I suck in a breath, try to replace my weakness for courage.

Vincit qui se vincit.

"Hey, Connor. It's me…"

CHAPTER 48
Ava

It's been a long time since I've just "hung out" in the hallways at school, and maybe that's why I feel like there are even more stares, more whispers than usual. I sit in front of Connor's locker, my legs crossed and my head down, waiting for him. I want to catch him after practice and before psych so we can at least get a few minutes to talk. I need to explain my stupid text.

I have my headphones in, but no music to accompany it. I wear them so I'll be left alone, but I'll still be able to hear Connor coming. Instead, I'm hearing people mock me as they walk past, and then two sets of feet, girls, stop in front of me. I don't look up when they giggle to themselves. Not even when one of them says, "I bet she has no idea what he gets up to when she's not around."

My head spins, my stomach does, too, and I don't… I don't understand what they're saying. All I know is that Connor wasn't home in the early hours of the morning. And so maybe they're right. Maybe I don't know him at all.

Another set of feet stops beside me, and I recognize them as Connor's. "Hey."

I take a quick moment to get myself together before looking up at him. His face is blanched, dark circles around his heavy eyelids. His body's slumped as if it's a task to remain upright, and I get to my feet, say, "Hey." I ignore the ache in my chest when he bypasses our usual morning kiss and goes straight for his locker, throwing his bag in without taking anything out.

He slams his locker shut, then leans against it, his hands in his pockets when he says, "What's up?"

His eyes are on mine, but the soul behind them… it isn't Connor.

I yank the headphones out of my ears and cross my arms over my chest. I feel so little, and I need him to stop making me feel like that. "I've been trying to call you," I murmur.

He shrugs. "I lost my phone."

My eyes widen. "What do you mean you *lost* your phone?"

"I mean," he says, looking down his nose at me, "I misplaced it. I don't know where it is."

"I know the definition of *lost*, Connor. You don't need to berate me."

"I'm not," he sighs out. His eyes drift shut, his shoulders lifting with his heavy inhale. When he opens his eyes again, he says, "Look, I just spent the entire morning running suicides because Coach thinks it's funny to punish a bunch of hungover kids, and so—"

"You're hungover?" I cut in.

He shakes his head. "No, I'm just really fucking exhausted. I've been pushing myself too far for too long, plus the constant lack of sleep—especially last night—and… everyone has their limits, Ava." His gaze bores into mine. "And I think I'm at my peak."

A stillness passes between us, seconds feel like hours, and we do nothing but stare at each other, like we're both searching for something that's no longer there. I look away when I feel the heat burning behind my eyes.

Connor pushes off his locker, his hand reaching up, and I close my eyes, wait for the moment his hand cups my jaw or his finger traces my forehead when he shifts the loose strands away... but nothing comes.

"Thank you," he breathes out, and my eyes snap open as I see him grasp the phone someone's holding up between us. I follow the arm to the person next to me: Karen.

"Where the hell was it?" he asks her.

"You left it in my car, *stupid*."

Connor chuckles. "No, you."

Karen faces me. "Hey, Ava."

All I can do is stand there, fighting back the hurt, the betrayal. I know she's watching me, they both are, and there's no justified reaction to match what I'm feeling, what I'm thinking.

I bet she has no idea what he gets up to when she's not around.

I look back at Connor, willing the tears away. "I'll see you in class."

◇◇◇◇◇

Connor and I say nothing to each other as we sit together in psych class. There's no hand on my leg, no witty banter.

There's just him.

And me.

In two very different worlds.

I grasp on to my textbook as I stare ahead, hearing but not listening to everything going on around me. The class phone rings, and Mr. McCallister pauses his speech to answer it. Back turned to the class, the conversation in the room picks up.

"Psst!" Rhys hisses, kicking the back of Connor's chair. "Where the hell did you disappear to last night?"

Connor shrugs but doesn't say anything.

I keep my eyes forward, watching as Mr. McCallister turns to the class, phone still to his ear, and then his gaze locks on me. He's nodding, his lips pulled down in a frown. My chest rises with my shaky inhale, and I sit up higher, my life source pumping rapidly as he hangs up, starts moving toward me. The world around me is silent, bar his heavy footsteps as he closes in.

I shudder an exhale.

And then Connor's hand finds mine on the desk, linking our fingers together.

Mr. McCallister squats down to my level. "Ava, sweetheart, have you got your phone on you?"

I pull it out of my pocket. The battery's dead because I hadn't charged it overnight. I spent the entire night walking the streets aimlessly, and I hadn't been home except to change into my uniform. I didn't plan on staying. I just came here for Connor...

"It's um... it's..." I drop the phone on the desk and look up at him. "What's wrong?"

"You're needed at home."

"Okay," I breathe out, feeling the first panic-induced tear slide down my cheek. I swipe it away. "Can I use the phone to call a cab?"

Mr. McCallister eyes Connor, and Connor says, "I don't have my car here."

Rhys speaks up. "I'll take you, A."

CONNOR

I'd been dreading seeing Ava all morning. When I saw her at my locker, I stood firm. I wanted her to know that she'd hurt me and that I was pissed, and I wasn't going to back down. The past few times we'd been together, I'd needed her, and she hadn't even been present enough to listen to what I was saying.

But when Mr. McCallister started to approach her in psych, I felt her fear, and I realized that I had no idea what had been going on with her. *Not really.* And it's not that I don't ask, but she never opens up about it. She never fully lets me in. Never tells me anything.

During lunch, I ask Rhys to take me to his house so I can pick up my car. He has no idea why Ava had to go home. He said that she'd been silent on the drive there and he didn't want to push her.

I send her a text, hope she's had time to charge her phone.

Connor: Is everything okay?

Ava: Yes.

I know I should head back to school, but once I'm in my car, the only place I can think to go is Ava's.

I stand on her lawn and send her another message.

Connor: Any chance you can come out for five? I think we need to talk.

The curtains part on Ava's front window, and a second later, she's stepping out and sitting on her porch steps.

I sit next to her, my heart heavy, mind clouded with confusion. I swallow my nerves. "Is everything okay?"

"Yeah, there was just no one available to watch her today," she says, her tone flat, her gaze distant.

I heave out a breath, keep my eyes on her. And I know it's not the right time or place, but I can't keep doing this. Going around and around like we are. "What's going on with us, A?"

"I don't know," she says, her gaze trailing to mine. "Why don't you tell me?"

"What does that mean?"

"Why didn't you tell me about Karen?"

"When?" I snap. "When would I have told you about it exactly?"

"I don't know," she deadpans. "This morning when I was standing right in front of you." She huffs out a breath. "What happened last night, Connor?"

I run a hand through my hair, tug at the ends. This isn't the conversation I was looking for. "With what, exactly? Me choking in the last five seconds of the game or you sending me a message proving you don't care?" There's a hint of anger in my tone that I didn't plan on being there.

"I tried," she whispers. "I watched the entire tournament and then my mom…" Her voice cracks and she sits higher, squares her shoulders. "What happened after the game?"

I sigh. "We went back to Rhys's, and we drank, and some of the guys couldn't drive, so Karen gave us rides home. That's why my phone was in her car." I don't know why I lie, and it's the first time I've ever done it, but none of this matters. That's not why we're here.

She's silent a breath, her eyes lowering. "What time did you get home?"

I shake my head, curbing my frustration in my fists. "I don't know. Like, midnight?" I know it was later than that. Much later. But I don't need her focusing on that because, again, it's irrelevant, and so I tell her that. "It doesn't matter what I did or didn't do last night, and Karen's not the problem. The problem is between us, A. You and me."

"Stop calling me A," she grinds out. "Only Rhys calls me that."

"Yeah?" I snort. "Was that before or after you fucked him?"

"Connor!"

I ignore her and keep at it, getting everything off my chest. "And while we're on the topic of not telling each other things, why is it that everything I know about you, I hear from other people?"

Her eyes snap to mine. "What the hell are you talking about?"

I count off each point on my fingers. "I find out about your mom through my dad. Then I find out about you and Rhys through Rhys. That your mom was a POW through Trevor. And even Peter fucking Parker seems to think it's—"

"My mom was a *what*?" she cuts in, her voice low, shaky.

Fuck. Everything inside me hardens, and I look up to see her watching me, her eyes brimming with tears, her bottom lip trembling.

My mouth opens, but nothing comes out.

"Connor?" she cries, begging for answers. "Was my mom… was she…?"

"No, Ava, she—"

"Tell me the truth!"

"Fuck," I spit, pressing the heels of my palms against my eyes. "Fuck, Ava, I wasn't supposed—"

Her sob forces a sharp inhale as she stares at me, her mouth agape. "Why would you keep that from me!" And then she breaks, her shoulders shaking. Those small hands I fell in love with cover her entire face, and she's crying, the loudest, most unconfined cry I've ever witnessed from her, and all the broken pieces of my heart fight for unity again because I remember everything about her, about us, everything I love. I fell in love with her vulnerability as much as I fell for her strength and "I'm sorry, Ava." I sniff back my own tears, watching her shatter in front of me. "I love you. I'm so sorry."

I try to reach for her, to hold her, to show her the magic… but she pushes me away. "Don't fucking touch me." She's on her feet and heading for her door, and I try to grasp on to her, but she's too… everything. She's too determined and too angry and too… too *damaged*. She slams the door between us, and I don't give up. Can't.

I turn the knob and push, but nothing happens. "Ava, please," I beg, my forehead against the door. "I'm sorry."

◇◇◇◇◇

I don't bother going back to school, telling Dad that I'm not feeling well, so he excuses me from classes for the rest of the day. I spend the time in my room, my phone to my ear, calling, calling, calling. My thumbs move faster than ever as I write out text after text after goddamn text, each one going unanswered. I stand at her door four fucking times with my fist raised ready to knock, but stop myself, knowing it could make things worse.

When the world around me turns dark and all hope is gone, I try calling her again. This time, she answers. But it's not her on the other end of the line. It's Trevor. "Stop fucking calling, Connor. You've done enough."

I stare down at my phone once he's hung up, anger and fear and disappointment hitting me in waves. Then I notice the voicemail icon and hope spikes in my heart. Maybe she's tried calling at the same time I have, and maybe Trevor's taken her phone because he's angrier at me than she is…

I hit play on the voicemail, listen to the intro timestamped 2:27 am. "Hey, Connor. It's me… It's umm… it's 2:30 in the morning and I'm at your window but… but I don't think you're home and I'm not really sure where you are… I just… I wanted to say sorry about my message. I watched the entire tournament and then with five minutes left in the final, my mom… she broke our TV… deliberately, and God, Connor, I got so angry with her. I yelled at her like I've never done before. And I… I'm just having a really shitty time at the moment. And I know that you are, too, and that's more important right now, so I'm sorry. I'm sorry I wasn't there for you like you've always been there for me, and I know that you're probably sick of hearing me apologize but… I don't know. I just thought… I thought maybe we could spend the night together, or at least a couple of hours. Because um… because I love you, Connor. I just love you… so much."

I throw my phone across the room, watch it fracture. And just like Ava before me, I *break*. As if I've reached my boiling point and the pressure's too much, and I explode. Erupt. Detonate. "Fuck!" I shout. My fist flies, goes through the drywall. Again, and again. And then my dad appears, his eyes wide, and I fall to the floor, my head in my hands. "Jesus Christ, Connor," he whispers, dropping to his knees in front of me. He grasps my hand in his, shifting the blood pooling at my knuckles. "What the hell are you thinking?" He inspects my hand closer, his eyes wide when he looks up at me. "This is your shooting hand."

CHAPTER 49
CONNOR

I DON'T SEE Ava at school the next day, not that I expected to. But I see her the day after, in psych, walking through the door. I sit higher in my seat and hide my bandaged hand under the table. I need to talk to her, to apologize. I've planned out everything I want to say. I need to tell her how sorry I am for the way I'd been acting, that it was never about her, and that it was all on me. That the pressure became too much, and I took it out on her. And I need to tell her that I love her, that I never stopped loving her, not even for a second.

But she doesn't look at me when she walks in. Instead, she goes to Karen, her mouth moving, but I'm too far away to hear what she's saying. Karen turns to me, her eyes sad, and then back to Ava. She nods, stands, and gives Ava her seat.

My heart sinks, and I look down at the table as Karen settles in beside me. "I'm sorry, Connor," she whispers. "I couldn't say no to her."

◇◇◇◇◇

The day is a blur, and I can't focus on anything. Not even basketball. After-school practice is a shitshow, and my injured hand only elevates my piss-poor performance. "It looks like it's healing well," one of the trainers says, inspecting my hand after practice.

"My dad's a paramedic," I mumble. "He made sure it was taken care of. Trust me, no one wants it to heal as fast as he does."

"Where the hell is my deodorant?" Oscar says from behind me. He's opening and closing lockers, searching.

"Just use mine," Rhys offers.

"I have sensitive skin, bruh."

"Check your car," says Rhys.

Oscar sings, "You're not just a pretty face, co-cap."

I watch the trainer wrap my hand again. "Your dad think it'll be good to go by the invitational?"

I nod. "It's just a minor sprain. No fractures."

"Good. Want to tell me how it happened?"

"Not really."

"Connor," Oscar says, his hand on my shoulder. "Your girl's out in the parking lot."

My brow lifts when I look up at him.

He shrugs. "She ain't waitin' on me."

Ava pushes off my car when she sees me approaching, her arms going around her waist. A few spots over, Trevor's in his truck, his eyes on me. Heavy-hearted, I motion toward him. "You bring a bodyguard?"

Ava's looking down at the ground when my gaze moves back to her. "He's just waiting to give me a ride home." Then she notices my hand, and hers reaches across, taking my wrist in her grasp. "What happened?"

I lower my hand so my fingers graze hers, taking hold of them. I say, my voice weak, "A wall came at me. I had to protect myself."

She looks up now, her eyes clouded. I squeeze the ends of her fingers, and it's as if she just realized I was holding on to her. She yanks out of my hold, hiding her hands in the pockets of her blazer. My throat closes in, my stomach twisting. Through narrow airways, I let out a breath and say, "I was hoping I'd get a chance to talk to you. There's a lot I need to say."

"Me too," she rushes out. "And I need to go first so that I don't…" she trails off, and I nod, my eyes on hers, my entire everything drawn to her.

She glances at Trevor, as if needing the courage, then back at me. "When we first started this, I warned you that nothing good can come of it. That there'd be no happy ending to our story…"

"Don't, Ava," I plead. "You're talking as if it's over."

"It *is* over, Connor."

I laugh once, incredulous, and look past her. "So I make one mistake, and that's it? You're done?"

"You didn't make any mistakes," she sighs out. "But we never should've started anything to begin with. We were so selfish to think that it would work." She pauses a beat, her voice dropping when she adds, "I wasn't made for this."

"For what? To be with me?"

"No." She takes a step toward me. Just one. But keeps her eyes downcast. "I wasn't made with the strength to do it all. Taking care of my mom is as much as I can do, and even then, I'm already spread so thin. You told me the other day that you were at your limit, and I think I passed that point a long time ago, Connor. I can't be trying to take care of her and trying to be focused on you and being insecure about us all at the same time."

I kick off my car, take one step forward and retake her hand. "You don't have to be insecure about us," I plead. "Nothing happened with Karen. I swear it, Ava."

Her eyes lift, lock on mine. "Then why did you lie?"

"About what?" I ask, even though I already know. So does my heart, because it's trembling in my ribcage.

"You're the only one who left with her. And you weren't home at midnight, Connor, because I was banging on your window—" Her voice wavers and she clears her throat. "If nothing happened," she says, tears welling in her eyes, "then why lie to me?"

I shake my head, sniff back the burn behind my nose, and look down at the ground, shame forcing my shoulders to drop. "Because I didn't want you to worry," I admit. "Clearly, I had my priorities wrong." I swallow the knot in my throat and peer up at her again. "But this isn't your reason is it, Ava? It's your excuse."

Her sob has me looking up, watching her wipe at her eyes frantically. "It's too hard," she cries out, her entire presence shrinking with defeat. "I can't..." The weight of her cries halts her words, and I exhale, wait for her to finish. "I can't be the person I want to be when I'm with you. I can't forget that... that my mom needs me more than I need you. And I did that. For one split second, I forgot. Because I love you, Connor. And I don't think I'll ever stop loving you..." She falls into me, her arms going around me, holding tight. "But I can't *be with* you."

I take in her words, breathe them into me. "You were my end game," I whisper, knowing she can't hear me through her cries. I wipe the wetness off my cheeks against her hair and clutch her head to my chest, her ear to my life source.

She quiets her sobs.

Waiting.

Listening.

But she won't find what she's searching for.

Because: "There's no magic in a broken heart, Ava."

To be continued in First and Forever

ALSO BY JAY MCLEAN

MORE THAN SERIES
More Than This
More Than Her
More Than Him
More Than Forever
More Than Enough

PRESTON BROTHERS NOVEL
Lucas
Logan
Leo

THE ROAD SERIES
Where the Road Takes Me
Kick Push
Coast

COMBATIVE TRILOGY
Combative
Redemptive
Destructive

BOY TOY CHRONICLES
Boy Toy Chronicles

DARKNESS MATTERS
Darkness Matters

THE HEARTACHE DUET
Heartache and Hope
First and Forever

ABOUT THE AUTHOR

Jay McLean is an international best-selling author and full-time reader, writer of New Adult and Young Adult romance, and skilled procrastinator. When she's not doing any of those things, she can be found running after her three little boys, investing way too much time on True Crime Documentaries and binge-watching reality TV.

She writes what she loves to read, which are books that can make her laugh, make her hurt and make her feel.

Jay lives in the suburbs of Melbourne, Australia, in her dream home where music is loud and laughter is louder.

For publishing rights (Foreign & Domestic) Film or television, please contact her agent Erica Spellman-Silverman, at Trident Media Group.

@JAYMCLEANAUTHOR

Printed in Great Britain
by Amazon